THE RELUCTANT WARRIOR

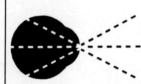 This Large Print Book carries the Seal of Approval of N.A.V.H.

THE RELUCTANT WARRIOR

MARY CONNEALY

THORNDIKE PRESS
A part of Gale, a Cengage Company

GALE
A Cengage Company

Farmington Hills, Mich • San Francisco • New York • Waterville, Maine
Meriden, Conn • Mason, Ohio • Chicago

Copyright © 2018 by Mary Connealy.
Scripture quotations are from the King James Version of the Bible.
Thorndike Press, a part of Gale, a Cengage Company.

LIBRARY OF CONGRESS CIP DATA ON FILE.
CATALOGUING IN PUBLICATION FOR THIS BOOK
IS AVAILABLE FROM THE LIBRARY OF CONGRESS

ISBN-13: 978-1-4328-5654-0 (hardcover)

Published in 2018 by arrangement with Bethany House Publishers, an imprint of Baker Publishing Group

Printed in Mexico
1 2 3 4 5 6 7 22 21 20 19 18

I'm dedicating *The Reluctant Warrior* to
my husband. He's my very own
romantic cowboy hero.

It's hard to know how someone will act
in high-pressure situations. Now I
know. You really came through for me
when I needed you most. Thank you!

CHAPTER 1

Sierra Nevada Mountains
April 1868

It was the silence that woke him.

Cameron Scott took in his surroundings before moving, before opening his eyes. He'd been a warrior for too much of his life, and some rules a man didn't forget. One of them was to find out all you could before they knew you were awake. The silence pounded in his ears. Then came the smell.

He snapped his eyes open. He was in his room in the bunkhouse at the Riley ranch south of Lake Tahoe. He'd been here, nearly a prisoner thanks to the weather, for the entire winter.

He awoke in this same room every morning. And never, morning or night, had the darkness or the silence felt so profound as right now.

Nothing moved. No subdued moonlight

slipping in through the tight shuttered window in his room. No wind. No blizzard. That was what he'd fallen asleep to. The blizzards hit now and then, but the wind was a ceaseless moaning that made him long to move to another climate.

But it wasn't the silence or the darkness that'd made him react as a warrior. It was the smell.

He swung his legs over the side of the bed and sat up. A wave of sickness struck that threatened to empty the contents of his belly.

His thoughts were sluggish. Danger was nothing new, yet he always trusted his lightning-fast reactions honed by war.

Right now, he felt like a doddering old man who couldn't clear his thoughts. Then he remembered he wasn't alone.

"Utah! Adam, get up. On your feet, men." Cam stood, and his knees buckled, taking him low to the ground. He knew instantly that the unfamiliar weakness had saved his life.

He shouted again, louder this time, and realized how accustomed he was to being obeyed, only now all he got was silence. He roared, "The bunkhouse is full of smoke!"

The darkness he couldn't explain, but the fire oughta shove it back. He crawled out of his room, looking all around. A few glowing embers in the fireplace were the only light.

"Utah, get up! Get out here!" Utah Smith was in the small room right next to Cam's in the newly built bunkhouse. And Utah reacted to everything fast. His room, door open, remained silent. They all slept with their doors open to let the heat in from the fireplace, the only warmth in the house.

If the smoke had overcome both cowpokes, Cam had his work cut out saving them. Wake up the men? Clear the smoke — if he could figure out how? Get the extra hands to work — unless they were unconscious and he wasted precious seconds?

Cam was a major in the cavalry and made life-and-death decisions in a snap.

The smoke first. He rushed to the tightly shuttered window between the fireplace and Utah's room. He flung the shutters open, swinging them inward.

Nothing.

No outdoors. Confused, addled by the smoke and the pitch-black, Cam reached his hand toward this solid wall where a window should be and touched cold. He crunched his hand into the cold and realized it was snow. A solid wall of snow higher than the window. He punched into the snow hoping it wasn't deep and he could break through.

He only drove his fist deeper into snow.

It all clicked into place in his foggy brain. The cabin was buried. Probably the smoke-stack of the chimney, too. The smoke from the dying fireplace was filling the cabin. Looking around, it was no trouble finding the snow shovels. Scooping snow seemed to be the main job they did these days. Still crawling, Cam grabbed the shovel, reached the fireplace, and scooped up a glowing log. He didn't know how he was going to dig out, but these hot logs oughta be able to handle the snow.

He stood, rushed to the wall of snow, and tossed the log right at it. It sunk out of sight. That opened a hole straight down to the ground around the bunkhouse. He stabbed the snow shovel deep, and it didn't reach air.

How deeply were they buried?

He carried a scoop of snow to the hearth and tossed it on the logs. They hissed and spat. Cam didn't wait for them to go out. He dropped low to breathe and found the steam coming off the fire was fresher than the air in the room. He sucked the air in, got plenty of smoke too, then grabbed more kindling, rushed to the open shutter and tossed the logs out. They melted their way out of sight.

Another scoop of snow dumped on the fireplace. Another scoop of kindling out the window.

He inhaled deeply. His head cleared as he rushed back and forth, snow in, logs out, back and forth.

"Utah! Adam!" He hoped the air was clearing some and they might wake up.

Neither of the men responded.

With the logs gone, Cam still had no tunnel out to fresh air, and with no more fire to melt snow or cast its red glow, he realized how smoky the room still was. He looked around, thinking, and saw a broom. He snagged it, rushed to the fireplace, and stepped inside. The rock floor of the chimney was cooled by the snow. He crouched to avoid the mantel and could nearly stand up straight in the narrowing chimney.

He poked the broom handle up and hit something solid. No snow fell. He didn't feel the chimney draw. Bracing his feet on either side of the fireplace, he climbed up as high as he could get before the chimney narrowed. He poked again and again, each jab harder, each more frantic. His thoughts became cloudy. His chest burned.

Something caught on the end of the broomstick. He yanked down, and a black

11

clump of something came down with it. And the smoke rushed past him — heat rising had found a way out. He coughed as he dropped to the floor and crawled out of the chimney. The smoke thinned enough that he thought it would clear out completely now. They were still buried, but not smothering anymore.

He ran to Utah's room. Utah slept like the dead.

And that wasn't a word Cam liked. He checked for a pulse in Utah's neck. It was there, but light and too slow.

Cam rushed to the window which, despite the melted spots, was still completely blocked, grabbed a handful of snow, took it, and rubbed it on Utah's face.

He yelped.

Cam dragged him by the leg off the bed to get him lower, to cleaner air. Utah growled as he hit the floor. Even with the smoke hopefully thinning, Utah needed every advantage he could get.

The cranky growl gave Cam hope.

"Wake up! The bunkhouse is full of smoke." Figuring Utah would make it, he ran for Adam's room, stopping to grab more snow.

"Get up, Adam, move!" he shouted. "We're trapped. The room's full of smoke, and the bunkhouse is buried in snow. We need to get out of here. On your feet!"

Adam rolled out of bed as Cam entered his room. By the time Cam was sure he was going to wake up, Utah came out crawling.

Utah's brain must've kicked in. "Dig in the window on the far side of the fireplace, the side near Adam's room. Last night, the snowdrifts were lowest on that side. Let's scoop out that way."

Cam grabbed his shovel. "The front door wasn't blocked last night. Why not go that way?"

"The wind was blowing in from that direction, and we'd scooped out a mighty thin path. It probably filled in deep."

Utah was still crawling. Adam moved faster, so he and Cam set to digging, throwing snow into the bunkhouse with no care for the cold they brought in.

"Cam, good thing you woke up, it saved us," Utah said as he grabbed another shovel and staggered to his feet.

"I got mighty lucky. It hit me about as hard as it hit you." He and Adam timed their digging to stay out of each other's way. And Utah got himself timed so he was scooping as fast as they were.

They all worked as hard as their aching chests and blurred vision would allow. The room began to clear some.

"The chimney was clogged — that's what made the room fill with smoke." Cam kept digging.

They dug on for long minutes, then Utah said, "The chimney on the cabin ain't any taller than the one we have."

The cabin . . .

Panic hit like a bolt of lightning. "My daughter and nephew are in that cabin!"

They all knew it. Cam's sister, Penny, was in there, too. And their boss, Trace; his wife, Deb; and her sister, Gwen.

Trace wasn't Cam's boss. Cam was here to get his daughter and nephew and take them home. That'd been his plan before he got trapped here in the first really big snowfall.

And before he'd found out his daughter and nephew hated him.

The hurt from that was like a wolf gnawing at his guts. And he was sure that pretty Gwen Harkness was doing things to the children so they'd keep hating him. Because she wanted those children for herself. The little kidnapper.

His digging went from hasty to frantic, and now it was salted with anger. Then the fear swept back over him. It didn't matter what he felt so long as it made him dig faster.

"They should be out there digging toward us if they're all right." Adam pushed his shovel deep into the wall of snow.

"Maybe not. We don't have one single idea what time it is."

Adam went out into the hole they'd dug and slashed at the huge drift. Suddenly he shouted, "I'm through!"

He dove forward and vanished through a hole in the snow. Light came in. It was past sunup, and the folks in the cabin should all be awake. If they were and could get out, they'd have seen the bunkhouse buried and come to help.

Cam's shovel went flying out next. Then he dove.

Adam was moving fast, and Cam figured Utah was only seconds behind him. He grabbed the shovel and got out of the way. Adam was wading through waist-deep snow. It was all powder-dry up here, blast it, and a man couldn't stay on top of it. But thanks to Utah, they'd found a spot the wind hadn't filled in quite so deep.

Cam rushed toward the cabin, only to see a massive drift that covered it over. From this angle he could just make out the tip of the chimney. It seemed clear and it

15

should've been okay, but there was no smoke coming out.

Utah charged past him and attacked the snow in a spot he must've picked out deliberately.

Cam followed and waded right in. "Why this spot?"

"That chimney should be belching smoke. No reason it's not. I think it's plugged. I'm digging to the corner. I can scamper up those crisscrossed logs to the roof and open the chimney."

"There was something in ours, and it wasn't snow. A bird died in there or something. I opened it up to clear smoke before I went to work getting you out of bed."

"Two birds?" Utah looked at Cam with fire in his eyes. "Two dead birds in two different chimneys on the same night?"

Cam scowled. "Not likely."

All three men worked on the corner. Utah hit it first.

"I don't need anyone else up on the roof." Utah was gone upward while Cam and Adam went for the back door.

"Let's get this door uncovered and opened!" Cam shouted the order, but Adam was already at it. Bad habit, being an officer.

A shout from overhead froze them worse

than the bitter cold. A shout of fear and pain.

CHAPTER 2

Cam rushed to the side of the cabin to see Utah falling, blazing like a torch. He landed in deep snow.

Cam fought his way to Utah. He got there and saw the fire had been doused by the snow. His coat was black, his beard singed.

"I seen him, Cam. I seen him!" Utah raved rather than talked. The breath had been knocked out of him, the explosion stunning. He struggled to get to his feet, but he was too confused to do anything.

"You saw who?" Cam grabbed him by one arm of his heavy buffalo coat and dragged him away from the cabin.

Utah shouted, "There's a fire in the cabin!"

You saw who?

Fire!

Cam tore back to the digging. Fire — he heard the crackle as flames ate their way through the small building.

What had Utah meant?

They dug toward the back door. If they could get to it, the door opened to a short hallway with the bedrooms on either side, and the hallway led to the main room where the fireplace was. If the fire started there, they still had a chance to save everyone.

The crackling grew to taunting laughter. A swirl of black smoke swept down from the roof. Cam prayed it was from the chimney and not a sign the roof had collapsed.

In the overcrowded cabin, his sister Penny slept on a bedroll in the front room. A sickening twist of his gut told him she'd die first. He dug all the faster. His shovel hit wood. "We're through! Clear the snow enough to get the door open."

Snow flew like fury from their shovels. They cleared the door enough to grip the latch. Trace had a sturdy one, front door and back.

Cam lifted it and it came free. Trace hadn't locked the door last night, and Cam counted that as a miracle because Trace was mindful of such things.

Cam shoved the door open and ran in. The black, choking smoke rushing for the newly opened door made seeing impossible. Every instinct in his soul told him to get his children first. But it had to be Penny. She was in the worst danger. He sprinted down the short hall, walls crawling with flames. They rolled over the wood like tiny orange waves.

He stepped out of the hallway into an inferno. The chimney and the floor around it were fully on fire. The flames were alive. Hungry, starving, eating their way along the walls, ceiling, and floor.

Cam took a few seconds to judge the room and saw a strange black object out on the burning floor in front of the fireplace, and the blackest wood seemed to be right on the floor as if that'd been on fire the longest. Maybe a log had rolled out of the fireplace, though by this hour of the morning that fire should've been down to embers.

"I seen him, Cam. I seen him."

Cam shook off the memory and turned to search for Penny in the dark room full of smoke.

Penny slept to the right side of the hallway, and the fireplace was to the left. Cam dropped to his knees and clawed his way to where Penny should be and found her still form. He gulped in the viciously hot air, better down low but still bad. He didn't try to wake her, although he longed for her to open those brown eyes so dark, like his own, and smile at him. He wanted her to say something grouchy, her usual tone. But there was no time for that.

He scooped Penny up, leapt to his feet, and charged for the back of the cabin. He sprinted down the hall, its walls now a column of fire, thinking of his children left behind. Then he burst outside, slipped on snow that was melting under the heat of the fire and turning to ice. He plunged toward the ground, twisting his body so he bore the brunt of the fall. Stunned, he forced himself to get up, keep moving. He placed Penny near Utah, both of them stretched out on a thin sheet of frigid water as the heat of the fire melted snow all around them. He shouldn't leave them in such a spot. The brutal cold would be deadly if they were soaked in the freezing wind. He'd seen plenty of men die from this kind of murderous cold.

He hoped Penny and Utah were far enough back in case the cabin collapsed, but he had no time to find someplace better. He had to get to Maddie Sue, still in the burning cabin.

Maddie Sue, his daughter! And his nephew, little Ronnie! He headed for the house and nearly slammed into Trace, who was running out with both children in his

21

arms. Trace and the children were coughing. The little ones were crying too, panic-stricken. Trace was hacking something awful and staggering.

Yet all three were alive.

Cam plucked the children away from Trace and took them to where Penny lay. He set them down, sick about leaving them in the bitter cold and icy water, but he had to get everyone else out. The four of them out here were soaked, him too. Cold with wet clothes on was as deadly as fire, though a slower way to die.

Utah gave Cam a sharp look and spoke with a voice that rasped like gravel. "I'll see to them. Get the rest out."

"We need to move everyone to the bunkhouse!" Cam shouted over the roaring fire. "Dried off, warmed up."

Utah began coughing again. Cam couldn't stop and help. He took off running again and met Adam carrying Deb, with an arm slung around Trace's waist. Trace stumbled and was close to collapsing.

Adam shouted, "The roof's caving in!" A part of the ceiling hit Trace on the head. "Gwen's still in there! The whole cabin is going!"

Cam dashed in to find Gwen. She was in the bedroom — unconscious, unmoving.

22

Cam scooped her up and turned. Pieces of timber rained down in the hallway behind him, striking him with each step he took.

He got outside to see Adam stumble and sink to one knee, hacking and coughing so hard he couldn't pull in a breath. Trace went down with him, flat on his face, soaked with frigid water. Then Trace shoved himself up, took his wife, and carried her away from the flames. Cam dragged Adam to his feet.

Without a woman to carry, Adam found the strength to stand just as Cam reached him.

A roar from behind them turned Cam's head to see the roof cave in. Flames drove out the door with explosive force.

Cinders slashed like shrapnel and knocked Cam, Gwen, and Adam to the ground. The fire stung Cam's back and legs like a swarm of bees. He smelled burning hair as he staggered to his feet, still clinging to Gwen.

Fire danced up the back of Adam's coat. Cam juggled Gwen to free a hand and rip Adam's coat off. Cam threw the coat on the ground to extinguish it. Then he caught Adam by the arm, still hanging on to Gwen, and dragged them all forward. He collapsed in sooty, blackened ice water by the other wounded.

There was sudden shouting as hands

pounded on him. He heard Trace scream, "Your hair's on fire!"

Trace grabbed snow in both hands and plowed it into the back of Cam's head.

Gwen was gone from him. Cam was pushed face-first into the icy slush, then grappling hands tore his coat away and turned him onto his back. He shivered violently, even with the blazing cabin close by. He was soaked front and back in ice water. A stiff breeze froze his fingers and face, and the rest of his body chilled with shocking speed.

He looked at the whirlwind of hurt and scared people. In all the action, Penny and Gwen lay motionless. Then Gwen coughed. It was deep and sounded painful, but it was a sign of life. Penny remained still as death.

Trace hauled Cam to his feet. "Your hair, your coat, most of your back were on fire."

Cam's blue army coat was shoved back into his hands and he pulled it on, even though it was as wet and cold as he was. He realized no one from the cabin had a coat.

Everyone on Trace's ranch slept fully clothed and kept their boots on to battle the cold. But the men in the bunkhouse had grabbed their coats. No one from the cabin was given a chance.

"We have to get the children warm."

Adam turned toward the bunkhouse, then stopped and looked back. "We put the fire out in there."

Cam's eyes went to Maddie Sue, shivering. Water dripped from her clothes. Ronnie was soaking wet and sobbing, his lips blue. Maddie Sue wrapped her arms around her little three-year-old body, shaking, crying. Cam met Adam's eyes, judged him to be fully alert, picked up Penny, and handed her over.

Cam noticed his sister had the leather bag she always carried slung over her neck and under one arm. She must sleep with it on. "Get her inside. She hasn't shown any sign of waking up, not even coughing." She was alive, though — he'd felt her breathing.

Adam took her and started running. Cam picked up Maddie Sue in one arm, Ronnie in the other. He rushed toward the bunkhouse as Maddie Sue clung to him and wept. For once, she was too upset to be terrified of him.

Deb shoved to her feet, stumbled but caught herself, then went after Adam, who slipped through the window carrying Penny into the smothering grave they'd just recently escaped.

Cam shivered until he could barely hang on to his little girl.

25

Deb climbed through the snow tunnel and dragged herself inside. Cam hated letting Maddie Sue go, but he handed her inside to Deb, then passed Ronnie through and turned back to see who needed help next.

Trace was on his hands and knees, still coughing and fighting for air. Cam rushed back to drag Trace to his feet and help him to the bunkhouse.

Utah was still on the ground and struggling to breathe. Cam suspected the older man was only partly conscious. Cam went to his side and helped him to his feet. It flitted through his mind, the brief talk he'd had with Utah that it was strange both chimneys were clogged.

"I seen him, Cam."

Cam was very afraid he knew what that meant. Then he remembered his little girl's weight and the strength of her cries. It all meant she was wonderfully alive and unhurt. Scared to death, miserable with cold, but alive. All of them were. Everything else could be fixed.

Which made him think of Penny. He prayed hard that he was right about them all being alive. He swept Gwen up in his arms, dragged Utah's arm around his neck, and headed toward the bunkhouse. The older man had a glazed look in his eyes.

"Get yourself through the window," Cam ordered. "Are you able?"

Utah nodded. Cam followed him in with Gwen limp in his arms. Soon all of them were inside, and a fire flickered to life in the chimney. Adam rolled the hard lump aside that Cam had knocked loose.

Trace closed the shutters to keep out the cold. As Utah sagged to his knees, Cam noticed the man's burns. He was singed all down his front.

"We need to get out of these wet clothes," Trace said.

" 'Ceptin' you don't have any dry ones," Adam said and knelt to add logs to the fire. "But I've got two changes. Mine'll fit you, Trace."

Adam's eyes went to the women and children. "Uh, I got another spare shirt. I can leave my wet clothes on awhile."

"Utah got blown off the roof by an explosion that came out of the chimney." Cam was worried about him. How deep did his burns go? "Adam, you're in the best shape."

That wasn't quite right. Cam was probably in the best shape, but he had a lot to do, and right now giving orders sped everything up.

"Help Utah into his room to get dry clothes on, then get him to bed. Check his burns. I don't think they're serious, but the explosion and fall stunned him bad. He needs to get off his feet."

Adam helped a feebly protesting Utah from the room.

"Trace, get changed fast. Deb, you look steady, get blankets from the bedrooms." Cam needed a dry outfit too, but not yet. "Deb, you, Gwen, and Penny are going to be wearing pants until your dresses dry. Let's get the children wrapped up and get some hot food into them. Utah made a big pot of soup last night — I'll start it heating."

The fire was just flickering to life. So strange, fire had nearly killed them, and now it would save them.

Cam nodded at a pile of snow inside the first shuttered window that he'd dug in but not gotten through. "The soup's under there."

"I'll get it," Trace said, coming out of Utah's bedroom with dry clothes on, carrying a stack of clothing. He coughed as he dug up the pot and hung it over the fire, now blazing.

Deb emerged from Cam's room with blankets.

Studying the fireplace and then their goodly store of food, Cam said, "Deb, tend the children while I see to Penny and Gwen."

He knelt down between the two, who lay close to the fire, both still unconscious.

Deb picked up the children, one in each arm, both wet and freezing, and started heading toward Cam's room. "How are they?" she asked.

Cam looked up at her. "They're breathing at least. Is there anything we can do for them?"

"Gwen always did most of the doctoring." Shaking her head, her face twisted with worry, Deb said, "Let them breathe clean air and warm up as best they can. I'll get myself and the children changed, then you men will have to leave while I get them into dry clothes." Her brow furrowed as she studied her sister and Penny.

Maddie Sue reached for Gwen and fought to get free of Deb's hold.

Trace got up and took Maddie from her. "You go, Deb. Get changed, then come back and help with the young'uns."

With one last near-frantic look at Gwen, Deb vanished through the door, closing it behind her.

By the time Trace had urged the youngsters closer to the fire and sheltered them with blankets, she was back, looking shocking in pants, even though Cam was used to seeing Penny in them. Trace's pretty, brown-haired wife looked all wrong in those trousers.

Trace held a blanket high to protect the children's modesty. Deb worked behind it and threw the wet clothes toward the hearth. Then Trace cuddled them both in the blanket while Deb straightened the clothes so they'd dry faster.

"As long as the clothes are already wet, they should be washed," Deb said, looking overwhelmed. "Everyone's should. We all reek of smoke, and no one's coughing is going to get better if we're breathing foul air."

"No time for washing clothes right now." Trace held the children in his arms while Deb rubbed their feet vigorously to warm them.

Adam came out from tending Utah and made coffee.

Gwen tossed her head, flipping her wet, bedraggled blond hair as she moaned. It was the first time she'd moved beyond coughing. Cam's heart lifted so high it surprised him.

A bit later Penny coughed and, harsh as the sound was, it was a thing of beauty to Cam. Her cough joined everyone else's. They all did their share of coughing, but

30

the unconscious women had it the worst.

As time passed, the worst of the chill was cut from the room. The children both started fussing and reaching for Gwen. A pot of snow was set near the fire to melt for wash water. The men left then so that Deb could tend to clothing for Gwen and Penny. Cam was back as soon as Deb allowed it. Then Deb rushed back to the children and held them as they cried for Gwen, their favorite. The heartbroken sobs filled the room.

It must mean the worst was over, because Cam was struck with jealousy over how much the children loved Gwen . . . and hated him. He'd had no time for jealousy before now.

The coffee began to boil. The smells of the beefy stew and steaming gravy added to the coffee and lifted Cam's spirits. They all took turns eating.

Before long, Ronnie cried himself to sleep in Deb's arms. And Maddie Sue looked heavy-lidded and began to fuss.

Trace picked Ronnie up and helped Deb to her feet. "Is it safe to put him to bed?" he asked.

Worried, Deb studied Ronnie's toes, then Maddie Sue's. "They were blue before, but now they look healthy and pink. They've stopped shivering."

Cam said, "By now the rooms are warm enough. Use mine." He watched his daughter being tended by someone other than him. Maddie Sue loved Gwen best, yet she adored Deb and was right fond of Trace. Penny had even found her way into the children's hearts.

The little ones liked Adam and Utah, too. It was only Cam who was the problem. He'd started things off on the wrong foot by being so overwhelmingly relieved to find them alive and well, he'd been loud and abrupt and tried to take them home with him the minute he got his hands on them.

And in the process he'd scared them half to death. But that was months ago. Why did they still hate him now? He was doing something wrong, but he didn't know what, and he didn't know how to change whatever it was.

What it came down to was . . . he knew nothing about children.

Trace took Ronnie to Cam's bedroom.

Deb walked the floor with Maddie Sue cradled in her arms and sang quietly over the sounds of the little girl's tears and the coughing women.

Cam thought of all he'd done wrong when he first found the children and decided it

came down to something simple.
He was an idiot.

CHAPTER 3

It was the hacking cough that woke her.

There was chaos. Motion, noise, coughing. Then she realized she was the one coughing. Only not just her. Her mind was fuzzy, and the activity around her had a dreamlike quality to it.

Her first thought, when she had one, was the children.

"Maddie Sue? Ronnie?" Coughing stopped her from saying more. She covered her mouth with the side of her fist. Her chest burned. Her throat was raw, and each cough was agony. She fought to stop, but she was too weak to make her body do anything.

A strong hand slid behind her shoulders and eased her up a bit, not so she fully sat up, but close. A glass pressed to her lips. She coughed and fought the hard rim of the glass, afraid to swallow, afraid the cool water would slice down her throat like a razor.

The strong hand persisted. A deep voice said, "Try and swallow. It might ease the coughing."

Cameron Scott, the man who'd come to steal her children.

She glanced to see his face, his worry etched there. Worry for her. His dark brown eyes met hers for a single moment. His dark hair, which hadn't been cut since he'd arrived, tangled almost to his collar.

The tin cup — that's what it was — pressed to her lips again. The water hit her tongue. Her mouth was so dry it seemed to soak up the small swallow so the water did not even reach her throat. She coughed.

Cam was her enemy, and every night she prayed fervently that she'd wake up in the morning to find out he'd rejoined the army and traipsed off to abandon his children once again.

Then she'd get up and start the day, and there he was.

His voice was too loud, his manner too abrupt. He treated everyone like soldiers under his command. That included his daughter, Maddie Sue, little Ronnie, and very definitely it included Gwen.

Cam's daughter hated him . . . a harsh thing to say, but facts were facts. Little

Maddie Sue didn't want him anywhere near her.

Gwen could see the hurt in his eyes. She had to steel her heart against it. He made that quite easy by being such a grouch.

"Try another sip. It will help." He was being really gentle and kind right now. He wasn't barking out an order that she drink. Instead his voice was soft and coaxing.

"My throat." She croaked like a bullfrog. And most bullfrogs would be offended by the comparison. "H-Hurt." She raised her hands to cradle her throat.

A second swallow reached the injured throat tissue and stopped the coughing long enough for her to get the water down. Another drink. This one she cooperated with and got a fair amount of water down. She felt it bathe her throat all the way to her stomach.

"What happened? Are the children all right? Where's D-Deb?" The coughing took over again.

"Don't try to talk. Everyone's fine." He gave her another drink. "There was a fire in your cabin. We got you out barely ahead of the flames."

"I-I don't remember."

"You were unconscious from inhaling smoke. You might never have even realized

36

what was happening."

He snuck in more water. So long as he kept pouring slowly, with many breaks so she could breathe, the coughing stayed back, helping her battered throat.

"You inhaled all that smoke. Penny's just now waking up. You two were the worst off. But we all got out — everyone's going to be fine. We're in the bunkhouse, and for now we're staying in here. The young'uns fell asleep. Deb and Trace took them into my bedroom to tuck them in."

"Penny?" Gwen wasn't thinking clearly yet. "Did the fire start from the chimney? Penny was much closer to it than I was."

"Yes, but we got her out."

A rough cough from beside her made Gwen push the cup back so she could turn her head and see Penny, her face black with smoke, her brown hair in a wild tangle. She was struggling to breathe. Gwen suspected her own appearance was the same.

Without the steady flow of water, Gwen started hacking again. Her throat hurt so badly, Gwen nearly wept.

Her eyes blinked fully open, and she saw Cam kneeling beside her, his arm around her. He was strong enough that he could hold her up with his right arm, his hand free. He caught her chin in a firm two-fingered grip and went back to forcing her to drink.

Right now, it felt like the only way she'd ever feel decent was to keep water trickling down her throat for the rest of her life. And as her thoughts cleared more with each passing moment, she started to think of all she needed to do.

"Stay down there." Cam wasn't quick enough, because Gwen was already up.

She wobbled a bit. He was on his feet, steadying her in seconds.

"You need to —"

She slapped her hand over his mouth.

Six months ago, he'd've court-martialed her for that. If she'd been a soldier under his command, of course.

Which she most certainly was not.

She used the other hand to swipe the tin cup from him and sipped. She studied the bunkhouse. When she turned back, he really saw her.

Gwen was a pretty little thing as a rule. But right now, her face was a sooty mess. Her hair was so knotted and scraggly it looked like it'd been combed by the claws of a rabid wolverine.

It flashed through his head that he might not look much better.

He'd washed up. His face and hands were clean, but even with that he might look worse than she did. To get Gwen out of the icy cold and wet clothes she wore, Deb had changed her into a pair of Cam's pants and one of his shirts.

An odd warmth swept through him to think of her wearing his clothes. It wasn't something he understood or had ever felt before, but it drove back his worry for the first time since the silence woke him.

She had the sleeves rolled up. Deb had stitched a quick hem in the pant legs. Penny was the same, except she wore trousers most of the time so they didn't look so shocking on her.

That left Cam with no clothes to wear. It was only sheerest luck he even had a change of clothes. He'd planned to spend a day fetching his children home and had only packed a change of clothes out of old habit to prepare for delays. Now his change of clothes was on that little child-stealing pest Gwen Harkness. It made no sense that he liked it.

He was still in the filthy, wet clothes he'd had on during the fire. But the bunkhouse, with a snowdrift for insulation, was warm, and his clothes were drying slowly, so he ignored his own condition to get everyone else cared for.

Between all the men, there was just barely one clean outfit for everyone. And it would take a long, hard day of laundry to get the women back in their dresses. The water was already heating.

"Gwen, we need to get you to bed." He caught her around the waist and swooped her up into his arms.

She sipped water and glared at him, then almost like an act of courage she held the cup away from her lips. "Put me down."

He obeyed as if a general had taken the field.

Once on her feet, she sipped again. "I see soup on the fire. A warm bowl would be just the thing to soothe my throat." She still croaked, but she was doing it with some spirit now. "And if it'd help me, it'd help Penny. I hear more coughing coming from the bedrooms. I need to get to work."

It flashed through his thoughts that he'd liked her better when she was unconscious.

"Let me up!" A roar from one of the bedrooms whirled Gwen around.

Utah charged out.

"What in heaven's name happened to you?" She'd been unconscious when she came in, and he'd been gone when she woke

40

up. His beard was burned black, and so was his hair, his face. Singed, she guessed. He must've run right through the fire.

Utah gave her a curious glance at her question, then hollered again, "Trace, get in here! Cam, Adam, pay attention."

Adam came running out of the room Utah had been in, as if he'd let his prisoner escape. "You're supposed to be resting."

"Shut up, everyone."

The children both erupted into wails in the bedroom to the north of Utah's. They came running out and threw themselves against Gwen's legs.

With a grunt from the impact, she staggered, then Cam caught her to keep her from going over in a tumble. She rested both hands on the little ones' heads, buried against these shocking trousers while she waited to see what had upset Utah so badly.

Utah rolled his eyes heavenward. "Well, maybe not them."

"Will you quit yelling?" Trace hissed, as if it weren't way too late to be quiet. "You're scaring Maddie Sue and Ronnie." Trace came out of the children's room with Deb right behind him.

Deb picked Maddie Sue up, and she squirmed and shouted, "Gemma!"

So far that was her word for Gwen. Ronnie

shouted it too, through his tears, reaching up for Gwen and bouncing as if he could leap into her arms.

Cam got a chair from the table and moved it by Gwen. He set it down with a firm thump and urged her into it. She picked up Ronnie and then reached out her arm. Maddie Sue threw herself at Gwen. Deb controlled the leap and settled Maddie Sue in Gwen's lap.

"I had my wits knocked clean out from falling off that roof, but my head's cleared enough I can tell you what I saw. Someone set that fire. Someone plugged the chimneys of both our cabins."

"I had to knock something out of this chimney, figured it was a dead bird." Then Cam remembered. "You said it before. You said how neither smokestack was buried in snow, and two birds sure as certain didn't dive into those chimneys and die at the same time."

"Yep, no chance of that happenin' by accident. But that's not what I remembered just now. I climbed up on that roof, and there was someone up there, just dropping something down. I think it was oil or kerosene or something. He plugged up both chimneys hoping it'd knock everyone out, then he set that fire. He'd've been back to burn ours down next. I saw . . ." Utah faltered in the telling of his story, his eyes narrowed. "I could swear I saw him sliding along on his feet like he was skating off the roof."

The room fell silent. The whimpering children were the only sounds in the room.

"Skating off the roof?" Gwen asked. "How can a man skate off a roof?"

"Let me think." Utah stared through the floor, looking into his memory. "Uh, what was on his feet? I climbed up there, and he was just dropping something. He had . . . he had another thing in his hand, not a lantern but a tin can. I think it was an extra one he had planned for the bunkhouse. He'd already maybe poured out some kerosene down the chimney, and he planned to use the rest on us. But he heard us coming and dropped it all into the cabin and ran."

Utah rubbed his beard, then jumped. He took hold of his whiskers, considerably shorter and blacker. "What happened to my beard?"

"It caught fire," Cam said. "You came off that roof like a torch. Landing in the deep snow put out the flames, or you'd've burned to death."

"Your beard is almost gone and bristly black." Gwen knew they all looked nearly as bad. Though most everyone — at least everyone who'd been conscious — had washed their faces and hands. "You barely have eyebrows, and the front of your hair is mostly gone. Your coat and probably your beard protected your skin long enough for the fire to go out."

"We've got to go after him."

"He's long gone, Utah," Adam said. "You've been passed out, or close to it, for over an hour."

Cam snapped, "We can track him." Cam headed for the window they could get out of, Utah right on his heels.

"Hold it right there," Trace interrupted. "We can read his signs, but we aren't going out on a long hike after that coyote."

Cam blinked, looking confused. "You don't want to catch the man who tried to murder every man, woman, and child among us?"

"That's not what I meant when I said *coyote*. Who around here do we know who's nothing but pure coyote?"

Deb plunked a fist on each hip. "Raddo Landauer, the man who led the massacre on the wagon train that killed everyone but Gwen, the children, and me. We've had him after us for a while, and he's always used a sneak attack. The worst kind of back-shooting, murderous dry-gulcher. Nothing but a low-down coward."

"And you, Deb," Trace said, "are the one who witnessed him burning that wagon train."

"You didn't witness the wagon train murders, Trace, but you saw him later and he knows it."

"He followed them back here, then kidnapped Deb," Gwen told Cam. They'd talked about this before, but now to think Raddo was back . . .

"He planned to use her to bait a trap for Trace." Gwen had almost lost her sister just the day before Cam and Penny had come for the children and gotten trapped by a blizzard. Raddo had sent one of his gang members to kidnap her, planning to force Trace to make a rescue attempt so he could be killed. Deb was the only witness to Raddo's murder at the wagon train. He would've killed her, too.

"Raddo! You're talking about the man who killed my brother? He's behind this?" Cam surged toward the window. "I won't be back until he's in my hands. Or dead."

Gwen knew Trace was a runner, but she'd never seen him move quite this fast. He dove at Cam and had him tackled flat to the floor.

The children whimpered and clung to Gwen, their faces buried against the front of her shirt.

"You just hold on. You're not charging out in snow deeper than a house by yourself. We go together. We learn what we can from his tracks, and unless we can figure out where he's going and it's close, we come back here and make plans."

Maddie Sue peeked out in fear at the tussling men. She saved her woeful glances for Cam, her papa. Gwen wanted to take the children out of the room — this was scaring them.

"You're being a hothead." Trace let Cam go but blocked the closed shutters by pressing his back against them, his arms crossed. "And that's not like you. Whoever did this, and it sure might be Raddo, could be holed up right now with a rifle trained right on the tracks he knows he left. If we follow his trail, the tracks could lead us straight to an ambush. This varmint didn't plan on a single one of us living through this, but by the time he ran, he knew Utah was alive and had to figure it was at least possible that everyone in the bunkhouse had gotten free and was coming to rescue us in the cabin. He started that fire to kill —"

"Trace!" Deb cut her husband off.

He gave the children an uneasy look, then glanced at Deb, nodded, and clamped his mouth shut.

CHAPTER 4

Deb urged the children out of Gwen's arms and into her own, then turned to leave the room.

Gwen wanted to go with them. She was a dab hand at calming the little ones. But she was still a bit woozy, able to function but not at the strength it'd take to mind two upset children. Besides, she liked watching Trace push Cameron Scott around.

"I'll go." Penny dragged herself up from the floor. Gwen lent her a steadying hand.

Penny caught up to Deb and the children. "The men can do their scrapping, and when they calm down, maybe we can plan how to live — all of us — in this one small building."

Penny went into the bedroom without relieving Deb of either child, which told Gwen how battered Penny was feeling, because she always did her share and more. Gwen thought of calling for her to wash up

48

a bit, but Penny might not be up to it. Which reminded Gwen that she was no doubt just as sooty.

When Deb closed the door, Gwen heaved a sigh of relief and stood, careful to make sure she didn't fall on her face. She headed to the washbasin. Washing turned the water black. With no mirror, Gwen couldn't begin to guess if she was decently clean. Her hair straggled across her vision, and it didn't even look blond, it was so dirty.

For now, she ignored the rest of her appearance and went back to watch the cranky men, glad Deb had gone out. The children didn't need to hear of such dreadful things as massacres, especially because it might remind them of how Ronnie's parents had died.

The children hadn't witnessed anything. They'd hidden in the tall grass when the massacre hit their wagon train. Deb had gone back alone to try to see the attackers. Deb knew she couldn't fight three armed men, but she could bear witness to their brutal crimes. Gwen had taken the children as far from the gunfire as she could, afraid the little ones would cry out and lead the killers into the grass where Deb and Gwen hid with the babies.

Trace still had his back to the wall, blocking the only way out. He said, "I agree we have to go, Cam. But calm down first. We need to think, and you were running out of here without a coat on. You don't have your rifle or your pistol. Think, man."

Cam nodded. "You're right — about all of it. Sorry." He rubbed one hand over his face. "I just came away from war. First the Civil War, then the frontier. I sleep light and have a gut instinct for trouble. That's what woke me up and got us out of here, but the same reflex to dive in fighting just about sent me into that snow unarmed. I'm a fool. I'm sorry I made it necessary for you to knock me down."

A smile quirked Trace's lips. "It's all right, Cam. I kinda enjoyed it."

Cam went and threw out the water in the basin, refilled it with hot water from a bucket tucked into the hearth, and as he scrubbed, one corner of his mouth turned up in a grudging smile. It even reached his eyes for a single moment before Cam turned grim again.

"I left the cavalry after six years of almost nonstop fighting. I wanted nothing but peace. I wanted to be a rancher somewhere, run some cattle. My real hope is to raise fine horses and train them well, to sell them. Now here I am, my brother dead, my sister-in-law dead. My little nephew orphaned. My daughter with no idea who I am except a man who scares her." His voice broke. Or maybe he just fell silent as he washed his face and hands a second time.

Gwen thought his voice broke. So rather than quit talking because he was out of things to say, he just couldn't go on. But that was a silly thought. Cam didn't have a soft side anywhere. He wasn't a man to start in weeping over his hurt feelings.

She thought of how gently he'd lifted her and urged her to drink. Maybe he did have a softer side. She should help him show that side to his children, but she didn't want them to like him. She wanted them for herself.

And that struck her as the most selfish thing a person could think. Had she done anything to help him get closer to his children? Or, she thought with shame, had she made it worse?

Trace stood away from the shutters. He went to the table that had been shoved aside from its regular place by the fire. Straightening it and fetching chairs, he sat.

"Let's do some thinking." He looked at Gwen. "We've only got four chairs, baby sister."

She grinned. Trace had called her that

some since he'd married her big sister, Deb.

He went on. "We don't mean to leave you out. I can sit on the floor if you —"

Gwen held up a hand to halt him. "I really could stand to get off my feet a bit longer. But rather than sit, I think I'll go help the women plan how we're going to live in this small space while you figure out how we're going to stay alive with a madman lurking in snow higher than the cabins."

"One thing about snow," Cam said as Gwen left the room, "it's mighty hard to hide your tracks."

Gwen turned back to take one more look at the motley crew. They'd been through a lot today. Trace and Adam were still hacking. Utah, good heavens, he'd been on fire! "Whatever you tough men decide to do, you shouldn't be outside until you've stopped coughing. Make sure you haven't injured yourselves while you were fighting for your lives. Utah, you most of all need to have those burns looked at. You should let me bandage them before you go outside. For goodness' sake, will you all just sit for a spell and recover?"

She left the room, figuring they'd head for the shuttered window before she had the door fully shut.

The last thing she heard before she left

was Cam say, "Sorry I lost my head. It makes me killing mad to think of my brother's killer running loose."

A fist slammed on the table, and Gwen looked over her shoulder to see Cam rising to his feet. "Abe shouldn't've even been on that wagon train. Delia's parents, Florence and Edmond Chilton, hounded Abe and Delia out of the country. They're as responsible for my brother's death as Raddo."

"Edmond, Delia is dead." Florence Chilton rushed into the office of her Philadelphia mansion, blurting out that bald truth.

She flapped the letter, which appeared to be written on . . . was it bloodstained? It looked like the paper the butcher wrapped meat in. She had little knowledge of butchers, of course. And it was written with a pencil, as if whoever wrote it was too ignorant of writing to use proper paper, pen, and ink.

Shaking her head, she threw it on Edmond's desk, glad to quit touching it.

"Dead, our daughter?" Edmond stared at the letter as if he couldn't bear to read it. "Our only child is dead?"

Breathless from the uncommon stress of running from the front hall, Florence gave Edmond a minute to absorb the information while she caught her breath.

And to grieve, of course. Yes, it was sad. . . . But, really, they'd had little or nothing to do with Delia since she'd betrayed them. The foolish girl had run off with their stableboy, Abe Scott, and they'd never let her forget it. They'd worked hard to break up the marriage after Delia and Abe's reckless elopement, and Florence had tried to convince Delia of the error of her ways many times.

They'd blocked any decent employment for her low-class husband. A few whispered words and many people who owned apartments and homes for rent had closed their doors to the newlyweds.

They'd been prepared to deny any requests for money from Delia unless she left her husband and came home. Their stubborn daughter had never come to ask. Florence had direly predicted Delia would come to a bad end. As usual, she was right.

"What are we going to do?" Edmond asked.

Florence had done most of the thinking for the two of them throughout their marriage, so this question wasn't unexpected.

"I read only the beginning," Edmond said. "Does it tell you where the boy is?"

"The writer, Deb Harkness, mentions a

town called Dismal, Nevada, and a man's name, Trace Riley. She says our grandson is there. This Trace Riley saved Ronnie." Florence sniffed. "The child's name is Cameron, but they call him Ronnie. I hate one name as much as the other. Cameron was Abe's ruffian brother, remember? Indians attacked Delia's wagon train."

"Indians? I didn't see that in the letter." Edmond picked it up and read.

"It says massacre. Who else does a thing like that?" Florence plunked her fists on her ample hips. "This letter is dated last fall and was sent from Nevada."

"I've never heard of Nevada. I have no idea where that is." Shaking his head, he looked to Florence, and she saw desperation in his eyes . . . which she herself felt.

Her husband, handsome years ago but now run to fat — a sign of prosperity, and she was just as proud of her own girth — rose from his heavy leather chair behind the massive oak desk. This house, the furniture, and the money to care for it had all come from her parents. When her mother finally died, Edmond and she had moved out of the smaller mansion her parents had given her when she married, and into here.

Florence tried to think logically. "Wherever Nevada is, we can't go ourselves. We'd be massacred by wild savages just as Delia was." Her real thoughts were of how uncomfortable long train rides were. "But we need to get the boy — we're his guardians now, his closest relation."

"That letter is from a woman who rode west with Delia and Abe. And she mentions our grandson's uncle. This Harkness woman also sent for him." Edmond returned to the letter and studied it more closely. Reading had never been his greatest strength.

"An uncle isn't as close a relation as a grandparent." Florence wasn't sure of that, but it stood to reason.

"He's Maddie Sue's father. That little girl who lived with Delia. But the uncle is in the frontier army. He won't want either child."

Florence kept on with her planning. "In case he decides he wants his own child and takes our grandson too, we need to beat him to little Cameron. Although the man won't want a stray child, and of course he has no knowledge of the child's inheritance. I'll send a note to the Pinkerton Agency right now. They can send someone out to fetch Ronnie."

Florence took a sheet of paper from Edmond's desk and scribbled out a request. They'd had occasion before to use Pinkerton agents, so she knew just where to send her note.

She found a boy loitering out in front of their house. There were always errand boys trying to earn a penny. They were mindful of the rich neighborhood and the mansions that could afford to pay.

The boy ran off with her note.

The only real money they had left was from Delia's trust fund, which they'd never told her about. Hard to bring a girl under a parent's control if she knew she'd inherit a fortune when she turned twenty-five. A birthday she had celebrated over two years ago.

A fortune that should have been Florence's if not for her wealthy mother who thought some money had to be designated strictly for Delia. A lawyer had wrapped that trust up so tight, Florence couldn't touch it. Unless of course she was raising Delia's son.

She went back inside lest the neighbors peek out of their curtains at her. She hoped none of them got wind of the financial struggles at the Chilton home. Delia's inheritance was their only way to salvation.

She mentally urged that boy to run faster, faster, faster.

CHAPTER 5

The minute Gwen swung the door shut, Cam headed for his rifle over the front door.

The rest of the men were just a step behind him — grabbing their coats, which had been drying beside the fire, and slipping into their rooms to quietly get their guns. Everyone was well armed. There was even a spare pistol, so Trace could have one. Cam didn't know if Deb and Gwen could shoot, but Penny sure as certain could. She had a gun in that leather bag she'd had hanging around her neck when he dragged her out of the fire.

It annoyed Cam that Trace got to the window first. Trace opened the shutters and climbed out. The rest of the men followed, one after the other. Utah came out last. He silently swung the window shut.

"I need a long gun," Trace muttered, hoping the women wouldn't hear him. "Mine's burned to a cinder."

"I've got another pistol in my room," Cam said as they hustled toward the burning ruins of the cabin, "but the women need it for protection."

Utah snorted. "As if that's why you didn't go in there."

The women would've caught him for sure.

They paused to look at the smoldering remains of the cabin. The sides and roof had collapsed and burned nearly to ash. The chimney stood like a tower in the center of the wreckage.

"I just finished building that cabin." Utah sounded like a wounded mountain lion, right down to the snarl and the bared teeth.

"No shortage of forest," Trace said, sounding disgruntled but resigned. "The Sierra Nevada Mountains have a way of teaching a man to pick himself up and go on, no matter the trouble."

"Gonna be a tight squeeze in that bunkhouse." Adam sounded worried. "That's the first time in my life I ever slept in a room by myself. I shoulda known it couldn't last."

"Once the embers cool from the cabin, I can get the cast-iron skillet out of there and some pots. Other things will have survived." Trace kicked at the snow. "I reckon my books are all burned to a cinder, too."

"I've got one, Trace," Cam said. "Remem-

59

ber you loaned it to me?"

"Me too." Adam rounded the cabin toward the deep snow, where Utah said the man had seemed to fly off the roof. "In fact, I have two. And one of them is your Bible."

"Yep, that's right. I'm glad not to lose that. You've got a couple, don't you, Utah?"

"One, and I ain't no reader so it's a wonder. You nagged me into picking it out of the box a couple of days ago, and your box was gettin' low. Sometimes a really thick book don't burn too well. Didn't your Bible have some char marks on it?"

"Yep, I found it in a burned-out wagon." Trace looked again at the smoldering ruins. "Maybe some of them survived. I hope so."

Trace looked around, assessing things. He was the owner of the High Sierra Ranch. But on the HS they all worked together, so when one of them had a problem, they all had a problem.

"It looks like the chimney's gonna stand," Adam said from the far side of the ruins. "Maybe if you rebuild on the same spot, you can use it again."

"Maybe." Trace frowned, looking glum, like a man expecting the worst.

Cam figured that here in the West, expecting the worst was usually just plain good sense.

"It's late in the winter, too," Utah added. "We could have a thaw soon."

"It's gonna be a long time melting," Cam said. "Ice Eater Winds are likely a month away."

"Ice Eater?" Trace looked up, his brow furrowed. "Never heard of that."

"The spring winds. Some call them chinooks."

"I heard of that one," Utah said.

Trace nodded. "I know about warm winds that blow over the mountains from the west."

"They named them after the Chinook Indians. I served in the army in the mountains around Oregon and Washington where the Chinook live. Those folks called the winds Ice Eaters, but in the army they'd taken to calling them 'chinook winds.' Those warm winds change things real quick."

"When the spring winds blow warm, the snow shrinks fast. Even so, there's a mighty big pile of snow." Trace looked behind him.

They all turned to study the bunkhouse with snow over the roof, packed in front, sides, and back. Cam shook his head at the little tunnel where they'd dug their way out. The chimney on the bunkhouse stuck well above the snow, and smoke curled out of it.

"That snow's gonna keep the bunkhouse

as warm as if we'd wrapped it in a buffalo robe," Trace said. "I'm in no hurry to dig it out."

"We might not have to wait for a thaw," Utah said. "The wind piled this snow in here overnight. One of these days we'll get a wind that sweeps it clean just as fast."

"It's gonna have to bring a mighty big broom," Trace said.

The snow had melted into slush, blackened with ashes. The drift that had formed around the cabin was pouring water still from the heat, but freezing as it flowed away. It formed an icy slick, making every step dangerous.

"A man seemed to go skating off the roof, Utah, is that what you said?" Adam had walked to the far side of the cabin's remains.

"Yep." Utah quit looking around and started moving.

Cam chafed because he liked to lead.

Trace's dog came running up from nowhere. The dog was a wolf, first and last, and he slept outside. But he hunted his own food and was gone for long stretches at a time. Cam wondered if he ran with other wolves part of the time.

Wolf hadn't shown himself during the fire, and the dog had the courage of a whole pack of wolves, so he'd've been here working to save his old friend Trace if he'd known. He was here now and paid little attention to the burned-out house, only fell in beside Trace to join their hunting party.

There was a crater formed from the massive snowdrifts melting around the cabin. The drifts that had nearly buried them were still there about ten feet back from the ashes, high and harder than ever to climb because the edges had become sheets of ice. The drift had melted and frozen again.

Adam pointed to the top of it, only visible because it sloped upward awhile. "See those two dents in the snow? They're the same depth, and they run alongside each other."

"Yep, that's where the man landed," Utah said. "Or at least I think so — I was probably being blown up about the same time he hit the ground."

Adam punched a fist in the ice coating the snow, broke through it, and had a decent handhold.

Cam shook his head. Trace was about the same age as Adam, and he started climbing next. Something about those kids tackling that ice wall without a thought made him feel every one of his twenty-seven years . . . and maybe a decade tacked on after that.

He got to the top of the drift after everyone else. Even Utah beat him. They were all standing and staring at the lines cut into the snow, yet Cam hadn't gotten a good look at them until now.

"I know what this is." Cam's eyes followed the parallel lines as they moved off into the nearby forest. "The man on the roof was wearing skis."

Every one of the men gave him a confused look.

Utah said, "What is 'skis'?"

"Have you heard of snowshoes?"

The men all nodded.

"Well, these are different than snowshoes but only in the shape. Rather than round to spread your weight over the snow, the skis are narrow and flat, and you can glide along on top of the snow. There was a man delivering mail wearing them at one of the places I was stationed. We called him Snowshoe Thompson."

"Snowshoe?" Trace said. "But you said these weren't snowshoes."

Good point. The corners of Cam's mouth twitched. "It was just his nickname, but he definitely wore skis just like this. Like a flat, narrow slat of wood, one buckled onto each foot. I saw him dodge around trees and rocks. Float over roof-high drifts. If a man gets used to skis, they're a mighty handy tool out here."

"Do you know how to use them?"

"Nope, but I watched Snowshoe plenty of times. How hard can it be?" Cam had a chill run up his spine that had nothing to do with the cold. It almost felt like a warning that his words would come back to haunt him.

"Are they gone?" Deb pressed her ear to the door.

"I think I heard the window shutters swing shut. If they're gone, they made quick work of escaping." Gwen shook her head and gave Maddie Sue a big hug. "They were quiet about it, though. I give them credit for that much."

Penny cracked the door open an inch. "Sure enough, the room's empty. I can't believe Trace tackled Cam to stop him from going, and then minutes later went with him. But I knew there was no stopping them. Maybe they at least took time to be a little bit cautious."

Deb pointed to the empty nails over the door where a rifle always hung. "They took time to put their coats on and grab their guns. That's probably as cautious as those half-wits are likely to be."

They went out, Deb and Gwen each carrying a child, to sit at the table that still had only four chairs. "All right, we need to

65

figure out how we're going to survive."

"Remember, it's April." Gwen shook her head. "Can you believe it?"

"I can't hardly," Penny admitted, then coughed for long enough a time that Gwen went and got her a glass of water. Got one for herself too, then Deb, all with Maddie Sue on her hip.

"Thanks." Penny sipped, then went on, "Yet we do know the days are getting longer, and the sun has more power."

"Right, because this bunkhouse is *buried* in snow," Gwen said wryly. She sipped her water as she returned to the table. "Welcome to spring in the Sierra Nevada Mountains."

"But like you said, it's April." Deb offered a sip of the water to Ronnie, who sat on her lap. "Spring is coming. If this had happened in January, we'd have to survive living shoulder to shoulder in this bunkhouse for months. As it is, we only have to survive a week or two. Or a month."

"Or two." Gwen smirked and hugged Maddie Sue tight. "But that doesn't change the point. However long we've got to survive, it'd be longer if this happened in January. Now let's stop whining and talk about where everyone is going to sleep."

Coughing again, Penny finished her water. "Maybe something warm will soothe our throats better." She got up and dragged the coffeepot out of the embers in the fireplace. She poured them each a cup of steaming hot coffee. "I lived in some cold country while I worked in the forts where Cam was stationed. Spring can come almost overnight, and I'd say we're due."

"Overdue," Gwen corrected. The coffee did feel good going down.

Penny grinned. "Overdue for a fact. The cold winds just change." Penny snapped her fingers. "Overnight, they get driven back up north. I remember being deep in snow and frigidly cold. This was in northern Montana Territory, as cold as I've ever been. The fort thermometer went down to forty below zero and then snapped in the cold. There was a nasty Canadian wind, always howling down from the north. Then one night it just went away, and a warm southern wind blanketed the fort by morning. Water started running. It was like the fort had been built in a river. Mud everywhere and running water a few inches deep over the mud. So yes, it feels like the depths of winter right now, but it will end soon. Then the men will build a new cabin, and everything will be back to normal. Now let's figure out how we get by in the short term."

Ronnie squirmed in Deb's lap. "Down.

Want down."

There was no holding him, so Deb put him on his feet. Gwen angled her chair so she could watch him if he toddled toward the fire.

"Down!" Maddie Sue echoed Ronnie and was set on her feet.

"The bunkhouse is built for a bigger crew than Trace has," Penny said, studying it. "The rooms are small, but each is big enough for two bunks. We'll have to build them, which can be done in the winter. Two of the men can take one room, the other gets one to himself. Deb, you and Trace can have a room. Gwen, you take the fourth room with the children. I'll sleep out here on the floor. More room for everyone, and I can feed the fire in the night so you don't all wake up to a freezing cabin."

"That reminds me. We only have the clothes on our backs and our filthy dresses. We need to do laundry." Deb looked between the two women. "When we survived that wagon train massacre, when Raddo and his henchmen —"

"Raddo struck with two other men. Now one's dead, one's in jail," Gwen added in case Penny didn't know the story.

Deb went on, "We had only the clothes on our backs then. And Adam — he had the fastest horse — rushed out to a little town south of here named Dismal and bought so much fabric we soon had new dresses and clothes. Now we're right back to what we're wearing."

"It's a good thing it's so cold we all sleep fully dressed," Penny coughed out. She took a drink of coffee. "Even our shoes. We'd be in trouble if we were barefoot."

Gwen sniffed. "As if we're not in trouble now."

"We'll be fine." Deb waved Gwen's worries aside. She'd gotten purely cheerful since she'd gotten married. "Trace's root cellar didn't burn, so there's plenty of food. I wish we had fabric, though, so we could sew ourselves new dresses and get out of these shameful trousers."

Penny laughed.

Deb clapped her mouth shut and gave Penny a stricken look.

Penny laughed some more. "I know my wearing pants is uncommon, and I didn't do it at the fort. It'd've been scandalous. But since Cam and I set out to find a homestead, I just put on a pair, and it's so much safer riding a horse without a skirt or working around a campfire. And so much more convenient for hunting and working around the covered wagon we had. I just kept wearing them. I don't give much of a hoot what anyone says."

"But you've always owned a dress," Gwen pointed out. "You wear one to Sunday services." The whole group had spent time every Sunday morning reading the Bible together. They'd say a prayer and sing a song or two. It was a good reminder to them who was really in charge around here.

"I'm sorry I said that, Penny. I've forgotten how to watch my words. I blame all the time spent with so many western men."

"Mostly I prefer blunt honesty, even if it might be rude, to all the fussing folks back east do. Don't worry about it." Penny had washed her face and had on clean clothes. But her hair was still a terrible, knotted, sooty mess. Her brown eyes shone, alive and intelligent in her pretty face.

Gwen wished Penny would adopt more conventional ways. She'd be pretty if she did. Well, she was pretty already, but for certain she'd be more womanly.

Deb went on assessing things. "Trace has still got chickens and a milk cow — the fire didn't change that. The men have their guns, though we lost some in the fire. Still, we have enough to hunt. When the fire calms, we can sift through the ashes — our cast-iron pots and skillets will have survived.

The tin plates and cups, the forks and knives. What else do we need?"

Gwen slapped the tabletop suddenly. "We put some of that fabric in the cellar when we first got it, remember? There was no room in the old cabin."

Deb grinned. "That's right, we did. And there's plenty down there. Enough to replace quite a bit of what we lost in the fire — including flannel so we can make diapers for Ronnie for bedtime."

The little guy used the privy well during the day, but the nights still called for a diaper.

"Before we do any of that," Gwen said, "I'd sure like to take a bath and wash my hair."

"Best time to do it is now with the men off on their hunt." Deb stood and went straight to a large basin hanging on the wall. Right below it sat a pail.

The women looked between each other and found their first genuine smiles of the day.

"It's time we quit feeling bad about all we lost and be delighted with all we saved," Gwen said. "We escaped without serious injury. I'm not going to complain about a thing. We've got work to do, ladies. Let's go."

CHAPTER 6

"Stop!" Cam hissed. "Get down."

They all dove for the snow, and the deep white powder let them sink in. It wouldn't stop a bullet, of course, but if someone was watching them and didn't see them dive, he might not be at an angle to see where they were hidden.

The men were silent as well as still. Even Wolf didn't move.

Cam kept his head down and spoke just barely above a whisper. "I saw those twin tracks lead straight to what must be a cave up the trail about one hundred feet. There's a dark area behind a stand of aspens. If he's in a cave and using the cover of those trees to watch our progress, then he might have his gun trained on us right now."

"Maybe he's living in it," Trace suggested. "I'm going at a flat-out run. I can reach the wooded stretch just uphill in a couple of long strides. I'll stay in those thick trees and make my way to the cave entrance and get the drop on him. If he isn't there, I'll holler and you can all come on up. If he tries to shoot me down, you'll have your chance at him."

"Trace, hold up, I can —"

"He's gone, Cam. He's got his dog along. He'll be fine." Utah's voice from off to his right stopped Cam from talking.

Sure, Trace'd be fine.

Cam braced himself to hear a shot ring out and end the life of his reckless friend.

There was no shot. Cam started breathing again. He realized what a hard time he had letting these cowboys make their own decisions. He was good at being in charge, though none of them seemed to admit it.

They weren't supposed to come after him because they were supposed to be dead.

That plan collapsed the second he heard voices coming from the bunkhouse. He'd figured to burn both buildings, but running out of time, he'd dropped the kerosene can into the chimney. He'd already poured a good quantity down and hoped it'd flowed out of the hearth and spread all over the floor.

Riley and that woman were in the cabin. They were the ones who'd seen him, so he'd plugged their chimney first and left them to smother, then skied overtop of the drifts and plugged the bunkhouse chimney. Then he'd gone back to the cabin.

He'd planned to kill them all and failed. In fact, he'd barely slowed them down. He saw them coming, including Riley. Raddo took careful aim just as they all dropped out of sight.

Had they seen him aiming? Raddo didn't think so, but maybe they felt his eyes boring into them. He'd heard such things could happen. He eased back a step, deeper into the shadows. He longed to put a bullet right through the heart of every single one of them. But five men? Even dry-gulching them, he couldn't win that fight.

He'd get a few, but they were knowing men. Spread out to prevent just such an attack, all out of sight right now in the snow. He'd never be able to kill every one of them. And the one he had to kill first, Trace Riley, who'd seen his face, had vanished just as fast as the others had.

Then Riley leapt into sight and tore up the hill.

Raddo brought his gun around just as Riley dashed behind one of the few old trees in that stretch of forest. Most of them were younger, skinnier. But the trunks were wide enough that with Riley now in the woods, he could slip around, making it hard for Raddo to get a clear shot.

Riley moved in and out of sight, ducking behind trees. Making his way toward Raddo's hideout.

Raddo would have to shoot into those trees and figure, after the first shot, there'd be bullets from five guns flying right at him.

The skis were on Raddo's feet. He'd kept them on even up on that roof, though that hadn't been hard with the buildings buried in snow.

Standing to fight was a fool's bet, and Raddo was no fool. Turning, he crouched and, with a hard shove of his ski poles, raced away, utterly silent, leaving a twin trail behind that he hoped the men saw as Raddo laughing at them.

Long seconds passed, then a minute, then two as Cam waited for Trace to open fire on Raddo or signal them to come running.

Or for Raddo to mow Trace down.

"No shots fired, and they would've been by now." Utah stood, then waved his rifle over his head. "Yep. Trace is past the cave. The trail must go on."

Cam was up and moving ahead of Utah. The cowhands fell in behind him. Trace, with Wolf on his heels, ran out of sight.

"He should wait for us," Cam grumbled.

"Ain't nobody better in the woods than the boss." Adam caught up to Cam's side. "When I got out here, he was doing well for himself. He'd been alone out here for years by then and knew these woods like a preacher knows the Good Book."

"I hadn't heard that before. He's still a kid. How long was he alone out here?"

Adam shrugged. "Four years, maybe five, I can't rightly remember. I found him living out here with a few cows he'd caught wild and locked up. I told him where a town was. He had no idea. He went and registered a homestead. Then it was the two of us for a few years. Last fall Utah showed up. He came right before roundup and the cattle drive. Before I got here, it was just Trace, his horse, and Wolf. They'd built that wreck of a cabin that's standing to the north of the new one."

"The horse and Wolf helped build a cabin?" Cam's voice rose.

"No, sorry," Adam laughed. "I didn't mean it that way. Trace built the cabin. But those two, the horse and Wolf, were his only friends and were good partners to him. I think they all three lived in that one-room cabin together. I helped him build the barn, and neither of us were what you'd call a hand at fine building."

Cam had seen the old cabin and barn. Cam could hardly believe Trace had survived for years living in that rickety old cabin.

He'd spent most days, when he wasn't shoveling, helping finish the new barn and working on the cabin and bunkhouse. They'd gotten the roofs up before the snow fell but not much done inside.

"Utah mostly built the cabin that burned down — with our help."

They passed the stand of aspens. The dark cave entrance Cam had seen was little more than a dip in the rocks. They could see the back of it easily. Cam had been tricked a few times by what was seen easily, though. He stepped into the dip and ran his hand along the back wall. No gap a man could slip through.

"Will you look at this," Trace said from ahead.

Cam looked up but couldn't see Trace. They hurried to where he stood and found the mountainside suddenly swooped down, sharply, with ski lines cut into the snow. Trace stood on the lip of a gorge.

Cam reached Trace's side to look across a twenty-foot gap at the bottom of the swoop.

The gap ended at a much lower level. On that level was a perfect parallel track.

"He jumped," Cam said — partly with disgust, partly impressed. Cam decided then and there that if he was gonna live in these mountains, he'd better learn to ski.

"There's no way across that gorge," Trace said. "Not for us anyway."

"Raddo surely does know how to ski," Cam said.

Trace crossed his arms and studied the tracks. "I know a way around this, but it'll be hours longer."

"Snowshoe, the man I knew, could go up and down, but he never could have jumped this gorge coming uphill. Raddo must've had another way up here."

Trace held up a buckskin-gloved hand. "Give me a minute. Let me think. I know this land better'n I know my own face."

"That ain't saying much," Adam said. "There ain't a mirror within a hundred miles."

Trace glared, and Adam just chuckled.

Cam knew Trace wasn't a real scary man to have as a boss. Here was the proof of that.

"I was going to say, I think I know how he got up. I doubt he used that cave where he was holed up as his hideout. He couldn't've survived the winter in that little dip in the rocks."

"He's a wily old coyote," Cam said. "He knew some of us survived and lay in wait for us to follow him."

Trace nodded. "He's a man who knows snow, judging by the way he works those skis. And he knows tracking and survival on the unsettled frontier. But I know my land. There's only one place he could ski in on."

"Where?" Cam asked.

"It's easier to show you, and we need to check anyway." Trace started out in a loping run. The rest fell in behind him. "We need to backtrack up the hill about halfway to my ranch. I want to see if a spot I know is drifted in. On skis maybe a man could just skim across, but it's no place a man could cross on foot, that I know for certain. The snow is so powdery, you'd sink in right over your head. But with skis . . . well, we'll see. Shouldn't be any mystery if he did it — there oughta be tracks, right?"

"Trace, have a care not to leave us behind," Adam said.

"Nope, not waiting. Our culprit is heading the opposite direction, so the only danger I can think of is if he circles back and heads for the cabin. I want to cut him off before he can do that. Follow my trail."

Trace picked up speed and left them behind, Wolf on his heels.

"Look at that man go, and in deep snow." Cam shook his head.

"You've never seen Trace run before?" Adam asked.

"Nope. Not much running around in this weather."

Utah laughed. "That's the plain truth."

"He's fast as a herd of mule deer running from a prairie fire, and that's just barely an exaggeration." Adam picked up his pace and talked as he followed Trace. "When I came out here, it took some gettin' used to, how much time he spent running. I'm a cowpoke and I never take a step if I can ride instead. But Trace spent a lot of time on foot. When he needed to cover some ground, he did it running."

Cam pushed faster. "We had forced marches when I was in the Civil War, but out here I was in the cavalry, so I've spent the last two years mostly on horseback."

"Trace enjoys running and he's mighty fast, so he still takes to the trail on foot plenty."

"Not a one of us should be out here alone. Trace should have waited. Let's pick up the pace, men." Cam winced when he heard himself snap out an order.

Utah muttered something Cam couldn't make out. It might have to do with Cam not being anyone's commanding officer. Despite his order, Adam was leaving them behind.

Cam made the best time he could, but it was slow-going. His boots stayed to the top of the drifts mostly, but once in a while he'd sink far enough that the others had to drag him up. He'd've been embarrassed by that if the other men didn't need the same help just as often. He saw Trace's stretched-out strides as they tracked him and wondered how the man ran in such conditions.

The land was as rugged as could be imagined. Trees, thick in some spots, scattered in others. Rocks, most of them almost buried by snow, but they created obstacles to get around. The snow seemed angry at them, trying to force them to go home. The steep terrain surrounded Trace's ranch yard and hid treacherous hidden cliffs, broken-off trees that could trip a man. The trees sometimes grew so close together they sent them on wide treks to get around them. Following Trace's footprints made it a bit easier.

Cam finally crested one of the constant rolls of forested, stony land and saw Trace standing about fifty feet ahead, staring at the ground. Cam saw ski tracks that headed for Trace's High Sierra Ranch. This trail wasn't as clean as the other, which had been two flat parallel lines cutting through virgin snow. Here the tracks were mauled, kicked around. The wind had tossed enough snow across them to make them harder to see.

Could Raddo have been trying to cover his trail?

"Is it the same man, Trace, or does he have help?" Adam asked.

Cam expected Trace to tell him that he couldn't tell much based on two almost filled-in lines in the snow, one of them badly stirred up.

Cam had learned by now that Adam had an unwavering belief in Trace's ability to do almost anything. It grated on Cam that he'd been put in the position of employee when he was mighty used to being in charge. But he'd been with these men for months now, and they were good men, wise to the ways of the frontier. Adam struck Cam as a man with plenty of skill and good sense to go along with it. When Adam trusted Trace, when Utah trusted Trace, Cam needed to respect that. And so he did.

The reason it chafed was because Cam figured himself for a top tracker, a top marksman, a man who knew how to live off the land and who had endured almost every condition, from winter in the northern Rockies to treks deep into the Mohave Desert to a summer in the swamps of Louisiana. And he'd commanded a lot of men and earned their respect and obedience easily. That wasn't happening here. Cam was out of the army, and none of these men knew him as an officer. He realized, somewhat sheepishly, that he'd figured himself for a natural leader, and other men could see that.

But maybe it'd only been his ability to send men to the stockade that had spurred their obedience. Just maybe he'd been a fool to think otherwise.

He didn't like feeling like a fool.

"Yep, same man."

How could Trace be so sure? Trace's wolf sniffed along the ski tracks. Maybe the dog could smell the same man and could signal that to Trace. Cam knew that wolf-dog was uncommonly smart.

"So just one, and he got across there?" Cam studied the tracks. They weren't broken up to his left, just two smooth tracks that wound left and right around boulders and trees.

"Why did you wonder how he got in?" Cam asked. "This looks so simple, I don't see why you'd question it."

"You're new to this land, Cam. And you would never notice it in the deep snow, but there's another gorge right there." Trace pointed to an especially smooth stretch with no trees or rocks. "It's not so deep as the one Raddo jumped, but deep enough that crossing it can be treacherous. This one fills in with snow. He just skied right across it, simple as you please. I came here because my land has a lot of trails that are broken up and tricky to pass, especially from this direction. I knew this gorge was likely snow-packed enough to let someone cross, but some years it stays open, so I needed to check."

Cam crossed his arms. Adam walked over closer.

"Don't anyone walk out where the snow is smooth," Trace called out. "You might sink in right over your head."

Adam stopped.

Trace added, "We'll drag you out if you do fall in."

Adam grinned, then crouched by the ski lines.

"I want a closer look, too." Cam wanted to figure out why that one part of the trail was so torn up. "Trace, tell me how you can tell two skiers apart. Is there a way to read

84

it like when you read a horse's tracks? Chances are a man can estimate a rider's weight and height and a few other things. But these skis . . . they don't tell me much. You say this is the same man, but is it because there's only one set in and one out, or can you see something in the tracks that you recognize? Teach me what to look for."

Cam had plenty of pride, though he didn't think it rose to the level of a sin. Even so, he wasn't afraid to ask questions of a man who was very clearly better at something than he was.

Trace was at his side. He glanced at Adam, then over at Utah, who came up beside them. Cam stepped into the torn-up snow to make room so that everyone could get close and hear.

"First, I do count it as a big clue that there is —"

An ugly *snap* cut him off.

CHAPTER 7

Pure agony lanced through Cam's leg.

He pitched sideways, the snow caved away, and Cam fell hard. Instead of hitting the ground, he sank into deep, powdery snow. His left leg jerked out straight, and he hung with his head down in the snow. His leg felt like Trace's wolf-dog was having it for a meal. Cam's weight tugged on whatever held him, and his leg tortured him with every movement as his weight wrenched his ankle.

"It's a bear trap!" Trace climbed over the edge of the gorge without hesitation, Utah right behind him.

"Stay up there, Adam," Trace ordered. "We may need help getting back out of here."

"Cam, we'll get you out," Utah said from his right. "Trace, pull down on this trap while I pull up."

Cam couldn't see anything but snow. "A

bear trap?"

The snow was soft enough that he wasn't smothering. He pawed at it and dug his head out enough to see.

Sure enough, the biggest bear trap he'd ever seen was chewing on his leg. Better than if it was a bear chewing . . . but only by a little.

"I'm alive. I'm fine." He wasn't fine really, yet he wasn't dead or anything.

Then he saw blood dripping down his leg. The teeth of the trap were mostly lodged in the tough leather of his boot, or it would have broken his leg, and he might've needed to cut his leg off.

Cam saw three very worried men looking down at him — Trace and Utah working the trap, Adam watching from overhead.

"I've got my side." Trace swallowed hard.

"Hang on careful, boss." Utah took a firm grip on the trap. "Don't let it snap back on him."

Trace got a grip, his face grim. He gave Cam a quick look. Cam kept his mouth shut and always would. A caterwaulin' man just made a chore harder for everyone else.

"Aren't you two afraid of sinking some more?"

Trace shook his head. "I know this gorge. We're at the bottom."

"Stay still," Utah said. "When we get the trap off, move your leg out of there fast. Ready, Trace?"

"Say the word. I'm ready."

"Now!"

Even with the borrowed coat on, Cam could see the muscles bulge in Trace's arms. Utah gritted his teeth, and his face flushed red from working on the trap. It gave a fraction of an inch, then a few more. Finally the teeth of the huge trap eased from his leg.

"Move, Cam."

Cam was ahead of him. He pulled his foot free from the trap as fast as he could.

"Close it slow, Utah. No sense letting it take a bite out of our fingers."

Cam's ankle felt like it'd caught fire. He looked for a way to help, but Utah and Trace had eased the trap so that only their fingers held it apart.

"Pull your fingers out, boss. I'll do mine at the same time, but don't just let it snap."

The two of them let the trap close tighter with every breath.

"I'm ready to let it go." Trace looked up. His brow was dripping sweat. Muscles bulged in his neck.

"Count of three." Utah then said with some speed, "One, two, three."

Their fingers jerked free. The trap bit into

Utah's glove and kept it, dangling by the index finger.

Both men, Cam too come to that, heaved to catch their breath. Trace called up, "Adam, look for a long branch! We'll need it to climb out. Then start cobbling a travois together — we'll have to drag him home."

Adam nodded, then disappeared from the ledge above.

Utah worked his glove free and put it back on. He began scooping with his arms, pulling aside a bushel of snow with every swipe. It was only then that Cam realized, though he'd dug enough snow away to uncover his head, the rest of him was still buried.

Trace turned to look at Cam's ankle. After digging it out of the snow, he touched it gingerly.

"You don't need to drag me home. I can — ahhh!" A cry of pain slipped out before Cam could clamp his mouth shut.

"It's mighty ugly." Trace quit poking at Cam's foot. "I'm gonna need to cut your boot off."

"Cam, you all right?" Adam yelled from a distance, reacting to the shout of pain.

"Yep." Cam didn't say another word because he'd have to start lying.

Utah pulled a bowie knife out of its sheath

under his coat and handed it over. "How bad does it hurt?" Utah asked in a low voice that wouldn't carry to the top of the gorge. Adam was gone, but it was hard to say just how far gone.

Cam looked up. Utah was studying him with his dark brown eyes. No pity, not even a lot of concern. The man appeared to be pondering how to handle a job and nothing more.

Trace handed the bowie knife back to Utah. "I've decided not to cut the boot. If I find out it's broken, I've got nothing to splint it with, nothing to wrap it with, and it's a blamed fool idea to take your boot off in this cold. Besides, a tough leather boot that reaches over your ankle is better than whatever brace we'd rig up. Back at the cabin, the boot'll have to come off so we can check if the leg's broken."

"I don't think it is. It hurts plenty, but not worse than the one time I did break it."

"Let's hope for a few cuts that'll heal right up, and nothing else."

"I found a long limb." Adam was tromping through the snow, dragging what sounded like a mighty big tree branch. His head appeared over the edge of the gorge. "Wolf helped me dig it up. I'll lower it down so you can just scamper right up it. Trace, you and Utah guide it. I'd hate to drop the bottom of this big old thing right on Cam's belly. He's likely had enough for one day."

Adam grinned before pulling his head back. A few seconds later, the butt end of a branch at least six inches wide shoved into view. Lots of sturdy-looking smaller limbs poked out in all directions.

"It'll be easy as climbing a ladder," Adam called.

The thought of climbing up that branch made Cam break out in a cold sweat.

The branch came down. Trace and Utah wedged it firmly at the base to form an almost perfect stairway straight out of here.

"I'm rigging a travois." Adam looked at them. "There was a stack of limbs big enough, it looks like floodwaters must've pushed them into a heap." He went back to his rigging.

Utah came to Cam's side. With casual disregard for Cam's injury, Utah tugged him to his feet . . . well, foot. Trace reached for his other side, and soon the two men had him standing.

Cam's stomach lurched, and for a moment he figured he'd finish off this morning by upchucking. His belly didn't feel completely opposed to such a humiliating thing.

"Let's climb out of here," Trace said, his

arm around Cam's waist.

Utah and Trace helped Cam hop the few feet to the tree branch. "Let me go up first," Utah said. "I can reach down and steady you from overhead. Trace can come from behind and do the same thing."

Cam clawed at the branch as his head swirled and his vision narrowed and turned dark. He found something to grab on to.

Trace clamped a hand on his arm. Speaking quietly, he said, "Your face just went bone-white. Give your head a minute to clear."

It must've been quiet enough because Utah went on up without a pause. He climbed fast and easy. Cam started to see a wider range again. It cleared his head to have an ankle throbbing like a ten-pound heart.

He said to Trace in the same low voice, "Somebody set that trap with us in mind." He turned to look at the man who'd given him and his children and sister shelter for the winter. And who'd stolen those children's hearts.

Nodding, Trace said, "Raddo. It has to be him — no one else was out here. And it was Raddo who tossed the snow around to disguise that he'd buried it. That's as deliberate as a man can get."

They both looked back at the trap. A chain ran away from it, up the edge of the gorge. It was anchored.

"We should take that trap with us." Cam got a better hold on the branch. He dragged his good foot through the snow, his left ankle bent back, hurting every time it moved. Well, it hurt whether he moved or not, but *more* when it moved.

He looked up the tree branch, probably no more than a dozen feet high. How in the world was he going to climb it, and then get all the way home? Frustrated with darned near every single thing in his life, he wanted to sink a fist into the big tree limb. But that'd get him nothing but a sore fist, and he hurt enough already.

"Can you do it, Cam?" Trace asked. "I can help you keep your balance. Or I can get Utah back down here. Or I can try and put you over my shoulder and carry you up that way."

"I'm not a man to lie, but I'm no complainer either. I'm probably gonna be able to do this, and I'd rather you not call for help if it can be avoided."

"Get going then. I'll be a few steps behind you. I'll try and keep you clinging to the branch."

Cam smiled. "Thanks."

93

He hadn't been keeping track, but it might've been the first time he'd smiled since he got the letter telling him his brother had died. No, it was before that. No smiling when he'd been driven off the range he'd claimed in California. No smiling, or little enough, in the cavalry with dozens of men's lives depending on him. Nor in the Civil War, especially after he'd gotten word his wife had died. Nope, this was about the first smile in years. And it didn't last longer than it took him to drag his good foot up to the lowest part of the branch.

His bad leg didn't bear any weight, but he had to use it to steady himself, and he nearly cried out in pain.

Reaching up as high as he could, he studied the smaller branches, picked one, and hopped his right foot up to it, letting his wounded left foot hang. Using his arms to bear all his weight when he drew himself higher, he advanced with miserable slowness.

Trace hung back, and Cam was glad. He felt like he was showing himself as a weakling by needing help. At least he hadn't fainted or emptied his stomach. A man can bear only so much embarrassment.

Every hop he took he'd wait until the burn in his leg settled to as close as it would get to bearable. Then he'd reach up for a new handhold, hop, and stop again. Before long he saw the top of the gorge come into view, and then his head was level with it.

Utah grabbed Cam's arms and dragged him over the ledge. He did it fast and without saying a word. Got it over with before Cam could tell him it wasn't necessary — especially since it probably was necessary. Cam concentrated on keeping his cut-up leg from getting banged around.

He sprawled out flat on the ground face-down, enjoying the snow that cooled the sweat on his brow and helped clear his dizzy head.

Then Trace was over the lip of the gorge. He didn't ask how Cam felt. That'd be a pure waste of time. "I'll get the trap." Trace followed the chain.

Adam came up with a travois rigged together. It was little more than two long sticks with Adam's coat buttoned around them. Which meant Adam was going to be freezing cold by the time they got home.

Nope, that wasn't true. He was freezing cold already.

Cam wanted to yell about making it on his own, but he didn't have the strength.

They loaded him onto the travois.

"Carry this." Trace set the big old bear trap on his stomach. Utah and Adam on one side, Trace alone on the other. They grabbed the long branches that made up the travois, and they were off.

It made him feel completely defeated, but the simple truth was that Cam was grateful for the ride. He tilted his head high and could see the three men dragging him.

Utah said, "Seein' as how I've pretty much been blown up today, and my beard's burned almost completely away — which means I don't have my usual blanket across my face — I'm glad to be headin' back to the bunkhouse."

"Gwen's probably the best hand at doctoring," Trace said. "She can wrap up Cam's leg and then see if she can find any burns on that face of yours."

"I don't want no woman fiddling with my leg. If one of you can't do it, I'll have Penny wrap it." Then he remembered why Penny couldn't.

"Better leave it to Gwen. She's shown some talent for it with the youngsters. Besides, if the kids see you being treated nice by her, they might stop screaming every time they see you."

The men started chuckling, and Cam wanted to beat every one of them to a bloody stump. But there was no sense pretending his children liked him, so they might as well talk about it. With these men it was either fighting for their lives, working, or jibing each other.

He wasn't up to working, and they were taking a break from fighting for their lives if his sore leg didn't count, so why not?

"We haven't done chores," Adam said. "No cow milked, no eggs gathered."

Utah added, "And we'll have to dig our way to the barn to find the milk cow and the chickens."

"I'll get Black out," Trace said. "If the trail is passable, I'll ride to the canyon to make sure the cows can get to the water and see if there's any grass for 'em."

"Sorry to not be ambitious, but I might wash up, let Doc Gwen have a look at me, then sleep. Trudging through this snow reminded me I took a beating this morning." Utah turned and looked over his shoulder at Cam. "The two of us make up a hospital ward, Cam. Maybe we can find time for a game of checkers. If we had any checkers."

"After chores, we'll sit and do some planning," Trace said. "And we're better off doing that in front of a fireplace than out here in the cold."

97

He picked up the pace again, and the other two kept up. Cam too, but not by any actions of his own.

"How'd you ever learn to run so fast, Trace?" Cam wanted something to take his mind off the agony of his leg.

"Not sure. I reckon I was born with speed. But I had to build up to the distance. I came out here with a wagon train that was massacred just like the one Maddie Sue was on. My pa and the whole wagon train were killed." Trace fell silent for a moment, then continued, "I've wanted justice for all of 'em ever since. Raddo set the fire today and did a lot of planning, what with burying that trap and all, and the distance he came. He meant to kill us. Deb saw him during the attack on her train. I saw him in Carson City, and then later Deb told me he admitted the crime to her. The two of us are the only ones who know his face. I knew he was dangerous, but I hoped he'd quit the country with one of his partners dead and the other in jail. I let down my guard."

"You just hoped he'd run off?" Cam fumed. He wanted to get out of this travois and land a war on Raddo's head. He kept his voice even. No sense snarling at the men who were carrying him home.

"I did. He's a lunatic if he thinks he can

kill all of us, and that's my other mistake. I figured all my plans to post a sentry to stand guard over my place would be in the spring. I never figured he'd cause trouble in the winter. I'm surprised he can get around in this deep snow. Skis." Trace snorted in disgust. "Who'd've figured? The Sierra Nevadas get mighty quiet through the winter."

"That's who killed my brother." Cam's fists tightened. He wanted to fight, but right now making a fist tensed his muscles all over and that included his leg. He forced himself to calm down . . . at least outwardly. Inside, hate burned with the strength of a house gone up in an inferno. "I want him. I want him caught, locked up, and hung."

"If I'm figurin' it right," Trace said, "and I am, Raddo rode with the men who killed my father all those years back. He's old enough to've been with them, and the crimes are too much the same." Looking back, Trace said quietly, "Cam."

Cam craned his neck to look up and forward. "Yep, I'm listening."

"You can't want him more than I do."

Brother? Father? Who had lost the most? Mighty hard to say.

Nodding, Cam rested back on the travois. The contortions made his leg hurt. "I reckon that's fair."

"Wolf. Home." Cam twisted to see Trace pointing for the ranch. The wolf-dog took off running. Trace then called over his shoulder, sounding anxious, "Sure as I am that Raddo was heading away from us at a high speed, I don't like the womenfolk and youngsters being home alone for so long a time."

The thought of the women in jeopardy got the men moving faster — even though they were acting as pack animals for Cam.

As Cam lay back on the travois, his leg throbbing, he prayed for the women's safety, for Raddo to be brought to justice, for his leg to heal right. His thoughts and prayers wandered to that pretty, child-stealing pest Gwen. Annoying as she was, he wanted to get back there fast to protect her.

John McCall drew the short straw at the Pinkerton Agency and hurried over as soon as he lost. With the Chiltons it was always urgent. Preparing to be polite while he was sent on some ridiculous investigation for the Chiltons, he settled into a chair in the ornate office of the majestic mansion of Edmond and Florence Chilton.

They had a history with the Pinkertons.

When they needed a detective, it was always urgent — that wasn't so unusual, but the Frantic Chiltons, as they were called, went so far with their urgency it had become a company joke. More seriously, a few agents had wondered if they'd been used to uncover scandalous things the Chiltons then used to blackmail people.

Since an agent had suggested that, the whole company had been wary of dealing with these folks, particularly Florence.

But they paid promptly and in full. The jobs were usually as simple as standing near someone in a crowd and eavesdropping, and what they learned had always been harmless enough that if people allowed themselves to be blackmailed over it, then they were too stupid to protect.

It came down to the boss liked their money, and John's turn was bound to come up once in a while.

"Our daughter has died. She was murdered." Edmond sat behind his desk, his hands folded into one large fist resting on the desktop. The man could almost be praying, except John had never noticed a shred of Christian charity in either of the Chiltons.

The statement drew John's full attention. He set aside how annoying they were and their strange need for detectives. This time they were hiring him to investigate a murder.

John sat in a heavy upholstered chair with thick flowered cushions. There was another beside him, both facing Edmond's massive oak desk. Florence sat on John's right, but her chair wasn't squared off with the desk. Instead it was slightly at an angle so she could easily watch John, while he had to turn to look at her. Her elbows were propped on the cushioned arms of the chair, her hands clasped together so tightly her knuckles had turned white.

Every time he looked over at her, she was watching him with her cold eyes, as if she were trying to bore into his brain and read his thoughts.

He sure hoped she couldn't, because he could hardly bear to be in the same room with the old bat. She didn't even bother to feign grief over the murder of her only child. Awful woman.

There was no sign of grief in Edmond's eyes either, but there did seem to be some strong emotion. John decided to at least give Edmond the benefit of the doubt.

"I'm so sorry for your loss," he told them.

Florence nodded without speaking. John knew she'd speak eventually — she always took over.

"Thank you," Edmond said. "Now, we have need of your services."

"The Pinkerton Agency sent me as fast as they could." That part was true. Word had only reached the agency about a half an hour ago. "Tell me what you need, and I'll get right to it. We will bring the killer to justice, Mr. and Mrs. Chilton."

Florence remained silent, but she sent out such cold disapproval, it chilled him to his bones.

"No, the killer isn't our concern. We're so far away, we can't begin to know how to solve a crime in Nevada."

"Nevada?" John decided then and there to shut up and listen. He had no idea what was going on. Their daughter had lived not too far from here. He clamped his mouth shut.

"Yes, Delia and that worthless husband of hers headed west on a wagon train."

John had investigated Abe Scott and found the man to be a fine Christian, devoted and true to his wife, and hardworking. But he changed jobs often and none of them paid well.

"What we need is for you to go to Nevada and fetch our grandson home. Ronnie Scott is the boy's name. He's under two years old." Edmond thrust a paper at John.

"Here's a letter sent to us by a woman who survived the wagon-train massacre, along with our grandson and two others. Deb Harkness is her name. Her location's written in the letter, also the name of the man who took them to his ranch. There's enough money in here to pay your fares and . . ." Edmond hesitated, and his hand extended almost as though he was forcing it forward, his mind divided about handing over the small black purse. "And there's one hundred dollars in twenty-dollar gold pieces to cover your expenses."

Internally John gasped. It was a huge amount to earn for a Pinkerton job.

"Any you don't spend will be yours to keep, and there will be one hundred dollars more when you return with our grandson."

"That's a fine amount, Mr. Chilton."

"It's a long journey, Agent McCall. We considered going ourselves, but we hoped a Pinkerton would have more experience in things of this sort. You'll be earning this money. In addition, if you make it back by the end of summer, September twenty-first of this year — that's within five months — we will add an additional fifty dollars to your earnings."

One hundred and fifty dollars! A man could live for a good long stretch on that kind of money — if he was careful. And John was. The one hundred dollars for expenses was more than it would cost. He'd save part of that, too.

"All we ask," Mr. Chilton went on, "is that you return with our little Ronnie. He's not safe out west, living with who knows what sort of people. Bring our grandson home, Agent McCall, and do it as fast as you possibly can."

It'd be the biggest payday of John's life. But he'd earn it. Along with everything else, John was supposed to travel the entire length of the country to bring back a two-year-old?

John didn't know much about kids, except they were little and leaky and cried over everything. And where in the name of heaven was Nevada, and how was he supposed to get there?

He planned to go to the office and punch somebody in the nose before he went home to pack.

CHAPTER 8

"They're back," Gwen muttered when she heard someone crawling through the tunnel. They could have used about four more hours to get all that needed doing done.

But they were finished with the laundry, had prepared a hearty meal, and all of them had their baths.

Gwen's hair was yellow again, like it was supposed to be. She'd changed out of the trousers the instant her dress was passably dry, Deb too. Penny had changed out of her borrowed trousers and into her own. They still needed to make her a proper dress.

They'd braved the outdoors, dug their way down to Trace's cellar, found fabric, and were sewing for the children. They'd done a poor job of shoveling snow, just enough to gather eggs, milk the cow, and hay the horses kept in a corral near the barn.

In a more normal voice, Gwen said, "Let's get the meal on. The men have to be starving."

Trace came through the shutters first, hopped down onto the bunkhouse floor, turned and reached back outside. Sounding grim, he said, "Cam's hurt. Someone — Raddo — buried a bear trap right on the trail."

Gwen tucked Maddie Sue into Penny's arms and rushed toward the window. "How bad is it?"

Trace was paying attention to the window. Cam moved inside under his own power. Gwen was glad to see him conscious and crawling along. Then she saw his face. Ash-gray, his mouth clamped shut so hard his jaw looked near to snapping.

"His leg's bleeding." Trace let Cam reach down for the floor as his body came in through the window. He caught Cam's legs, though, one of them soaked in scarlet.

Gwen helped steady both his legs while Trace carried him over to the fireplace. Together they laid him down gently.

"I'm all right, just torn up a little." Cam's voice was barely loud enough to hear through his gritted teeth.

"A bear trap can break a man's leg," Trace said sharply, overriding Cam's protests. "It can even rip it up so badly you could lose it. We're not taking your word that it's all right."

Adam came in next, then Utah. Wolf leapt through the window last, and then Utah closed the shutters.

Wolf went straight for Maddie Sue, who squealed and begged to be let down. The wolf-dog shook snow off his coat. The half-wild critter was quick to bare his teeth and lay back his ears, but not around the little ones. He let them maul him without complaint.

Deb set Ronnie on the floor and trusted Wolf to keep them from wandering too close to the fireplace.

Utah said, "We're just gonna warm up for a few minutes. We haven't even done morning chores yet."

"The cows are milked, the eggs gathered, and most of the animals are close to fed." Gwen talked as she tried to get a good look at Cam's wound. "We dug a path to the barn, although it's a real narrow one."

Trace nodded. "Thank you. That makes the day easier."

"Come. You should eat something." Deb bustled toward the fireplace and the table in front of it, all loaded with the food they'd gathered from the men's stores and from the cellar.

"We had stew for breakfast, so we made breakfast for dinner. Biscuits and bacon. We've got the skillet hot." Penny was on Deb's heels, giving Cam worried looks but not offering to tend him. "I'll fry up some eggs, and after you get Cam to bed, Gwen can tend him while you men eat."

Even Penny knew Gwen was the one to help.

"Should we keep him out here near the fireplace?" Trace asked.

"No." Gwen shook her head. "The snow is perfect insulation. The bedrooms are as warm as out here. The whole bunkhouse is warmer than it's been all winter."

"Fine." Trace shed Adam's spare coat and hung it up, as did the other men. Then Trace came and helped Cam get out of his. "Yep, he'll be warm enough even after he shucks his pants and boots."

"No one's taking my . . ." Cam's eyes darted back and forth, not unlike a cornered rat. His voice dropped to a near whisper. "No one's taking my pants off in front of all these women." Speaking normally, he added, "Gwen, you can't check my leg. That wouldn't be proper. One of the men can do it, or . . . Penny?" He sounded uncertain all of a sudden.

"You know better than that, Cam," his

sister spoke up. "I'm no hand with doctoring. Remember the time I checked a bump on your head and accidently set your hair on fire?"

Gwen flinched and exchanged a look with Deb, who arched a brow.

"We got the fire out before it hurt me," Cam said in her defense.

Penny plunked her hands on her hips. "Didn't I once check a finger you broke, and the swelling was so ugly I had to leave the room and empty my belly?"

"But you came back after you were done upchucking."

"A long time after I was done. After someone else straightened your finger and tied it to the next finger so it'd heal — and then came and found me where I was hiding."

Cam looked at his slightly misshapen middle finger on his left hand. "You were gone a long time. The men finished with me and got worried about you and had to hunt you down like you were a maverick calf."

"You know blood bothers me."

Cam scowled to curdle milk, then glared at Gwen. "Well, it can't be her."

"Gwen's a hand at injuries, Cam." Trace gave the injured leg another worried look.

"We'll make sure you're . . . um, decent."

Gwen noticed Trace's expression. He wanted to get Cam's leg checked, yet Trace took modesty seriously — he would see that things were done proper.

"I have no more wish to see your unclothed person than you have of allowing me to. I'll wait until you're covered fully, all but right at the wound. Then I'll come in. Will that suit you?"

Cam gave her such a grumpy look, she almost expected him to admit that nothing suited him. Nothing ever did, and particularly nothing about Gwen. He resented how close she was to the children, and it made him hostile . . . and she was fully sick of it.

She caught herself thinking of her prayers that he'd rejoin the army. Maybe she shouldn't pray for that. Maybe the hostility wasn't all on his side.

Trace nodded to his men. "Grab him." He looked at Gwen. "We haven't even looked at it yet. We didn't want to uncover his leg outside in the cold."

"Prepare it, and do it as fast as you can. It looks like he's lost a lot of blood, and that robs a man of his strength. The sooner we stop the bleeding, the faster he'll mend." Gwen watched them carry Cam away.

As the men left the room, all her confidence vanished. Gwen turned to Penny and Deb, who were working together to set food on the table and help keep the little ones back from the fire.

"It looks bad," Gwen whispered. "Penny, are you sure you can't help?"

The color left Penny's cheeks, and she reached for the table to steady herself.

"Don't faint. I'll do it." Gwen poured steaming hot water from a pot they kept in the fireplace. Basin in hand, she grabbed a cloth. "I'm not sure if they've got anything to use for bandages. The dresses we're wearing are the only ones we have — we don't dare tear strips off of them."

"There's fabric here, but we need it to make more clothes." Deb's eyes slid from the bedroom where the men went to the shrinking stack of fabric. "I think we can make enough bandages using scraps."

"I don't want to go in before they're ready. Give me the bandages while you and Penny cook."

Gwen groaned as she thought of her meager doctoring skills.

Cam groaned as they laid him on the bed.

"I'm going to cut your boot off now, Cam," Trace said.

Utah drew his bowie knife again and

handed it to Trace. "It's razor-sharp, oughta hack through leather slick as anything."

"These are the only boots I've got. You're not cutting them."

"Your foot's so swollen, I don't think I can get the boot off without cutting it."

"Figure something out. There aren't any spare boots around here, and I can't function without 'em."

Trace looked up at Utah, who stood close to Cam's head. Adam was behind him. There really wasn't room in here for all of them.

"I'll try." Trace put down the knife and reached for Cam's foot.

Cam braced himself.

Trace did his best, but he had himself a fight getting that blood-soaked boot off Cam's swollen foot and leg. By the time he was done, Cam was weak and trembling. His stomach stormed around, and his vision got narrow and dark. He lay panting on the bed, doing all he could to quell the shout of pain that wanted to get out.

His pants were next. They hurt a whole lot less than the boot, but it was bad enough. Then his shirt had to go so they could remove his long johns, which was mighty embarrassing. Not even in the close quarters of the Civil War had he been this unclothed in front of anyone.

Utah whistled quietly. "Looks like the war was hard on you, Cam."

"One bayonet stab in my gut. One saber slashed down my leg. The bullet wound came in from the back and went right on out the front, low on my side. I got hit by pretty much every weapon they had." Cam didn't list the cannon that had peppered him with shrapnel. He was just glad they couldn't see his back.

"The blood has dried your long johns to the wound, Cam." They had his long handles off everywhere but the one leg. Trace stood there looking at that leg doubtfully. "It stopped bleeding. I don't want to cut the drawers off. There's no sense in it — we're real short on clothing, what with every stitch of cloth in the house being burned up. But the fabric's gotta come off somehow, and tearing it loose from the wound might start up the bleeding again."

Trace stared down at Cam's leg, then gave Cam an uncertain look. Cam wondered just how bad it was. At that moment, Gwen came into the room.

Utah quick tossed a blanket over Cam.

"Hey, get out!" Cam clawed at the blanket, spreading it over himself.

Trace whipped around to block Gwen's

view. "We're not quite ready for you, Gwen, but we can use the water."

Trace relieved her of the basin she held. She had clean rags with her too, and he took them. "Go on back out while we wash away the dried blood and make sure he's decent." He turned her and urged her backward so fast she didn't have time to protest. Trace shut the door firmly in her face.

Cam heaved a sigh of relief.

Trace worked on cleaning the wound for a while. Finally, his teeth gritted, tugging a bit too hard for Cam's comfort, he got the drawers free.

"You don't need me in here," Utah said and left the room.

Cam was pretty sure he did it because if Cam was gonna go to whining and moaning in pain, Utah'd as soon not witness him disgrace himself. Or maybe Utah had a weak belly like Penny.

A moment later, Adam went after him. He had to slip past Trace to get to the door. "Gwen, he's ready," Cam heard Adam say.

Cam wasn't ready. He wasn't ready for nuthin'. But sure as certain not for a maiden lady to see his bare leg. Before he could figure out how to put a stop to that, Adam disappeared and Gwen came in.

"Help me sit up a bit, Trace." Cam

propped himself up on his elbows. Every movement made his leg hurt all the more, no matter that he hadn't involved it one bit.

"I'll get more blankets to put under your shoulders," Trace said.

"No, I'm —" But he was gone. All of the men had run from the battlefield and left the wounded behind.

Cam looked up, sorely afraid he was blushing, and saw Gwen's brow furrow as she studied the wound. Her lips curled into a frown. She dipped her cloth into the hot water and wrung it out. Then for the first time she turned and looked right at Cam. "I'm sorry this happened to you. That man, he was after Deb and Trace."

"Better me getting hurt than them."

Their gaze held.

Cam saw only compassion. She might be a child stealer, but she loved them. She treated them well. Heaven knew she was better at handlin' them than he was.

He looked into those blue eyes and felt them touch a place inside him that had recently awakened, bruised and lonely and in love with the daughter he'd abandoned.

"Maddie Sue loves you and hates me." Then he said something even harder to admit. "And that's all my fault." He was a long time speaking words so overdue.

"Thank God in heaven that you were here to care for her when she was in such need. I was nowhere to be found."

"She doesn't hate you, Cam. She just doesn't know you."

Cam dropped flat on his back. "I feel like the most useless member of this whole unit." He shook his head. "No more feeling sorry for myself."

One corner of Gwen's pretty lips managed to curl up in a smile. "No better time than when a man's had a bear trap take a bite out of his leg."

"Yep, if not now, then never. But I'd as soon it be never."

"I've got a blanket you can use to prop up your head." Trace was talking as he came in with a bedroll. He eased it behind Cam's shoulders, took a quick glance at Cam's leg, then left the room just a little too fast.

Gwen pressed the cloth on his shin. "There's only one really nasty gash — really nasty. Deep. There's another not-so-deep slice on the outside of your leg. It's not bad enough to be a worry, though. All the bleeding has stopped."

She freshened her cloth and returned to her meager doctoring. "I'll delay the stitches. You have to have them, but it's too swollen still. I'll let the swelling go down a

117

day or two first. Of course, if I delay too long, it's more likely to get infected — so maybe not. And it might not heal right. Maybe sewing it up, even swollen, would lessen the chance of infection and help the wound to close more quickly, and certainly with less of a scar. But the swelling will calm down, and the edges of your skin will come back together. Maybe I don't need to put in stitches at all. With a tight bandage, that might be enough. Yes, that might be for the best."

"What kind of doctor are you?" Cam asked.

She swallowed again. "I learned the way of it on the wagon train. We didn't have a doctor, but one of the women with us had healing skills, and I helped her. She thought someone else should learn in case something happened to her. I cast a broken arm. I sewed up cuts."

"So you're no kind of a doctor."

Gwen sighed, plunked her hands on her hips. "I'm the best doctor you've got. And if I'm a poor one, you're just going to have to be content thinking of me as better than nothing."

Cam managed a smile. That was two in one day. "Yes, Miss Harkness."

Gwen grinned at his prim obedience.

"I know nothing myself about doctoring, which makes me worse than nothing, so we'll do it your way."

Nodding somewhat frantically, she went on, "I'll check the swelling regularly and sew it if I decide that is what's called for. Cold cloths will make the swelling go down faster."

Cam shuddered. "I've had about enough of the cold."

She cleared her throat overly loud.

He held up both hands in mock surrender. "But you're in charge."

"Good of you to notice."

"Walking is going to be beyond me until someone builds crutches or a cane. I reckon I'm stuck here for a couple of days at least."

"Probably more like three weeks, maybe a month judging by one badly sprained ankle we had on the wagon train. This has to qualify as a sprain. By then the snow will —"

"A month! I was hopping around in a couple of days when I was a kid."

"You probably shouldn't have been."

"I'll go out of my mind if I do that much lazin' around."

"I can see where the trap clamped on to you. Your boot protected you, but not completely."

She was ignoring him, and she wasn't going to get away with it. "I'm not a man to lie abed for a month while others do all the work."

Cam's shouting brought Trace into the room with his arms full of cloth. "Don't worry about the work, Cam. We'll be fine. If it weren't for the snow shoveling, it'd be a mighty easy time of year. We've just eaten. As soon as you're done in here and you're up to it, Deb'll bring you in some fried eggs."

Trace was referring to hard labor, every day, hours of it, just to reach the barn and the canyon where his cattle herd stayed. Yep, except for that.

"If you stay in bed, do you mind if I take your spare clothes? Mine burned. Deb is washing yours right now. They'll be dry soon enough. And you probably need a bath — you're still sooty."

Cam was silent, possibly because his jaw was so tight that talking was beyond him.

"I tanned a few deer hides earlier," Trace said. "They're down there in the cellar. We can make coats. Gwen, Deb said neither of you has worked with deer hide, but Cam would know how."

"We can learn."

"Penny can do it," Cam said. "And yes, so

can I. While I'm sittin' around, I can help. But it's not gonna be a month."

"We're gonna need those coats, so the more hands the better." Trace thrust a stack of rags at Gwen. "We tore strips off an old sheet we found in Utah's room. I've gotta get on. Adam went out for chores, though you ladies have done a lot of them. Utah admitted he's seeing two of everything, and just now, hunting for this sheet, he got so dizzy we had to catch him. That was finally enough for him to confess he's played out."

"Go. I can handle this and see to Utah, too. I'll holler for Deb if I need help, and Penny can watch the young'uns."

"She's still coughing bad. We convinced her to lie down too, and the little ones are napping. But she's here if you need her." Trace left again.

Approaching him like she might a wounded cougar, Gwen said, "Lay flat now and close your eyes."

"Just do it," Cam said. "It ain't gonna hurt any less no matter what I do."

"Unfortunately, I'm afraid that's true."

Gwen resumed her doctoring while Cam concentrated on keeping his mouth shut and his pain to himself. He closed his eyes so that Gwen wouldn't look at him and see white all around like a panicky horse.

"I don't think I've thanked you yet for saving us all," she said.

That opened his eyes.

"I am just now hearing about what happened this morning. The men said you figured out the chimney was plugged here in the bunkhouse."

"That seems like days ago. I did most of it while my head swirled from lack of air."

"Then you got the fire in the hearth out before it smothered everyone. You opened the chimney, woke all the men up, and helped them dig out of here to escape. Then you all came for us in the cabin, ran into a burning building, and helped us all out just before it collapsed."

"That's not brave — it's just what any decent man would do."

She gave him a gentle smile, not letting him be humble for a second. Instead, she went on talking nice about him. Gwen really hadn't spent a lot of time being nice to him, so it was noticeable.

"We all lived because of you, Cam. Thank you so much." Her hands never stopped binding his wounds.

He forced his thoughts from the pain and concentrated on her sweet, soothing voice. He couldn't remember the last time someone had thanked him for much of anything.

Maybe when he passed the salt.

What did a man say in such a situation? He pondered this while she poked at his leg, until finally he came up with, "You're welcome."

A man doesn't say please when he's giving orders. And when the men obeyed him, it wasn't his way to waste a lot of time with thank-yous. But his ma had pounded some manners into him a long time back.

"Utah said you woke them all up, and it wasn't easy because they were closer to unconscious than asleep. Then you drove them to dig out when they all wanted to collapse."

"Utah wasn't too bad. Adam woke up before I got in his room. Neither of 'em were in the smoke as long as you were."

"Don't make light of saving us, Cam. You ran right into the teeth of a blaze, carried Penny out, then came back for —" Her voice broke.

"Stop, Gwen. I was lucky because I woke up. Or blessed, stirred by the hand of God maybe, but not through my own doing. Every man here would've known just what to do after they smelled that smoke. And every man here rushed into that fire — well, maybe not Utah, but he'd just been blown up, so that's a mighty good excuse. What I am is the careless one who stepped his foot right into a bear trap. I should've realized that torn-up snow meant something was buried there. I was a reckless fool and I should've —"

Her hand came down gently on his lips. She didn't have a spare hand when she was tending his leg, so she must've finished up with her bandaging.

Her fingers, strong and soft, touched his lips, but they seemed to touch something deeper, a wound in his mind where he'd had to learn to live without the softness of a woman. War did that to a man.

He had no idea he'd been so lonely for a gentle touch.

CHAPTER 9

Gwen stepped out into the main room, leaving stern instructions with Cam for him to rest.

Trace climbed through the window. He was coated in snow. "I got a few more supplies from the root cellar."

Deb rushed to him and took the stack of things from his arms, including more fabric and food.

"Utah had an extra coat in the barn. I borrowed guns, too." He gave Deb a sound kiss. Maddie Sue ran to Trace and clung to his pant leg. Ronnie toddled toward them with a grin on his face.

Trace gave Deb another kiss, then turned his attention to the little ones. He scooped them both into his arms and tickled their necks with noisy kisses and his cold, scratchy beard. The youngsters giggled and pulled his hair.

Cam, fully dressed, stepped to the doorway of the bedroom, all his weight on one leg. He opened his mouth to say something, but the words never got past his throat. He silently looked at his children playing with Trace. Every bit of his love and regret and hurt showed in his eyes.

Gwen knew her dislike of him wasn't fair. And she especially knew it since the heroism of this morning.

But he wanted Maddie Sue. There was no honorable reason a woman could have for wanting to keep a man's family from him and send him down the road forever. Except that she loved them with all her heart, and they loved her and thought of her as their mother. Add to that, Cam Scott's tendency to snap orders scared the children.

But right now, none of his commanding officer behavior was on display, only his hurt. Gwen remembered how he'd said the children loved her and hated him. She couldn't stop herself from feeling bad for him. He loved these children — his daughter and nephew — and he wanted them to love him back.

But he didn't know how to begin to win their love.

Cam watched his children being happy and sweet to Trace while Cam had no idea how to win their love. His heartache was nearly as painful as his leg.

He was a man with a lot of skills.

He was a top marksman.

He could ride hard all day and march for miles on half rations.

He could read signs like the written word — and that included tracking Indians, and those folks knew all the tricks of hiding a trail.

He could charge into battle with a rifle and a fixed bayonet and not hesitate, not for one second consider running.

He could make hardened soldiers stand up straight and obey him.

But he couldn't make his daughter love him.

He thought of his wife, Madeline. They'd named Maddie Sue for her. He'd barely seen Madeline in the years they'd been together. Their courtship was short, and their honeymoon shorter, because he'd gotten called back to the fighting.

He'd seen Madeline briefly when she was expecting Maddie Sue, then once again he had to return to war. When word reached him that his wife had died from a fever, the funeral was long over. He'd been marching with Sherman, toward the sea, burning as much of Georgia as they could along the way. There'd been no way for a soldier to get leave. Instead he'd written and thanked Abe for minding Maddie Sue.

When finally he did get back home, he found his brother now had his own child, besides Maddie Sue. The little boy named for Cam. Little Cameron . . . Ronnie.

Abe lived in an attic with one bedroom with his wife, Delia, Cam's toddler daughter, Abe's infant son, and Penny. Cam had the offer to head west with the cavalry. He and Abe planned out that Cam would go and, once there, serve out his time, then find a homestead for all of them. Penny had asked to go along. She could work at the fort as well as in a shop in Philadelphia. She'd send part of her pay home, and she and Cam would claim land. The weight that'd take off the overcrowded household was a relief to everyone.

Cam and Penny had gone west. Through it all, Cam had carried his love for his daughter in a special place in his heart. But no child could understand someone loved her from such a distance.

Now here was Cam, at last ready to be a pa to Maddie Sue, and she couldn't stand the sight of him. Both children ignored him, for the most part, if he stayed back from them. And if for some reason they got too close, they burst into tears and ran to Gwen.

He tried to remain calm and easy when he was nearby, but he also knew he felt near desperation to claim them and take them home with him. And even trying his best not to show the urgency he felt, it must've shown regardless.

And now he stood here watching the easy way Trace had with them.

How did he do it? What was the trick?

He watched his child love on another man while not bothering to say hello to her own pa.

Gwen took a second to be grateful he'd put his pants back on. Then she stepped between him and the children before he said something stupid. The man was a master at approaching the children in the worst possible way.

Wolf had stayed inside, and the children were practicing being gentle with him. They weren't very good at it, poor dog.

"Go on and get back in bed," she told Cam. She laced the words with kindness. It was true he was a grump and made every word that came out of his mouth sound like an army officer ordering his troops. But his love for that little girl glowed in his eyes.

"No, she's in a good mood. Maybe now's

a good time —"

"Cam, get back in there. You've got no color in your face. I can almost see the pain pounding in your leg. Let yourself heal. I'll help . . ." It hurt bad to say it. She had to force the words out, yet it was only right. And the man's pain was impossible to ignore — the pain in his heart, not his leg. "I'll help you become Maddie Sue's father." He gave her a look so full of longing, tears burned in her eyes. "Now let's get you off your feet before you fall in a heap." She pressed a hand flat to his chest.

He tore his eyes from Maddie Sue and looked at Gwen. "I don't need you to —" He cut off the angry words when a whimper from Maddie Sue got past his temper. Wolf moved to place himself between Maddie Sue and Cam.

Gwen flinched. Wolf acting like Maddie Sue needed protection from her pa was a hurtful thing for Cam.

Whispering, Gwen said, "Come on, Cam. Back to bed." She patted him on the chest again and marveled at the iron-hard muscles. The width of his shoulders, the dimple in his scruffy chin. None of the men shaved much in winter. Even more quietly she said, "I have an idea that might help you get to know Maddie Sue better. Maybe together we can solve the problems between you two."

"Do you really think so?"

She'd never heard him sound so vulnerable. "Yes, I really do. You just got off on the wrong foot with her. I think I can help her get over that." Her hand still resting on his chest, she added, "She needs to learn you're her papa and you love her, and she needs to fall in love with you. When better than right now when you're trapped in the house for a while?"

Cam nodded, turned, and hopped the few steps back to his bed. All his weight was on the one leg, and the good knee wobbled for a second. Lurching forward, he caught himself on the bed, sprawling facedown. He bumped his leg, and a groan escaped.

Gwen barely heard it because his face was buried in the blankets. Then Cam gathered himself and gingerly rolled over, protecting his foot. He sat up, scooted down the bed, and eased himself to his back with the bedroll for a pillow.

"So, what do we do? Tell me."

Gwen went to great lengths to straighten the blanket, covering his legs, making sure he was comfortable. As she worked, she thought fast. Giving him a shaky smile, finally she said, "Well . . . we can try a few

131

different things, Cam."

Dear God, what things? she prayed. *Help me!*

Truth was, only one thing came to her. She could start with the blunt fact of the matter, but it asked too much of him. And he was so badly injured, it was unkind to lay such a weight on him. She hesitated and prayed even more desperately, but God was not forthcoming with any other ideas but the one.

"Um, you could . . . that is, you need to . . ." She decided then to plunge ahead. "The way I see it, you have to pretty much, uh . . . change." She cleared her throat. "Change your whole, um, n-nature, Cam."

Dead silence reigned for a long moment.

Then Cam said, "How do — ?" He paused.

Gwen watched him fight for calm.

"Change my nature. My nature? Isn't a man's nature, well, isn't that who I am? You want me to change who I am? Come up with some false way of acting and talking, so the children will love that pack of lies?"

She shrugged one shoulder a bit helplessly. "Yes."

Silence again. She hovered near his feet where she'd spent about ten minutes tucking in a blanket that would come loose again the minute Cam lost his temper and ripped it off and threw it on the floor.

She went to the head of the bed, rested a gentle hand on his shoulder, and leaned in far too close. She had to admit, reckless though her behavior was, it drove his temper away.

"I'm afraid that's what I want, Cam. And remember, you asked. I don't think of what I just told you as advising you to lie. To stop snapping out orders, to learn that a little girl wants smiles and patience and sweet words — that isn't lying. In fact, it doesn't even mean changing everything about yourself."

"I'm afraid that's just what it means," he muttered.

Gwen smiled and shook her head. "It means finding the father inside yourself. The tenderness. You've been living among rough men, in charge of dangerous battles. You've been doing it a long time, and I'd bet you were very good at it."

He shrugged. "There were some who said I was among the very best."

"Now you need to set that part of yourself aside." She patted his chest. "You use a different part of yourself with children. And that's not easy for anyone. We all need to learn to watch children, see how our words and actions are affecting them. We gentle our voices and touch them as if they are very fragile. You need to get down on their level. Talk with them instead of giving orders. Tickle them . . . only maybe don't do that until they've started to be more comfortable with you."

"You really think the day will come when my children will be comfortable with me?"

"I do. They're sweet and you love them. We just need to work on it a little." She smiled.

He smiled back. "Considering that this day has been a nightmare up until now, I can't believe how much you just helped."

"Good." Gwen straightened away from him.

Cam caught her hand, and it startled her. At the same time she marveled at his strength, even after all he'd been through.

"You've given me hope, Gwen. Thank you. The most hope I've had since I found the children. And the first real happiness I've felt since I got word that Abe was dead. I've thought this whole time that taking charge and barking orders was a sign of strength, but now you're telling me to behave in a way that seems like weakness. It reminds me of a Bible verse."

"You know the Bible, Cam?" She held his

hand tight and felt a connection to him she'd never felt before. She'd almost go so far as to say she was starting to like the man.

"My folks did a lot of Bible reading when Penny, Abe, and I were growing up. And I've always kept to their strong faith. The verse I remember is, 'My strength is made perfect in weakness.' "

"I've heard that verse. It makes absolutely no sense."

"Nope, never did to me either. But here I am, laid low, weak as a newborn foal, and I've never needed God's strength more. Maybe it's time I showed a little weakness to win my daughter's love."

"It has to be in the Bible for a reason. Maybe this is the right moment for it."

"I'm going to need help, Gwen. I'm going to need someone to kick me when I'm saying the wrong thing."

"I'll aim for your good leg."

"Or you can just slap the back of my head those times when I bark out an order."

Gwen gasped in mock pleasure. "I have your permission for that? Because I would dearly love slapping you."

Cam narrowed his eyes, but they were lit with humor. Gwen gave him an unrepentant grin.

"I'll want you to jab an elbow into my gut

135

when my temper flares."

"Why, Cameron Scott, it would be my greatest pleasure to do every one of those things. In fact, I can see that it's gonna be almost pure fun! I believe I can give you, right here and now, my most solemn pledge to kick, slap, and jab you whenever I think it's called for."

Gwen smiled as she walked out of the room. She was surprised to hear Cam laughing behind her. She thought it might be the very first time she'd ever heard him laugh.

Keeping Cam in bed for the last four days was harder than keeping the snow from falling.

Harder than asking the sun not to rise.

Harder than his stubborn head.

"I swear I'm going to tie you right to that bed if you don't lie down." Gwen had gotten the job of tending him.

Penny, the toughest woman Gwen had ever known, got the vapors around her brother and his ugly leg wound, even though it was completely covered by a bandage.

Deb seemed more inclined to smack him over the head with the cast-iron skillet. Which she resisted by refusing to deal with him.

The men just laughed and left the cabin to work. They had a fine excuse to escape from the growling.

That left Gwen, and she hadn't ruled out the skillet entirely. She went into his room to get the plate from the noon meal she'd brought him.

He was sitting up, legs swung over the side of the bed. "I am ready to be up, Gwen. Just help me to a chair in the kitchen and let me do *something.*" His voice dropped to a whisper. "I swear you're going to come in here and find me with every hair on my head ripped right out if I can't get a look at something besides these four walls."

Gwen started to snip back at him, then paused. She looked at his terribly messy, overly long dark hair. She was shocked at how badly she wanted to run her fingers through it to smooth it down.

"It's been only four days since you were hurt. Two days since I put in those stitches. You're such a wretched patient, you are always asking for something you shouldn't get. So, I've gotten in the habit of saying no to everything. But this time I'm saying *yes.* The men are out in the barn building chairs from some scrap wood. There is work for you to do in here, and later, Trace said you could help do the finishing work on the chairs. The children are both napping, so we don't have to deal with them crying right now."

Cam flinched at that.

"Yes, I think it's time. Let's get you out of bed and out to the kitchen table."

"Go slow. Every time I stand, my head spins until I'm afraid I'll pass out." Cam grabbed the edge of the bed.

"Slow? I thought you were desperate to get up?"

"Just sitting here, my vision went slowly black. I had to let it clear before I could eat. It always happens when I sit up, then stays that way a few seconds before it starts to clear again."

"And that's why you want me to go slow?"

"Nope, that's not why. I want time because, between now and the minute I hop out there to the table, I've got to change everything about myself. I doubt there's enough time in the world, but I'll at least be glad for a few minutes."

And Gwen would be glad if a new, kinder, less bossy Cam Scott sat down in her kitchen. She decided then to give him all the time he wanted.

Cam gripped the wall above the little cot he slept on, using that to balance himself as he stood. "Let me stand here for a minute.

My vision clears quickly." He breathed in and out until he could see. "All right, I'm ready. The throb in my leg has settled down to hammer blows."

Gwen slid her hand around his waist. "I'm so sorry you're hurting."

He glanced down at her, his brown eyes laced with pain, yet they seemed calmer than usual. "Let's go present to the world the lying weakling, the smiley wimp of a man, the new Cameron Scott."

Gwen was tempted to take her arm away and let him fall on his face. *Bet he'd be hard-pressed to be smiley then,* she thought.

"Cam, remember when I said earlier you've got to completely change your whole nature?"

"Yes?" He was definitely growling.

"You should go ahead and start right now."

"All right, fine. Consider me changed."

Instead of following her instincts and dropping him, she held on tight, shook her head, and muttered, "I'll believe it when I see it."

CHAPTER 10

Penny could be heard quietly singing in the room where the children slept. Deb sat at the kitchen table with pieces of cutout leather before her, pushing a needle hard to get it through the tough tanned hide.

Gwen helped Cam to a chair directly across from Deb.

"Where'd you get the fool notion to sew leather like that?" Cam sat down at the table and scowled.

Gwen slapped him on the back of his head.

A surprise laugh escaped from Deb.

It was such a shock that Cam didn't even think about hitting back — which of course he wouldn't have done anyway. "You know, none of the men under my command would've ever dared to swat me."

"Well I'm not one of them. I suspect you've noticed that, but a reminder may be in order." Gwen stood at the head of the table, her back to the fireplace. Cam sat on her left, Deb on her right. She put her hands flat on the tabletop and leaned so close to Cam, they almost touched noses.

She whispered, though Cam thought it sounded more like a hiss, a snakelike hiss. He braced himself in case she started to rattle.

"Listen to what you're doing to the children," she hissed so that only he could hear her.

And then he focused on the room closest to the shuttered window they'd climbed out that first day.

Ronnie was sobbing. He'd been quiet before.

Maddie Sue said something, but her little voice was so quiet that he couldn't make out words, only that she was upset.

Penny made cooing sounds. "Don't be scared. He's not mad. His leg just hurts."

Cam saw Penny's fingertips slowly swing the door shut to keep the noise down. Cam regretted being loud. At least Penny was on his side, which wouldn't stop her from slapping him, too. He'd never managed to get her to obey him.

"Sorry," he whispered back. He then turned to Deb. "Sorry," he said again.

He reached out his hand for the needle.

She nodded and handed it over. Deb hadn't gotten a single stitch in yet. Cam saw one of her fingers was already bleeding.

He whispered to Gwen, "Get my saddle-bags out from under my bed. The leather one with 'US Army' stamped on it."

He watched.

She watched back. Hands still flat. Finally she arched a brow. He had no idea what she wanted, but then a notion that seemed ridiculous, and yet possible, flickered through his head.

"Uh . . . please?"

With a jerk of her tensed jaw, she turned and left. He envied her two working legs.

"Cam," Deb said.

"What?"

"Can I slap you, too?"

Gwen was back before he could think of what to say to Deb and her request. Good thing. He took a vow of silence . . . unless it got to be too much of a nuisance.

Penny went back to her singing.

He took out a small cloth packet out of his saddlebag and unrolled it to find his sewing tools. He picked up the leather from Deb. One glance told him she was sewing up the side seams of a large coat. It must be for Trace. He was the only man who'd lost clothes in the cabin fire.

He took out his sewing awl and a spool of heavy thread that'd stand up to this work. Deb had a regular spool of thread, fine for sewing a dress or shirt, but that was about all.

With a quick look at Deb, who studied the awl and seemed fascinated by it, and Gwen, who hadn't hit him in nearly a minute, he showed them how to make a coat out of buckskin — all without saying a word.

Maybe not speaking was the change Gwen was looking for. Cam would keep it up as long as he could. It helped that he could really do some good here, considering these women had no idea how to sew leather. And obviously he was a hand at it.

But it hurt to sit with the women. He wondered how long it'd take to be healthy enough he could go back to being tough again. He preferred that.

Then he thought of the children and knew he never could.

Whatever his future held, he'd better watch out, or he'd be living it alone.

Raddo slipped close enough to the cabin to scale some high rocks and see if he'd killed the woman he wanted dead. He knew Riley had survived. Through his spyglass he saw

143

the blackened skeleton of the cabin.

He lowered the glass and settled in. He was a patient man, dressed for long hunts. His skis were still on — he almost never took them off when he was out and about. He wasn't that far from where he'd wintered. He had plenty of food until the snow melted. Raddo knew the ways of the Sierra Nevada Mountains and could tear his own survival out of them, but the living was hard.

Spring had a fight on her hands driving winter back north. Even so, she'd win out. She always did. While he didn't want to wait until then to act, he might have to.

He'd hoped to smother them all with smoke — bunkhouse and cabin. Then set the fires with no one even waking up. The house mattered most. That was where the folks who'd seen him lived. But he'd figured to burn to nothing the bunkhouse, too.

He should've had plenty of time with the smoke smothering them all quietly. Yet somehow those men in the bunkhouse had woken up and gotten out.

Thanks to the skis, he'd escaped to safety. Only he hadn't been able to see if he'd killed the witnesses. With Riley still alive . . . well, he could only hope he'd gotten the woman.

Raddo had been there at his perch for

hours when two women climbed out of a window of the bunkhouse. He watched their every move, studied them with his spyglass, but he couldn't make out their faces. They were bundled up with scarves with their coat collars pulled high.

He could barely recognize the window, because the back of the building was buried in snow all the way to the roof with only the chimney showing, which was now belching out smoke.

Raddo had skied right up to the top of the roof of both the bunkhouse and the cabin, easiest thing he'd ever done, even carrying kerosene and scraps of wood and stones to plug the chimneys with. And he'd thought it'd be enough, especially since he never figured for 'em to wake up.

They hadn't dug the rest of the bunkhouse out of the snow, but why would they? Deep snow would keep them warm.

He pondered how he might use that against 'em while he watched.

Just as the women reached the privy, they both unwrapped their coats enough for Raddo to see two heads pop out. The women each carried a child.

There were only three woman — two of them and both young'uns had lived — and he'd studied them from this look-out long enough to know the women and children were all in the cabin. Everyone had survived. He hadn't thinned the herd by even one.

Which meant he needed to try again. They'd killed Meeks, his saddle partner. Dalt sat in a jail cell, a tough man who'd done prison time before. Raddo didn't think he'd talk because Dalt prided himself on his toughness. Besides, to talk about his saddle partners would be to admit attacking that wagon train. Turning on Raddo would only earn Dalt a noose.

If it'd been the other way around — Dalt dead, Meeks in prison — Raddo would've had to find a way to bust Meeks out or, failing that, kill him. The man was a weakling who'd point hard and fast at others in hopes of saving his own hide.

He grunted. As if there was any saving for men who'd massacred innocent folks riding along on a wagon train.

Raddo had abandoned his partners to save himself, just like any savvy outlaw would. It'd left him on foot with only the clothes on his back and a few supplies stashed in a hideout cave, where he and his gang had lightened their load. He was lucky he had a habit of grabbing his pack and rifle, and that included the spyglass. He'd had a couple of days' worth of food and mighty little else, not with winter coming on.

He'd lived out here long enough to understand the ways of finding shelter and meat. He didn't dare leave killing the witnesses until spring. Once the snow loosened its grip, the woman — that one small, weak woman, the one he'd had in his clutches for a short time who'd been there as an eyewitness to his crimes — that woman would spread word of Raddo far and wide.

He clasped and unclasped his hands. He should've killed her dead the minute he had the chance. But he'd wanted to use her to lure in Riley. Except Riley hadn't witnessed the crime — he'd only known Raddo was guilty because of the woman. If Raddo had just killed her when he had the chance, he'd've been content to ride away.

Now he intended to kill them both, because he knew Riley would be coming for him. Or sending the law after him. To think he could've slipped out of this whole mess had he just killed that woman . . . He'd been a fool by making things too complicated.

And he'd pay dearly for that if either of them survived.

Raddo studied the ranch yard and thought of the one man he knew had the clout to help him out. Luther Payne. But Luth wouldn't wanna be dragged into Raddo's trouble.

Luther Payne, what a name he'd chosen for himself. Raddo shook his head and smiled. Luth had turned honest, or rather his crimes weren't committed with guns these days. And Luth had gotten himself very rich. He'd shed his outlaw skin like a snake. Yet Raddo knew Luth was just a different, sneakier kind of snake now. Luth wouldn't like word getting out about who he really was, and Raddo was the one who could prove Luth's crimes and send him to the nearest hanging tree.

Raddo saw men coming out of the barn. There were a few footprints wading in, but now they all came out — one of them carrying two pails, milk probably. The man took both pails to the hole they'd dug out of the bunkhouse and went inside. Then the rest of men got to shoveling. Just like any other day.

Raddo studied them. He knew Trace Riley well enough by now, and Riley was the man who most needed to die. Those were tough men down there, though, four outside working and one more who hadn't come out in a while.

Raddo had seen the spot where he'd left that bear trap and knew he'd gotten one of 'em — a man, not a bear — yet he also knew that man was still alive and healing well enough to step outside and, with a lot of help, get himself to the privy. That made five men in all. Every one of them as determined to protect Riley, the women, children, and each other as Raddo was to see a couple of 'em dead. Raddo very much doubted they'd let someone shoot Riley dead without a fight.

Somehow he had to cut Riley and the woman out of the pack.

Raddo knew that wouldn't be easy. If he couldn't do it on his own, then he needed more men. And he doubted he could find the help. This was Raddo's mess, and he didn't see any money to be made out of it. If he couldn't silence these witnesses by himself, then Raddo would need the kind of assistance only Luth could give.

Raddo intended to make very sure Luth knew exactly how high the stakes were. As high as a gallows.

CHAPTER 11

"Boss?" Utah came close to Trace and scooped.

Trace glanced at him and saw that Utah was focused on the snow and talking low. Taking the hint, he kept on scooping. "What is it?"

"I saw a flare of light up on top of that bald knob to the west of us."

"Flare of light?" Trace's mind rabbited around.

"Yep, a spyglass maybe or a —"

"Rifle scope." Trace didn't have to look at the spot Utah had referred to. "That's out of rifle range."

"Which is why I'm thinking spyglass. We're being watched, boss."

"Raddo." Trace wasn't asking. "We knew he'd come back."

"I've scouted enough to know it'd be nigh on to impossible to climb up the slope from this side to where he's set up without being seen." Utah scooped again. "You know this land better than anyone. Can we swing around, come up on him from behind?"

Trace thought out the land. "Nope, no way without riding for miles through drifts we can't cross. I know the way that'll clear out first when the snow melts. We can leave before dawn and reach that spot."

"Even if he's not there, we can trail him back to where he's holed up."

"We'll plan on it after the chinook arrives." Trace thought of the warm west winds that brought spring with them. But then right back to that varmint watching them. He knew Deb was Raddo's main target, but the man was a villain right down to the soles of his feet. He'd kill whoever got in his way. Man, woman, or child.

"I'm starting to believe there is no spring, Trace. It's all a tall tale told by desperate men."

Trace straightened from his scooping. He'd reached the door of the barn. They did this every morning, and even as he stood, snow sifted down. Fat flakes today, so big they'd almost knock a man down.

"We're dealing with someone desperate to keep any eyewitnesses from testifying. I wonder if it's just the massacre, or is there more? But what more could a man face other than multiple murders? And why doesn't he just clear out of the country? With those skis he could've gotten out in the winter. Seein' he's still here, we know he's been able to live off the land."

"Some arrogance there."

"He must think he can escape prison if the evidence against him is weak enough. Like he's got an ace hidden up his sleeve."

Utah jammed his shovel into the snow lining the trench they'd dug to the barn. "But what could that be?" Utah rubbed his chin.

"And Cam is mad enough about his brother's death," Trace said, "that we're going to have a hard time bringing that varmint in alive anyway."

"Well, we gotta try. But if someone's shooting at me, boss, I s'pect I'll be shooting back."

Nodding, Trace went into the barn. Utah got a pitchfork while Adam caught up a horse to go check the cattle in the canyon.

Trace told Adam what was going on so he could keep an eye out. The group did their work somberly that day. But they'd been grim since they'd almost died in the fire, so not much had changed.

Cam had turned into a teacher.

Strange.

Oh, he'd taught lots of people lots of things. He'd taught raw recruits how to shoot. He'd taught men how to shave out of a cold stream. He'd taught soldiers how to salute, stand at attention, and say "Yes, sir" loud and clear. But he'd taught them by yelling, by threatening, and sometimes by throwing a poor learner into the stockade.

Yet he'd never taught a woman how to sew before. And sure enough never when he was under the threat of crying babies. He had a fear of crying women too, though none of the women here had ever cried in front of him. Women on the frontier surely knew better than to cry.

He was afraid to find out.

Penny knew the ways of an awl and how to cut and sew sturdy leather into a coat. As he'd suspected, Utah and Adam each had a sewing kit with an awl. Penny and Trace both had one too, but they were buried under what remained of the cabin. Penny should've kept hers in her leather bag, but it couldn't hold everything.

Even without those two, he had three kits, enough that he and two of the three women could work at the same time. The third woman kept busy cooking, tending the children, or sewing on regular clothes.

By the end of nap time on the third day,

the first coat was done, and it'd been a week since Cam had been caught in the bear trap.

He had Gwen and Deb working because they needed the practice. The sisters faced each other, one on either side of the table, with himself on the fourth side farthest from the fireplace and closest to his bedroom. They were all working on a section of the second coat while Penny stitched on a pair of pants for Maddie Sue.

Ronnie started crying.

"I'm between seams, I'll get him." Deb jumped up.

"Wait a minute, Deb." Gwen stopped her.

"What is it?"

Gwen turned to Cam. He sure hoped she didn't expect him to go and get the little ones. They'd be so upset, it'd be all afternoon settling them down again. Not to mention he didn't know if he could carry a baby and hop at the same time.

"Cam, you and I need to get down on the floor with this coat. I want the children to see you calmly sewing and working with me. Penny, you stay seated at the table. Deb, you come and sit down with us and hold Maddie Sue and Ronnie. Cam, no talking."

He realized what she was doing, helping him to get the children to like him, so he listened to her every word.

"You be as close to invisible as a six-foot-tall man can be. We're not going to win them over in a day, but maybe in a week's time they'll stop screaming at the sight of you."

Cam scowled at the harsh but unfortunately true description of how the little ones behaved in his presence.

She caught him by his collar and jerked on it. "And you hear me well, Cameron Scott, if one of those children jumps up and down on your leg, you never make a scowling face, and you don't make a sound. *Is that clear?*"

He hunched his shoulders and nodded. "Yes, ma'am."

He slid off the chair and scooted over to sit in front of the fireplace, his leg paining him with every move. He started wondering just how hard it was gonna be to stand back up.

Penny stayed where she was. Gwen joined him on the floor and sat at a right angle to him like she had at the table.

Deb headed for Ronnie. Before she got to the door, Maddie Sue hollered, "I want up." She chanted it as if it were a song.

He'd've liked to have one child at a time. When there were two, if one of them forgot to hate him, the other would be sure to remember. One at a time, he had a better chance.

As Deb left the room, Gwen hissed, "Be careful with that awl. If the children get hold of it, they could put their eyes out."

Cam paused to look at the innocent little tool and shuddered.

"Have you ever heard of Braille?" Gwen asked.

"No, is that a person?"

"A Frenchman actually. He blinded himself in one eye when, as a child, he accidentally stabbed himself in the eye with an awl. Then he got an infection that spread, and by the time it was all over, he'd lost the sight in both eyes. Braille invented a kind of writing that the blind can read. It's a series of raised dots formed in a certain way that they can be read by touching them. Deb wrote an article about him for the paper."

"He put his eye out with an awl?" Cam grimaced. "That's a terrible story."

"It is," Gwen said with a sharp hiss. "I'm hoping it's the kind of story that makes a man be careful with sharp tools around children."

Nodding, Cam tried to get comfortable on the floor. The sewing was harder because now he held the awl so tightly — for fear the little ones might snatch it away — that it was hurting his fingers.

Deb came out with the children, one riding on each of her hips. As she talked to them, Maddie Sue giggled and wrapped her arms around Deb's neck. Ronnie had his head rested on her shoulder, his eyes heavy, with a crease from a wrinkle in the blanket across his right cheek.

Ronnie's eyes opened and, without lifting his head, scanned the room. Cam went back to focusing on his work before Ronnie caught him staring.

"Let's get a drink of milk and some bread and butter for you both." Deb went about getting Maddie Sue and Ronnie an afternoon snack.

Cam listened to every word spoken but kept his eyes on his work and his hand on the awl. He realized he was pulling the threads too tight, causing the seam to not lay flat. So he had to go back and fiddle with the thread to smooth out the seam.

Finally, Deb came back and sat on the floor at the end of their rectangle with Gwen on her right. Cam could lift his eyes and look straight at Deb, but he didn't. Instead he glanced sideways at Gwen a couple of times, and then she'd glare until he looked back down.

Deb didn't start her sewing back up. Cam

was relieved. He was afraid he was going to have to knock the awl out of her hand, and that would upset the children for sure. She entertained the little ones until they climbed off her lap and began wandering the room. With Cam's back to the fire, he could block the children from getting close to that danger.

Cam realized they hadn't started crying at the sight of him. He must've finally managed to be near them without scaring them half to death.

And all he had to do was never speak, never look them in the eyes, just generally ignore them.

For the rest of his life.

Nice welcome home for Papa.

"There's no more track?" John McCall ripped his hat off his head and whacked himself with it on the leg. "I thought I could take this all the way to Nevada. The agent who sold me my ticket told me the railroad is almost done."

The man selling tickets rolled his eyes. "It is almost done. We've come near to six hundred miles, and we've only got about four hundred more to go. This railroad'll be done within two years."

John looked down at his ticket with disgust. No one had made it clear that the train tracks were two years away from being fully built. Clearly, John hadn't asked the right questions.

This trip was being sidetracked by tracks, of all things, or in this case, the lack thereof.

The whole trip had been a struggle. The train had stopped for ice and hail. A blizzard stopped them on the cold train for three days in the middle of Nebraska. The food had run low by the time the blizzard ended, and John and the rest of the passengers helped dig the train out on short rations.

The fact that the train carried plenty of shovels was all the proof John needed to know this happened regularly.

The conductor kept assuring them it was spring and the bad weather was just an oddity. It was a lovely time to travel. But the farther west they went, and the higher altitude they reached, the worse the conditions got.

Now there were no conditions at all. "How do I get to Nevada, then?"

The man behind the ticket counter, a man who only sold tickets for folks heading east apparently, furrowed his weathered brow. "Nevada? Is that a new state? It sounds familiar."

John would have thought the man was stupid, except everything he knew about Nevada he'd learned only since heading for the place. "It's the last stop before you get to California."

The man chewed on the corners of a droopy gray mustache while he considered that information. "Most folks don't stop, I reckon. They just go on to California and never even mention Nevada."

"How about the Comstock Lode — have you heard of that?"

The man perked up. "I surely have. Is Virginia City where you're goin', young feller? Why didn't you say so? Rough life in a silver camp, but they're haulin' millions in bullion out of there."

"The Comstock Lode is close to where I'm going. But I have to go on farther west. I'll head out if you'll tell me how to get there."

"You can't get there from here."

John was silent for a few long seconds. "And why is that?"

"Everything past Virginia City is filled with snow above the treetops. The California Trail passes over the Sierra Nevada Mountains west of Virginia City, and it's closed down for the winter and that's that. It's the reason the Union Pacific has to lay one thousand miles of track, while Central

160

Pacific only needs six hundred miles. We got the easy part so we had to do the greater share. We didn't have to figure out how to lay track through the Sierra Nevada Mountains. They're a fright."

"What do I do? There has to be a way through."

"You could get on with a wagon train, if you wait for spring."

"It's April! Spring was a month ago." John was usually a little calmer than this. The western frontier was a different sort of place than he'd been before. All his skills seemed to be useless out here, and this long, harsh journey was wearing him clean out.

"Wouldn't matter. The wagon trains set out from St. Louie in the spring, but they come through here midsummer."

"So I don't need to wait for spring; I need to wait for *summer*?"

"Well, I reckon you could go on the wagon train trail." The man chewed his mustache again.

John felt the hundred dollars the Chiltons had promised him slipping through his fingers. And the bonus of another fifty. He'd be lucky to ever get to this boy, and then he'd have to hightail it home, or the winter would stop him again.

"You'd have to go alone, on horseback to

where it splits off to the California Trail. That'd get you to Virginia City, but not beyond. Rugged land out there for a man alone."

John felt his stomach sink. "Rugged?"

The man shrugged. "You know, Indians, blizzards, rattlesnakes, grizzly bears, avalanches of both snow and rock. And your general outlaw bands. There's a reason folks go in big groups."

John thought of why he was on this trip: because a wagon train had been massacred. What chance did he have going alone?

"Is there a sheriff in Cheyenne? I'm a lawman myself. He might be able to advise me on what to do to get there fastest. Sheriffs often transport prisoners and such."

The old man gave directions to the sheriff's office that were much better than the ones he'd given to Nevada.

Gwen made Cam sit on the floor every day between meals. It took another week before she gave him permission to look up. The children gave him wary looks, but he smiled and didn't speak and kept sewing.

Trace's coat was done, and three more for Penny, Deb, and Gwen.

Utah made him crutches, though Gwen didn't want him clomping around on them.

162

She was afraid the children would find it scary. So he sat.

By the end of the second week, Cam was allowed to sit at the table and work on finishing chairs so they could all eat at once.

In the third week the swelling in his leg went down, and the ugly cut looked fully healed. Gwen said she'd take the stitches out if he'd swear to go easy on his leg for one more week.

He wasn't sure how she'd define "go easy." He decided he'd be the judge of *easy* and made the promise.

And he talked to the children now. One day, Gwen made a cake and let Cam offer tiny bits of it to the children. Pure bribery, but the little ones let him share his food. He felt like he was gentling fractious horses by offering them sugar. And in fact that was just about what he was doing.

At the end of week four, he woke up in the middle of the night and smiled. He'd become a smilin' fool in the last month whether he wanted to be or not. But this was worth smiling over. The cabin was strangely warm, and he heard a sound that made him sit up and think of all that was possible.

Spring had finally come to the Sierra Nevadas.

■ ■ ■ ■

Gwen heard a sound that almost sent her into a panic. She sat up in bed, thinking of the fire and the man who'd attacked them.

Save the children!

She didn't start screaming and running, though. Her brain started working in time. Though who could say if she had good instincts about things like fighting for her life?

Yes, she'd had an overly large dose of fighting for her life lately. But most of her life had been as calm as a frozen lake.

She hadn't appreciated that nearly enough.

She studied the noise. It wasn't fire she was hearing.

She felt Ronnie stir beside her and sat still as a rock, not wanting to wake the boy. While it was always dark in her room, usually she could see a bit with her door open and the embers of the fireplace glowing.

Ronnie stopped shifting. She felt him settle deeply back to sleep.

Then, an inch at a time, she slid her legs out of bed and stood. As always, she slept fully clothed right down to her shoes and stockings. Even through the soles of her shoes, she knew instantly what was different, besides that unusual noise of course.

The floor didn't send waves of cold up her legs.

She slipped out of the room. And then she figured it out.

The sound was water dripping.

No, not dripping. It was water running, pouring. Rain?

She inched open one of the shutters. The mountain of snow burying them was pouring down! She still looked out a short tunnel leading to the ground, then on through the snow. But she could see the ground now, which glistened with running water under bright moonlight.

She smiled as she stood before that open window. There was a breeze, but it didn't hurt. For the first time in months, the wind felt mild. Winter was losing its battle with spring. A chunk of snow splatted down from the top of the tunnel, and water poured from drifts that grew pointy with miniature icicles.

Movement whirled her around. A shadow approached, but the panic was from being startled. She wasn't afraid of anyone in the cabin. Then she noticed the slow, uneven way the newcomer moved. Limping.

She whispered, "Morning, Cam. The

snow's melting."

Gwen smiled so big she felt the curve of her lips lift her heart. Cam couldn't see her so it didn't matter to anyone but her. She turned to face out the window again.

He came up beside her and stood close enough that their shoulders brushed against each other. "It's a chinook wind."

"Chinook?" Gwen's brow furrowed.

Cam nodded. "Chinook people call it the Ice Eater Wind, the warm wind that blows over the mountains from the ocean, after a whole winter of winds coming from the north. We'll watch that snow shrink like a wool shirt in boiling water."

A large part of the outside edge of the snow tunnel collapsed, and they could see the moon surrounded by a sky lit with stars.

"Spring has finally come." Gwen sighed at the thought.

"It can turn cold again, and it'll almost certainly snow again, but yes — spring has come." He slung an arm around her waist and smiled down at her. "We are winning the war against winter."

"War is a fine way to describe it. A war fought with shovels instead of guns."

She didn't protest his arm around her. It felt like the two of them were in this together. Surviving the winter. Welcoming the spring.

And then she remembered what else she'd noticed. "You're walking on your poor beat-up leg. Do you think that's wise?"

"It's not hurting too bad. It's about back to its normal size. Ugly scar, but it isn't my first one."

It'd been over a month since the bear trap, and Gwen had removed the stitches.

"I've been careful since you removed the threads. The wound looks well healed now. The pain's mostly gone. In fact, I didn't notice I'd left the crutches before I'd walked a fair piece. Tomorrow I'm getting back to work, and the crutches stay behind."

"Maybe you should wait a bit longer."

"No, I've been a layabout long enough. I'm not gonna —"

"Hush now." She patted him on the chest. She'd thought a few times that touching him calmed him. Like petting a nervous horse. "It's not about your work, Cam. It's about how things are going with the little ones. The children are getting better with you. Maddie Sue smiled at you yesterday and took a bite of cake right off your fork. And Ronnie called you Papa."

"Yep, I'm his papa too now. My brother's son is taking me into his heart. I see no reason to explain that he and Maddie Sue aren't brother and sister, not when they're so young yet. I want them both to know about Abe, but not until they're older."

"Should you give your leg another week or two just because you're near a truce with your children?"

A chunk of snow the size of a man crashed down from overhead, hit the lip of the vanishing tunnel, and opened their line of vision even wider.

Gwen could see the snow disappearing at the same time she could see there was a lot left to go, but she loved the sight and sound of rushing water.

"The drift swallowing the bunkhouse might well be gone by morning."

He turned his face to hers, and they were too close.

And they stayed too close.

"For the first time I have hope that the children will come to love me." His eyes never left hers. "And I owe that to you, Gwen. The advice you gave, the times you swatted me to get my attention when I was upsetting them."

"Getting your attention is often a challenge."

A smile broke over Cam's face. "I'll bet that's the plain, bald truth."

How many times had she seen him show even the faintest sign of cheer? She'd never seen a full genuine smile like this one. Oh, he'd been smiling at the children, but she could see it was all forced, not a full out, happy, honest smile like this one.

He was so much more handsome than she'd realized. His time inside had earned him a haircut and a close shave. His clothes stayed clean. He'd stopped rapping out orders. Why, the man was halfway to civilized.

She could think of no earthly reason to look away from that smile.

The moonlight, the unexpected warmth — well, warmth relative to what they'd been having. The sound of spring pouring over their house. A man who, for all his grouchy ways, had just been kinder to her than her own father had ever been.

And then that smile drew closer for a hovering second, two seconds, five. Then he stumbled back.

He rubbed the back of his neck and inspected the floor between his toes. "Um . . . well, you might be right about M-Maddie Sue and Ronnie and my l-leg . . . uh, resting it more."

He was talking more to his leg than to her. Which was just as well because her head

169

was kind of fuzzy from whatever had just happened between them.

He said, "We should go to bed."

A rush of shocking heat swept through her.

He gave his head a violent shake, then took a wild look at her and snapped his eyes right back to the floor.

"I mean *I'd* better get to bed, and you too, but not . . . we. N-Not, that is, w-we shouldn't do anything. Not t-together. We . . ." He looked up again and whirled to face his bedroom. "Good night."

He moved to that bedroom at a mighty fast pace for a limping man.

CHAPTER 12

Cam rushed to finish his breakfast, washing it down with coffee hot enough to leave a scorched track the length of his throat. Then he got up and left the house through the window, all in a hurry.

He barely spoke to Gwen, never looked her in the eye, and sure as certain never touched her. Enough of that'd gone on last night. He'd decided he would stay in the house a bit longer, until that one long moment when he'd forgotten about most everything in the whole world except how pretty she was and how the moonlight bathed her skin and blond hair until she looked like an angel. An angel with tempting lips.

Cam was sorely afraid thinking that was a pure sin.

He strode — well, strode to the extent he was able — toward the barn, thinking about Gwen and how everything about her was a bad idea. His boots dragged through the slushy snow. Little of the ground had been uncovered yet, but before long much of it surely would be. They'd have mud every-where by nightfall, with a river running through the yard for days most likely.

"You coming with us?" Trace spoke almost into his ear and way too loud. Cam had the feeling it wasn't the first time Trace had asked him that question.

"I'm ready to work. Check the cattle for newborns, fork dirty straw out of stalls, feed chickens, milk cows — anything that needs doing. Wait, what do you mean, coming with you?"

The barn was just ahead. Cam had slowed, and all the men caught up with him. He saw Trace look over his shoulder at the house. None of the women were in sight.

Cam thought Trace was looking for Gwen. Somehow he knew about last night. Some-how —

"Utah saw someone watching the place from high ground."

Trace was whispering. He knew nothing about an uncommonly close moment be-tween Cam and Gwen. Instead he was just trying to make sure the women didn't hear him.

Just because Cam could think of nothing

172

but Gwen didn't mean anyone else was thinking along those lines.

"We couldn't reach the lookout spot from here, not without a fight through high drifts and up an ice-covered slope. Otherwise we'd need to go around a huge mountain, and going around means the same sort of drifts."

"Wait, hold up. Lookout spot? How long have you known this? It has to be Raddo. Why didn't you tell me? Why didn't we — ?"

Trace punched Cam in the arm. Not too hard.

Cam raised a brow. "That reminds me a little of Gwen swatting me on the head."

"And what do you do then?"

"I shut up and listen."

Trace nodded. "Good. Now let me finish. We couldn't tell you because the women were always around and we didn't want them to worry. We didn't go when we first saw him because we couldn't. We decided to wait until the spring melt. That's today. We're headin' up there to find Raddo, and if not him, then his trail, and follow it to where Raddo's hiding out. It's time to put an end to the trouble stalking us."

"The fool's probably sharing a cave with a hungry grizz," Utah muttered, sounding glum. "The bear'll think that Raddo is his friend, and we're his first meal of the spring."

"Adam went to the canyon to check the cattle," Trace said, ignoring Utah. "There are enough chores to keep you both busy for the day."

Utah added, "By tomorrow the snow oughta shrink enough that we can start chopping down trees. We can have that cabin back up fast. But I want the man who brought it down — I don't aim to build another cabin for him to destroy."

"We're wasting time." Cam turned toward the barn and picked up speed. Soon he had a horse saddled and was waiting for the others. His leg hurt like a sore tooth, but that was mostly from his not moving much for a month. He didn't feel any weakness under the new scar, nor deep muscle pain.

"Lead the horses awhile. It's quieter. And just keep walking — don't look at the cabin," Trace said. "Even if they're outside, we'll pretend like they're inside. So long as we don't make eye contact, we can keep right on moving."

"That sounds mighty hopeful, and it's probably not called for." As they started across the yard, Cam found himself holding his breath and looking away from the bunk-house with such determination that it made his neck ache.

"You stop right there." And then his neck really did ache. The hand around his collar was way too familiar, and the voice — hard as the ice still clinging to the eaves — was the final proof.

"I'm not staying in that house for one more day." Penny. His sister didn't like being in the house too long.

He'd forgotten that.

"I've barely been out of the bunkhouse, nor the cabin before it, except for trips to the —"

Cam slowly turned to face the inevitable. Penny's cheeks pinked a bit as she looked past Cam to Trace. Then her voice dropped to a whisper.

"— trips to the privy" — not a whisper but a hiss — "for months." Not a snake hiss either. More like a stick of dynamite burning fast through its fuse.

Then she went back to talking in her normal loud voice. "I've been inside all day every day. I've been caring for adorable children, working alongside very nice women, and tending men I respect." Her blazing dark eyes didn't match her sweet words. Not one speck. Especially when she tightened her grip on his collar and started twisting and shaking, like a mama might

when sending a naughty child to his room.
Except Penny was real pleasant to the little
ones — just not her big brother.

"And if I don't get out of that bunkhouse
soon, it's gonna go up in smoke just like the
cabin did. Only this time you can lay the
blame right at my boots, because the fire's
gonna be caused when my head explodes."

Her eyes sharpened. Penny was a smart
one. She saw the tracks of horses leading to
the canyon. Noticed Adam was gone and
that Trace had already started up a trail no
one but him could see.

Cam didn't know how she'd noticed all of
this. He just knew his sister. She had learned
a lot of things living with army troops for
two years. And one of them was how to
judge a situation in seconds. He'd depended
on her, and now he was regretting just how
savvy she was.

"Where are you going?" She finally let go
of Cam's collar and looked from Trace, in
the lead, to Cam, then to Utah, who'd
frozen in the doorway of the barn.

Cam made an assessment of his own.
Utah had been trying to sneak backward,
one silent step at a time, hoping to escape
unnoticed just in case Penny blew.

He'd failed.

"I'm going with you," Penny announced.

"No, you're not." Trace had to get involved. It was almost like the man wasn't afraid. Which meant he was stupid. Because anyone who knew Penny for more than ten minutes and didn't fear her flashing eyes and that dynamite-fuse hissing tone was dumb as a snowdrift.

"Watch me." Penny was in no mood to discuss it.

Cam hoped Trace knew he'd made a lucky escape. But just in case, he said, "We can't stop her."

"She can't go." Trace got a stubborn look on his face.

Utah jumped out of Penny's way as she charged into the barn. So, Utah was thinking straight.

"She's going, Trace. We can ride on, but she'll just trail behind us. We can't get away from her." Cam realized he had the forlorn voice of a man looking at life from behind a jailhouse door. He practically heard the sound as the bars clanged shut.

"You just go right on in there and stop her."

Cam led his horse forward so he could speak clearer to Trace and get past the man's muddled thinking. Utah came along as if hoping someone had a plan.

"My sister can out-track all of us."

Utah snorted. "As if following the trail of three horses over snow takes any skill."

"She can outride all of us."

"No one can outride me." Trace's jaw clenched.

"Now's not the time to get your manly pride knotted up. I'd stop her if I could. And I'd try too, if I didn't know her." He sighed. "Let's just get going."

"No!" Trace practically howled the word as he swung up onto the back of his black mustang stallion.

Penny came striding out of the barn at that point. She must've figured out what Trace was howling about, because she mounted up and rode right toward them. She could out-stubborn any man, woman, or child any day of the week and twice on Sunday.

"Why can't I go? Are you afraid I'll slow you down?"

"No, I've seen you ride." Trace's hands tightened on the reins, and his horse stomped and tossed its head. Almost like it was telling Penny no, too.

"Then is it because you're going to search for that low-down skunk Raddo and you're afraid I'll get shot?"

"No. I don't care if you get shot."

Penny's fierce expression turned murderous. "You don't?"

"I didn't mean that!" Trace slapped himself on the forehead and talked fast. And he sounded sincere. "I just mean you wouldn't get shot, so I'm not — not *worried* that you'll get shot. We're just looking for his trail."

"So you admit you're hunting *Raddo.*" Penny's eyes turned to razors.

It wasn't like Trace to crack under questioning. Cam would've been disappointed in him, except Penny was a wily one. If there'd been any hope of keeping her home before, it was gone now. But since there had been no hope, it didn't matter much.

"Trace, she's going. Not because I want her along, but because she's coming with or without our permission."

"You can't. I won't allow it. I absolutely forbid it!" Trace bellowed.

"For heaven's sake, why are you so worked up?" Cam asked, bewildered by Trace's near-violent protest.

"Because" — Trace did some hissing of his own as if he didn't want anyone to hear, although there was no one else around — "if she goes with us, then —"

"Trace, honey, is something wrong?"

All the rigid anger went out of Trace at that moment. His shoulders slumped. His head dropped low.

Cam had his back to the bunkhouse. He turned around, already knowing what he'd see.

"Penny said we all need an outing." Trace's pretty wife, Deb, had her head out the window. Smiling for all she was worth. Ronnie was in her arms, waving bye-bye. "She's going with you today, but she said if I wanted a turn, I could go tomorrow. Do you think it'd be good for the baby to come along, too?"

Cam wanted to laugh.

Deb still had more to say. "Gwen and Maddie Sue can ride with you the next day."

Cam lost every ounce of humor. He glared at Penny. "I'm not takin' Maddie Sue to track down a killer. You think it's a good notion to take a baby to a gunfight?"

"So you *are* heading for a gunfight."

Cam's shoulders slumped to match Trace's. He noticed Utah had gone on up the trail. He must've known where Trace was headed. He'd been around before the snow started piling up, which gave him an edge Cam didn't have.

"And if we stand here much longer," Penny said triumphantly, "maybe we can bring all three women and both babies to this gunfight. Good thinking, Trace."

"Tomorrow's your turn, Deb." Penny waved, then reined her horse around and followed Utah. Cam went after them. Let Trace stay and try to douse this fire by himself. It'd even be fine to leave him, if Trace wasn't the only one who knew where they were going.

"See you later, Deb." Trace called a moment later, sounding downright dispirited. He caught up to Cam and passed him.

Normally Cam liked to lead, but he couldn't lead when he didn't know where they were going. Trace pushed past Penny, who had her nose in the air and ignored him. Next, Trace rode past Utah, and even from where he rode in the back, Cam could hear Utah laughing.

Trace snapped, "You're fired!"

Utah laughed louder, and for a minute it looked like he was gonna fall off his horse right into a snowbank. But he managed to hang on.

Then a thought struck Cam that sent pure terror coursing through his veins. "Hold up!" he shouted, his army voice right there handy. He thought maybe he'd lost it while trying to win over the children this last month.

CHAPTER 13

Cam drew back his reins so hard, his horse tossed its head and neighed. The bridle jingled, and the three people leading him wheeled around.

He took a second to note how they all obeyed him and took some satisfaction in that. Then he remembered why he'd stopped. "Penny, you've got to go back."

"Cam, we've already had this talk — I'm *not* going back. You're only wasting time."

"It's not that I don't think a woman should go with us, Penny. I just realized we're riding off and leaving Gwen, Deb, and the children without a guard."

Penny smirked. "It's all —"

"You're right. We can't leave them." Trace looked scared. "I've been riding out to check cattle without giving it a thought because, Cam, you were there with them. Now Adam's ridden off, maybe for hours. What was I thinking?" He turned to face

Penny. "You think you're tough enough to protect them?"

"She's as tough as any of us here."

"I'm more than tough enough, but I am absolutely not going back. It doesn't —"

"Then you go, Cam. Go take care of them."

"I've been shut up in that bunkhouse for just as long as Penny. I'm not going back either. You go back, Trace."

"I can't. I'm the one who knows where we're headed."

"I saw it, boss." Utah rode up but kept some space between them. Clearly a man looking to make a break for it. Which made Cam think . . . "Utah, you go back."

Utah laughed in his face, turned his horse, and rode on up the trail.

Cam and Penny glared at each other.

"As I was saying," Penny said loudly, "no one has to stay with them."

"They do, too," Trace said, pulling his Stetson off his head and slapping it against his leg.

"What is going on in your head, Penny?" Cam's hand fisted on his reins as his horse skittered sideways.

"No one has to stay" — Penny went on as if she'd never been interrupted — "because

183

I taught them how to take care of themselves."

Trace and Cam fell silent. Cam looked at
Trace, who seemed too confused to talk.

"How'd you do that?"

"You think we've just been sitting in that
house all day every day all winter?"

"I never saw you teaching anyone anything," Cam said. "And I've been in there
for a good part of the winter."

"We did it before the fire, and since the
day you came, we did it during your nap
time."

Cam felt his cheeks heat up. "You make it
sound like I'm one of the youngsters."

Penny snorted and went on. "We've had
the rifles and handguns out. I've taught
them how to clean the guns, load them, and
take aim."

"I haven't been that far from the house
doing chores. I would've heard you." Trace
slapped his mangled hat on his head.

"Oh, I never let them pull the trigger. We
don't have enough bullets for that."

Cam crossed his arms. "You really think
that's enough?"

"I know it is."

"Why didn't Deb tell me?" Trace asked,
anger flashing in his eyes.

"I advised them to keep it to themselves

until we were ready to talk about it. I didn't want one of you men discouraging them because it isn't ladylike."

"It *isn't* ladylike," Cam reminded her.

"You shouldn't have done that." Trace sounded mighty discouraging.

Penny snorted. "You need tough women in the West."

"You mean tough woman who don't faint at the first sign of blood?" Cam loved reminding her of that weakness.

"Not sure what's in my head that makes me do that. But I can shoot the ace out of a playing card at four hundred paces. I can kill, skin, and butcher a deer."

"Why doesn't that make you faint?" Trace asked.

Penny shrugged. "Don't know. For some reason, it's just human blood that sends me into a spin."

"That's just stupid." Cam shook his head.

"Then I can use the deer hide to make a teepee and live in the wilderness."

"You don't know that. You've always lived at the fort."

"Just because I haven't done it doesn't mean I don't know how. You could do it too, Cam, and you've never done it."

Trace looked over his shoulder and

shouted, "Utah, you're taking the wrong trail!"

Utah stopped and just sat there in the saddle, staring at the ground.

Cam looked Penny hard in the eye. "Do you swear those women will be all right? You're sure enough you are willing to ride away from them?"

"Yep, I'm sure." And she sure as the sunrise sounded confident.

Cam said, "All right. Trace, let's get on."

Shaking his head and muttering, Trace pushed his horse on up the trail, turning off before he reached Utah, who fell in behind him.

Cam felt his heart pounding hard, worrying about the women. But if ever a person could be believed, it was Penny. And besides, Adam should be back home from the canyon after a while. Then he'd spend the day doing chores close at hand.

Trace picked up the pace, and they all stuck with him.

The snow had thawed enough that it wasn't hard going. They rode steadily upward, and then it got steeper and they really had to climb. It was an hour of that. Their horses were all mountain born and bred, so they were surefooted critters. Finally they had to abandon their horses and went on afoot on the treacherous slopes.

"It gets me that Raddo's still running loose, trying to kill witnesses same as before," Trace said with disgust. They were close enough together to talk after riding in a line that spread them out.

"You think it was him watching you from the mountaintop?" Penny asked.

"I've got to figure it was. From Utah's description, it was definitely him who burned my cabin and tried to kill all of us."

Trace looked back at Utah. "Did he realize you saw him? Because if he did, I reckon you're on his list, too. Though it seems he's not opposed to killing us all."

"I s'pect he knew I was up there, yet he was running mighty quick. He might believe I couldn't point him out to a judge, and I prob'ly couldn't."

Cam went on, "We've gotta figure he set that bear trap in the hopes of doing serious harm to anyone tracking him. Now he's keeping watch with what we hope is a spyglass."

Penny's brow furrowed. "Why do you hope that?"

" 'Cuz a spyglass is a whole lot better than a rifle scope." That earned Trace a long moment of silence.

"Doesn't matter what he's watching with.

187

I reckon he's got a rifle." Utah grabbed a rock with the ice melted off and pulled himself along.

"We're almost there," Trace said. "Pay attention. If he came to do his spying today, we might catch him red-handed. That'd save a lot of time." He gave Penny a stern look. "Try not to get shot. Deb's not gonna like it if I bring you home with a bullet hole. Don't forget it'd make you faint from the sight of blood. And on this mountain, if you faint, you might still be falling next week."

Penny rolled her eyes and kept climbing.

The man who killed Abe might right now be at the end of this trail. Rage washed over Cam like blizzard winds. When he thought of his brother, he was filled with both anger and guilt. It was Cam who'd talked Abe into coming out here.

Now Abe and Delia were dead, and all Cam could do was avenge them. Although he knew that wouldn't end the guilt. Nothing would.

Even so, Raddo wouldn't ride free while Abe was cold in the ground.

Cam's hand slid to the butt of his six-shooter. He wanted to find the man who'd killed his brother. He wanted it bad. So bad he knew it for a sin. He heard the small voice in his head telling him that hate was always wrong. Vengeance was for the Lord God alone.

Fighting back the desire for revenge, he went back to using his hands for climbing, yet his fingers itched to find his target, aim, and shoot.

Gwen found her target, aimed, and shot.

No bullets, so she didn't really shoot, but Penny had assured her it was good practice all the same. And necessary because bullets were hard to come by.

As Deb came out of the children's bedroom, Gwen glanced up from where she lay flat on her belly shooting at the fireplace. Sort of shooting.

Deb nodded at her, encouraging the practice. Gwen had the rifle that always hung over the front door. Which, now that Gwen thought about it, was silly, since for the last month the front door had been snowed shut. What were the chances that danger would come from that direction?

She considered suggesting they move the rifle to above the window they came and went through, except it was a little late now. The way things were melting, they'd soon be back to using the front door.

Gwen rose from the floor. Deb was examining the pistol to make sure it was unloaded. She was careful to point it downward at all times. That had been Penny's first and most insistent instruction, and Gwen knew it was a good rule. But neither gun had been close to a bullet for a long time. The bullets were all carefully stored out of sight in Trace's room. Well, every man had his own gun and bullets, so they were all over, but the point was, none of those bullets were in this gun. They were doing the careful aiming at the floor for practice, too.

Gwen hung up the rifle, then got out the tin coffee cups and filled them with the piping-hot coffee they'd made fresh after breakfast. It'd been a strange morning. She'd gotten used to having Cam around. Penny too. The work was doubled, but being alone with Deb felt familiar, and she liked it.

"Do you know where the men went?" Deb asked quietly. "I saw them ride up the hill behind the barn."

"Adam headed for the canyon earlier," Gwen answered. "I stepped outside just now and saw him doing chores around the yard. He'll eat the noon meal with us, and Adam told me not to expect anyone else. Did Trace tell you what he was doing?"

"He said he had some tracking to do."

Silence hung between them.

"I can't believe they let Penny go." Gwen sipped her coffee thoughtfully.

"I overheard a little of it. I don't think she gave them much of a choice." Deb grinned. "I want to be just like her."

"Work up to it slowly, or you'll scare Trace." Gwen laughed, and Deb joined in. Then they both broke off and looked nervously at the children's room. The silence was reassuring.

Deb set her gun aside and picked up her coffee cup. "Did something happen between you and Cam?"

Gwen jerked and splashed coffee on her fingers. She set the cup down and waved her hands to cool them, then stood to get the towel that hung near the washbasin, and dried her hands with it. The coffee wasn't burning hot, but she had a sudden desperate need to be busy.

"I'm going to assume from your reaction that something *did* happen. And it must've been last night because you acted normal all day yesterday."

Gwen hung the towel back on its nail and straightened it until it was painfully tidy. Then she turned, her lips pursed, to stare at her sister.

"What happened?" Deb suddenly lost that

stream of humor. "Did he scare you? Or hurt you?"

Short of running out the window, she saw no escape, and she'd always told her sister everything. Of course, she'd never had much to tell her before. The two of them, alone in the world, were very close. Gwen shook her head and came back to the table and sat.

"It was just the opposite. He was . . . umm . . ." Gwen cleared her throat. "He was extremely nice to me. And I to him."

"Nice?" Deb's brows arched nearly to her hairline. "What do you mean by 'nice'?"

"Shhh!" Gwen didn't think Deb had really spoken that loud. And after the little ones had been asleep for about ten minutes or so, they settled in and rarely stirred. Gwen was just trying to think of what to say.

"Nothing improper happened, if that's what you are fretting about. We just . . . well, I've wanted to ask you about it. We . . . that is, I heard the water running in the night. It was such a strange sound. I couldn't figure out what it was. I got up to look outside, and Cam came out and said it was an Ice Eater Wind. He also called it a chinook — the warm spring wind. Anyway, we stood at the window together and watched the water run."

192

Gwen shrugged. "Perhaps we were a bit too close for a time. I wondered . . . I think maybe he almost . . . ." Gwen paused to scratch the back of her hand. "Maybe he almost k-kissed me."

She took a quick glance up to see Deb's mouth fall open. Then it snapped shut. There was a flash of temper, but Deb fought it down and asked with a sharp hiss, "Do you want him to kiss you?"

Gwen had to think on that for a while. "Yesterday I'd have told you no."

"And today?"

"It was just so out of nowhere." Gwen pondered her cooling coffee. "The breeze was warm, and it was hard not to yearn for spring. We were watching the snow shrink, the moonlight stream down. My spirits lifted. I doubt I'm the first woman to stand with a man on a moonlit night and find a bit of romance in that." Gwen swallowed hard. "And then he smiled at me."

She looked at Deb and really hoped her big sister — her married big sister — could give her some advice. "Right at that moment, yes, I wanted him to kiss me. And now it's daylight and the men are all gone, and Cam's leg isn't fully healed, so he should *not* have gone with them." She felt the worry and temper rising and ruefully accepted that she cared about him more than just as a patient. "He's worrying me to death."

"A bit of an exaggeration," Deb said with a smirk.

Gwen nodded. "And the worry is aggravating, which makes me remember he's a man who snaps out orders so briskly I feel like a lowly army sergeant. So now I'm not so sure I want him to kiss me." Gwen picked up her tin cup and set it down with a sharp *click.* It eased the worry so she did it again, then found herself tapping out a rhythm with it. Staring at it, through it, and thinking how handsome Cam was in the moonlight.

"Now I'm curious and . . . and . . ." She tapped faster. "And yes, yes I think I do want him to. Is that just crazy?" She looked up and searched Deb's eyes. "He's the same grouchy man he was yesterday. So why do I feel differently?"

Deb reached over and stayed Gwen's tapping. The two stared at each other.

"I'm trying to decide what's best. Trace did convince me to marry him." Deb looked up, smiling. "Remember when we climbed in that wagon with Abe and Delia, how determined I was to run a newspaper in California? I was going to stand on my own, go to work for myself after a life of serving our father. But it was always different for you."

A tiny shake of her head went on too long. "How is it different?"

"Well, we're no longer going to California. When I gave that up, I gave it up for both of us because I'm the one who always pushed for it. And I don't see you going on without me, a woman alone. The two of us alone was reckless enough."

"I did want to go west, but it was mostly to stay with you and get away from where we were." Gwen thought of the newspaper they'd run in the small town near Philadelphia, and how Pa had made them do all the work.

Pa was the big man around town. He talked and charmed the leading citizens. He played cards until all hours, spent every penny they earned eating fine meals and wearing handsome clothes. When he died, he left them with nothing. Deb would have gone on running the newspaper, but the town didn't want a newspaper run by a woman — even though Deb had been running it for years.

Deb had sold out before they went broke, and it hadn't left them much.

They'd heard things were different out

west, women had more opportunities. They'd signed on to assist a family going west who had two little children to care for. The kindly Abe and Delia Scott had taken pity on them. And it had all led them right here, right to this moment.

"Cam is determined to take the children." Deb sipped her coffee. "And we have to admit that Maddie Sue is his daughter, Ronnie his nephew. He doesn't know them, but his claim on them is undeniable."

"And he loves them," Gwen added, rising from the chair, so impatient to understand her confused thoughts that suddenly she couldn't sit still. "He really does. He's dreadful at showing them, but I've been working with him."

"I know. I've tried to help, too. But isn't that all part of admitting he's going to take them away?"

Nodding, Gwen finished her coffee in a single gulp, shuddered at the bitter taste of the cold brew, then headed for the basin to wash the cup.

"And," Deb went on, "if you're going to be kissing him, well, when soft feelings grow between adults, that often leads to marriage."

Gwen gasped. "Deb, for heaven's sake."

Deb shrugged almost helplessly "You're

adults. That's what kissing leads to between proper men and women."

"Not after one day and one almost-kiss." Gwen felt her cheeks burn and knew she was blushing bright pink.

"No, of course not, but think of this, baby sister. If you did marry Cam, that is your chance to stay with the children. And that's the best hope that the children won't be confused, hurt, and scared when they leave us."

"Why does it feel like you're trying to blackmail me into marrying him?"

"I'm not. In fact, this whole thing shocks me. I never considered the two of you as any kind of match."

"Is protecting those children a good enough reason to marry a man?"

Deb grinned and brought her own cup to be washed. "Protecting children you love is the practical reason for letting things grow between you and Cam. The less practical reason is wanting to kiss him. Less practical, but very good luck."

Gwen didn't respond, but she was having a hard time feeling lucky.

Cam didn't like bringing up the rear.

He'd been in the army too long — or maybe he just hadn't been out long enough.

197

Admitting that, he didn't try to pass anyone. The trail was so narrow it would have been impossible. That probably helped him decide to stay in line more than knowing he'd look like an idiot if he took the lead . . . especially since he didn't know where they were going.

He had a feeling God was reminding him he had a long way to go, and a desperate need to get there, when it came to being humble. The children liked him better when he behaved with some humility. Which meant he needed to get better at it. That might also be why his leg was throbbing like a sore tooth. It wasn't bad enough to make him go back, but it made the going hard, uphill on a slippery slope.

It kept him humble. But God wouldn't use a bear trap on a man, would He?

Probably not, but once the bear trap snapped, God was there in many ways. Cam was healing, which honestly was a miracle. But it had laid him low for a long time. That gave him a chance to get to know his daughter and nephew.

Nope, Cam did not believe God snapped that bear trap on his leg. God had an overriding interest in souls, not legs. If God did such a thing as set a trap, He was going to try and trap a soul. And that was a gift from heaven.

"This was where I saw the glint." Utah stopped beside a boulder the size of a house.

"He was definitely here. Look." Trace pointed at something over the far edge of this peak. Cam reached his side and saw how trampled down the snow was, and with a couple of steps he saw the boulder was on the edge of a steep downward swoop. There was plenty of mountain left that went way higher, but from this spot, they had to go down to get up.

The mountains rose and fell, sloped up, then down for a time, then up again. It was all broken up by boulders, trees, and cliffs.

"Look at this." Cam tapped Trace on the arm, but he was already turning. Utah and Penny came to Cam's side.

"Multiple parallel lines made by skis. He's been up here a dozen times," Trace said quietly, thinking, planning.

"Yep," Utah said. "Those are the same marks as we saw the day Raddo burned down the cabin."

"Skis." Penny stared at the marks. "I've heard of skis for getting around on snow. Look at the way he coasts along the top. I am going to learn to ski. This is a great idea." After a short pause, she added, "It

199

burns my chaps that I'm learning something useful about getting around in the mountains from tracking this varmint."

"We can follow him right back to his hideout." Cam started forward. The land on this side was steep but smooth. The snow was still thick but packed enough that they could walk on it.

Trace caught Cam's shoulder. Cam turned impatiently.

"Let me lead, Cam. I know this trail. It's got some narrow spots and plenty of places that fill in with snow and become treacherous." He looked at Utah and Penny. "Stay in my footprints near as you can, or we'll be digging you out of a ditch."

Controlling his irritation, the humor of it then struck. Cam could barely keep from smiling. Strange how it felt as if God himself were stepping in for Gwen and slapping him on the back of the head. "Go. I'll bring up the rear." A rear guard was always important. Cam doubted it was in this case, but he'd stay alert regardless.

Trace picked up the pace, downhill suiting all of them. It was impressive how fast the man went. Utah came behind and did a good job loping along. Penny, in her trousers, kept right up. Cam had seen Trace run like the wind. Cam was grateful his friend was using some restraint in his running speed by setting a pace that let them all keep up.

Cam was doing the worst of all, falling behind more with every pace. Every running step strained his leg. Stretched out muscles that'd been still too long. He started thinking about just how far he'd have to go to reach his horse. He'd be sore tomorrow, but for now the thought of the man who'd killed his brother, right at the end of this trail, helped him set aside the pain and keep going.

The trail rose, then fell, then skirted around a mountainside. Trace slowed to a walk now and then, and he made some surprising choices in the trail. Cam figured that was to avoid something that the rest of them couldn't see.

Everyone was careful to follow Trace closely.

Trace reached the top of a rise and vanished. Cam didn't like it and pushed harder to keep him in sight. Utah passed over and was gone. Penny was next, but Cam was close enough behind her that she never left his sight.

As he passed over the rim, a hand grabbed Cam's shoulder and dragged him to the ground.

■ ■ ■ ■

John found Nevada.

The sheriff in Cheyenne knew a freight wagon headed that way. They didn't take passengers, but they agreed John could ride along behind them.

And the freight wagon had other outriders — armed men and plenty of them. John threw in with them and offered his rifle to help with protection.

He'd finally reached Virginia City. From there he'd gotten directions to a trail that sent him on to Ringo. Now John stood and stared at a trail that only existed if a man had a powerful imagination.

Considering he was staring at a snowdrift that stretched as far and wide as he could see and reached twenty feet high.

John sat on his bay thoroughbred. He led a blue-roan packhorse, and he thought of how he'd fought his way across the country to this point. Philadelphia to Virginia City, on his way to Dismal, Nevada. A town no one back east had ever heard of, no map had considered worthy of mention, and no one in Virginia City could recall.

The best advice he'd gotten was to go to

Carson City or Ringo and ask. Ringo was closest.

He'd considered all the possibilities and then turned back to Virginia City. And now he was here in this huge boomtown, trying to think his way around a snowdrift.

He didn't make it today, and he silently apologized to his faithful bay for even thinking of going up that trail, because John had stood there and considered it. Maybe if he went into the forest? But with some inspection, he saw the forest was deeper and more impassable than the trail.

But was the snow crusted? Could the horse walk over it? He'd checked, and it wasn't.

Should he abandon his horse and walk in?

He sure didn't see how.

The Chiltons had been very generous in what they agreed to pay. And they'd promised a bonus if he got little Ronnie back to them fast.

He thought of that little tyke.

Those Chiltons made his blood run cold.

They wanted the boy, Cameron Scott, their grandchild, but had no interest in his girl cousin, also a survivor of the wagon train. Florence Chilton had told him emphatically that if he brought her back, it was his problem and he'd need to find her a home.

If they'd treat a three-year-old girl with such coldness, how well could they be expected to treat a little boy? Blood was thicker than water, of course, but the Chiltons' cold blood seemed almighty thin.

Florence Chilton's gleaming, heartless eyes made his gut twist. But she and Edmond were Ronnie's grandparents. They were better than nothing. And that uncle was coming, and John had surmised that the little girl was his child, so she'd have a home after all.

Later, he stabled his horse and walked into the wild bustle of Virginia City. Now that he thought about it, that storekeeper had a twinkle in his eye when he'd given directions. He'd known good and well John couldn't get up there. Maybe he could pass some time by punching him in the nose.

John walked along facing a warm breeze. Winter was waning. Water ran in all directions. It wouldn't be long until the snow would melt and he could get through.

And up until the drift stopped him, he could see that in better weather, the trail was a busy road, so they'd probably get it opened as early as they could.

It was the path the California Trail took,

and all those who came and went between San Francisco and Virginia City's silver mines of the Comstock Lode. It also led to Carson City, Nevada's new capital. A big road for big commerce. Everyone would make more money when it was passable.

But that wasn't today. It chafed, but John hoped at the rate the snow was melting, he'd get in there soon.

Or maybe there was another way. He'd looked at the main trail, but if he could find someone who knew of less-traveled trails, maybe a man on horseback could handle them. Maybe he could get through.

He strode along the streets of Virginia City and picked out a likely diner. He'd ask better questions this time. If there was another way through those mountains, someone would know. *If* it was possible, he'd get through. He had a job to do. Find little Cameron Scott and take him home to the bosom of his family.

Poor kid.

CHAPTER 14

Cam turned, ready to fight. Utah had him.

Utah, dragging Cam down, hissed, "Quiet! Trace found Raddo's hideout."

Nodding, Cam dropped onto his belly. Penny was facedown, peeking through tall brush, staring down a slope for all she was worth. Cam peeked right with her and saw parallel ski lines leading straight to a cave mouth.

Then he thought back. Trace had found one of Raddo's hideouts once before, only the man had been gone. "Let's go," Cam said. "No one's standing watch. We'll close in on the entrance and trap him in there."

Utah shook his head. "Trace said to wait. He'll signal us."

"That's what we did before, and we lost him. But then the hideout was such we couldn't see if Raddo was standing watch. This time the entrance around that cave is clear. Let's go."

Cam moved quickly. He felt Utah grab at him and miss. He hurried straight down the slope. Purpose quieted the pain in his leg as he followed the trail worn down by the passage of skis.

No one stopped him. No one yelled or signaled him in any way. He rushed the entrance of the cave, a small black gap in a solid white wall of a cliff. Cam, gun drawn and cocked, dove in. A bullet exploded overhead. Seeing the man who fired, he brought his gun around. The man threw himself backward just as Cam pulled the trigger.

Raddo — it had to be — scrambled out of sight toward the back of the cave.

The man who'd killed Abe. The man who'd killed a whole wagon train of good, honest people. Cam went after him, planning to chase him down like a rabid skunk. He saw a tunnel in the shadows of the small cave. Behind him someone came in. Cam figured it to be Trace, but he didn't look back. He plunged into the narrow opening at the back. The tunnel was big enough that Cam could run flat out.

It wasn't a long tunnel. Light poured in, though he couldn't see a mouth at the end. Then it curved.

Cam rounded the curve, saw the aimed

gun, and threw himself backward. He rammed into Trace, and they both fell to the tunnel floor. Bullets whizzed past the spot where he'd just been standing. The ricochets whined and buzzed like a deadly swarm of wasps. Cam dragged himself on his belly to the curve, reached his gun around the corner, and fired.

Suddenly the shooting stopped. Trace climbed to his feet. Cam saw Utah and Penny behind him. He tore off his hat and waved it around the corner. Only silence. Cam jerked his head out and back fast. Raddo must've run on. He rushed after the outlaw, fury building as hot as forged iron. Raddo would not get away this time.

Cam slipped around the curve again, but no gunfire met him — only an opening to the outside, big enough to light the tunnel's length. He skidded to a stop, poked his head outside, and saw Raddo plummeting down an incline so steep that Cam didn't consider stepping outside. "He's skiing away!"

Blasting away with his gun, Cam saw Raddo fall. But he twisted on the skis and somehow got back up without hardly losing any speed. Cam had never seen anything like it.

"I saw you too, Raddo!" Cam shouted. Cam fired again, but hitting someone moving downslope was always hard. With a six-shooter it was nigh to impossible. "I'm a witness now!" Cam roared after Raddo. "I know what you look like, you yellow-bellied murdering filth."

Trace pushed up beside Cam.

Cam flung out an arm. "Don't step out."

Raddo looked back, and Cam emptied his gun. It was futile. He was only wasting lead.

Utah and Penny came up and looked over Cam's shoulder.

Trace said, "Look! He's goin' over that cliff."

They watched Raddo fly out into midair. The man soared forward as he dropped. The ground was steep enough that they could see him fall all the way to the bottom of the cliff.

"It has to kill him, a fall like that," Penny said.

But Raddo hit the bottom smoothly, then skied on until he vanished from their sight.

"Look at the cave floor." Penny snapped them out of their trance watching the man fly like that. They all looked down.

"Blood." Cam crouched down. "I'm not hit." He glanced up. "Are any of you? A ricochet you didn't notice maybe?"

"Nothing," Trace said. The others shook their heads.

"It's his." Cam, still hunkered down, pivoted on his boots to get a better look. "You can see he left blood on the trail. He's bleeding pretty good."

"Still seemed to have plenty of energy," Utah muttered.

"Yep, he escaped again." With bitter regret Cam rose and pushed off the edge of the cave's entrance, back onto the dry floor of the tunnel.

Together they charged for the front of the cave.

"We risked the women's safety for nothing!" Cam said.

"Hold up, Cam."

"No, we've got to get back." He stomped on, thinking of Gwen and Deb and the little ones, all alone. He knew his frustration at missing Raddo was fueling his fear. And his anger.

Trace jerked him around so hard he stumbled against the wall.

"You headlong fool, I said hold up!" Trace shoved him back into the cave wall, hard. "Why'd you charge the cave like that?"

"There was no one standing watch — it was safe to go in."

"I told Utah to wait and make you wait, too."

Cam shoved back. "You took off last time,

210

circling around, and he got away."

"I know this cave. I was going to cover the back of that tunnel. We would've had him too if you'd've just let me get into position." Trace pushed again, causing Cam's head to hit against rock.

Cam clenched a fist. Then he heard what Trace said. "Wait. You knew there was a back way out?"

"He's lived out here for nigh on to ten years. Why would you be surprised he knows this land better'n you?" Utah snorted with disgust and headed for the front of the tunnel.

Trace almost growled.

Penny came up beside him. More quietly but laced with scorn, she said, "The children aren't the only ones tired of you barking out orders."

"I don't have time to be lectured to. Raddo's on the move. He's wounded, and that makes him dangerous. We need to get back to the cabin."

"Go then." Trace sounded furious.

It was enough to stop Cam and spin him around.

"I mean it, go," Trace repeated. "As for me, I'm looking around this cave. If Raddo left anything behind, I'm taking it. I don't want him to have even a bite of jerked venison if he comes back up here."

That held Cam in place for a few seconds. "Good idea, but I think I will go back. I'm worried about leaving the women and children at the bunkhouse. Even if Penny did teach them to shoot."

Although without any bullets.

Penny smiled and looked smug. Cam figured she'd probably done a good job.

"That's a good idea. Go on. Don't go alone, though. Either Penny or Utah should go with you. I won't be here long."

Cam hesitated, then waved a hand at them. "Look, I know I'm in a bad habit of giving orders. And I know you're good men, smarter'n me in most ways when it comes to living out here. You don't need a commanding officer." He was silent for a while because humble pie tended to stick in a man's throat. "I'm sorry. I reckon Gwen isn't the only one who oughta slap me on the back of the head when I'm acting wrong."

"I'd as soon use a fist." The red anger faded some from Trace's expression. "Most of your orders don't bother me overly, because you're ordering me to do something I'm planning to do anyway, but today you messed up our best chance to end this, Cam. You should've stayed put." Trace shook his head. "Head back to the bunk-house. You're right — the women and children shouldn't be alone." He turned and walked back through the tunnel toward the cavern.

Cam turned to Penny, who said, "I've been wanting to slap you in the head for years. I'll help train you to be out of the army."

He didn't share her glee but nodded regardless. "I made a big mistake today, and I did it out of rage and arrogance. I'm so killing mad at Raddo, it's a sin and there's no denying it. Help me, Penny."

With a nod, Penny said, "Let's start for home."

Cam headed out with Penny following him. He let her catch up — not that hard with his sore leg. When they were side by side, Penny seemed to be more set on a stroll through the snowy woods than a forced march back to the horses and a race back to the bunkhouse.

With his leg near to killing him, Cam decided to let her set the pace. They walked together for half a mile in silence. Out of sight and earshot of Trace and Utah. And then Penny started talking, blast it all.

"So, what's going on between you and Gwen?"

Cam turned too suddenly. His feet, stuck in the snow, didn't turn with him, and he fell over sideways. The snow was fluffy enough that he sank in until his head was buried.

Penny laughed.

He'd never had a speck of luck getting sympathy from this woman.

She crouched beside him and brushed the snow from his face. She was none too gentle about it, neither.

"Well? What's going on between you and Gwen?" She acted like she had him captured and wasn't letting him go until she got answers. This had happened to him twice in the war. All she needed was a Springfield rifle and the gray uniform of a Confederate soldier.

"Where'd you get a harebrained notion like that?" He sure hoped she didn't notice that he was asking a question right back.

"That's not an answer, and we both know it."

"It is too an answer. When the question's a foolish one."

"You never met her eyes this morning. You always try to have at least one moment with the children. Although today you ran out of that bunkhouse like a rooster with his tail feathers ablaze."

"I did not." Cam let too much time tick past as he tried to recall details from earlier this morning. He swallowed hard. "Did I?"

"You most certainly did. And I heard you tell Deb good morning, and then you nodded at me like your usual poorly mannered self. But you ignored Gwen and the little ones altogether."

"They were busy eating, all three of them."

"So was I."

"And I'm not poorly mannered." Cam had been trying mighty hard not to be that way anymore.

"Not around the children maybe. With them you've changed of late into a fine, easy-talking gentleman, and it's been strange being around to see that. Then this morning you were *not* a fine, easy-talking gentleman. Instead you were your usual poorly mannered, grumpy self. Especially around Gwen. So, tell me what happened between the two of you."

Cam met her eyes. Though she never wore a dress if she could avoid it, and did nothing to enhance her looks, she had fine bones in her face and was pretty right down to her fingertips. Under that, she looked a lot like him. She had the same brown eyes Cam had, as well as the same brown hair with too much curl to it. They had oval faces and skin that tanned easily. They were of a type very much like their father. Abe, on the other hand, had been light-haired with Ma's blue eyes.

Cam watched Penny, his only family, not counting Maddie Sue and Ronnie. Those two counted also as family, except of course they weren't one speck interested in joining the Scott clan.

"Would . . . should I . . . uh, things would go much better if . . . no, not if, *when* we leave here and t-take the children, uh, I mean if Gwen c-came along." And that was about the hardest thing he'd ever said out loud. He let his head sink back under the snow just to rest.

Penny grabbed him by the hair and lifted his head. "Gwen came along? You mean to hire her to watch the children?"

Oh, if only that was what he'd meant. "No, well, yes, to watch them." Cam cleared his throat, took a deep breath. "W-What happened last night was, we watched snow melt for a while." That just made him sound like an idiot. "In the moonlight, together, alone. And I got some notions about her that . . . that surprised both of us, Gwen and me."

"I'll join you and be surprised, too."

"Nothing happened." Except he almost

kissed her. "But maybe inside my head something did happen, and now I'm confused, and it was awkward seeing her and so . . . like a low-down coward I ran instead of acting normal. Or maybe I was normal instead of acting nice, like a 'fine, easy-talking gentleman.' "

They stared at each other for a long moment.

He finally asked, "What do you think I should do about it?"

Penny's eyes widened like his question scared her. Well, fine, it scared him plenty, so why shouldn't she be afraid, too?

They'd spent the last two years together, just the two of them. Cam had been given officers' quarters at the western forts rather than having to live in the barracks with dozens or hundreds of soldiers. Penny had stayed with him. She'd cooked for him and washed his clothes. She also had a real paying job cooking for the fort. And she'd worked in the washhouse, doing laundry for all the men when she had free time.

Because of that, they knew each other very well. Cam really did want to know what she thought.

"I don't know what you ought to do." Penny stood and extended a hand. He grabbed it, and she dragged him back to his feet. He sorted out his tangled boots, and they started walking again.

"I mostly want her help in getting the children to like me," Cam went on. "But last night, for a few seconds there" — it'd been about five — "I was drawn to her. I reckon I'd not had much time to think of women before Madeline, nor since. Of course, I've been in gun battles for most of my adult life. Now I'm thinking, though, and my thoughts are of Gwen."

They passed the place Raddo had set up to watch the ranch. It was steep for the next stretch, until they finally got down to where they'd tied their horses. Mounting up, Cam got the weight off his leg and sighed with relief.

It was still slow-going, the trail slick and treacherous. Running water over ice. They paid attention to the trail until it widened and the going got easier.

"I think that if you feel something for Gwen," Penny said, "and considering how much the children love her and she loves them, you probably ought to marry her."

Another stretch of silence followed, which had nothing to do with the steep trail and everything to do with Cam not knowing what to say next.

"Our folks were good partners in their

marriage, and we always knew they held much affection for each other. And that strong union helped make a good, steady life for us. 'Course, I don't know if that's the way it'd be with Gwen."

"We'll be riding out in a few weeks." Penny reined her horse around a boulder where the trail leveled some. "We'll build cabins, get settled, and then you can come a-courtin'. Take her out riding. Pick her some spring posies. Compliment whatever it is you like about her. Go to Carson City and buy some candy for her and the little ones. Then maybe all three of them will love you."

"I'm not leaving here without those children. Once I'm gone, with all the work ahead of us building a cabin and tending a cattle herd, training horses and putting up fence, I wouldn't be able to get over here much. The children would forget me, and Gwen would think they were all well rid of me."

"You can't take them, Cam, and you can't leave them." Penny closed her eyes. Her horse seemed fine with picking its way along the trail.

"Unless I take Gwen with me." Cam saw the trail had reached a dry stretch. He loosened his hold on the reins and pressed the animal with his knees. Instantly his horse picked up the pace. Cam wasn't sure why he'd be in a hurry to get back and face Gwen, but he rode faster even with his doubts.

Penny had to pick up speed to catch up to him.

Before long they reached the ranch yard to find pouring water coming from every drift, and there were a lot of them. In fact, the whole world seemed to be a melting snowdrift.

As they rode to the barn and dismounted to lead their horses inside, Penny hissed at him, "I think you should do it, Cam. Propose. I'd like to have her come along. Maybe the two of us, Gwen and me, can keep you in line for the first time in your life."

Cam scowled. He thought of about ten things to say, every one of them similar to an army officer barking orders. He clamped his mouth shut. He had to change. He was going to change toward everyone. He led the way into the barn. Cam was eager, despite common sense, to get in the house and see Gwen.

CHAPTER 15

Gwen looked up and saw Penny climbing through the window. Her heart sped up, but not because of Penny. It was for her brother, who climbed through the window right behind her.

Her eyes dropped to the floor, and she wanted to slap herself. *Stop being a foolish child.* She lifted her chin, hugged Ronnie a little tighter, and Cam looked her right in the eye. Something he'd not managed to do this morning. Although Gwen couldn't be sure about the morning because she'd been too busy trying not to look at him.

Finally, Cam tore his eyes away and shed his snowy boots and heavy coat. He moved to the pegs on the wall where they hung the coats and where the boots got lined up as close as they could get to the fireplace.

Ronnie said, "Papa."

Cam's eyes came back up and locked on his nephew. No, not his nephew. Not anymore. Ronnie was his son now. "Hi, Ronnie. Papa's home."

Maddie Sue was under the table playing with a cloth doll, sewn together and stuffed with scraps. She looked up at Cam and crammed the doll into her mouth.

The doll was her only toy. Gwen had sewn it for her after the fire. The few she'd had before were similar to this one or carved out of wood. Cam should've found the time to whittle a toy soldier for Ronnie and a little horse for Maddie Sue. Gwen would see to it that he started tonight.

Cam smiled at Ronnie.

Gwen almost giggled at the sight. He was trying hard to be soft-spoken around the children, yet it sure didn't come naturally to him. Although didn't every person on earth change their tone a little when speaking to children? Why had it taken Cam so long to figure that out? Why had it taken so long for her to help him?

Because she'd been jealous. Gwen shoved aside those thoughts. They could only go on from here. Cam was trying hard to be a good pa, and Gwen was through wishing he'd leave without the little ones. It wasn't going to happen, and she'd just be wasting her time.

Instead she stood and enjoyed watching

Cam and Ronnie get to know each other. Cam moved slowly toward Ronnie.

"I went on a horse ride, Ronnie." He took a quick peek at Maddie Sue, who had stopped chewing her doll and silently watched Cam with wide eyes. "Would you like to go riding sometime? I could take you."

Cam looked under the table. "I'd take you with us too, Maddie Sue."

She slowly crawled out from under the table. "I like horsies, Papa." Then she stuffed the rag doll back into her mouth.

A natural smile came to Cam's face. "You're a pretty little girl, aren't you, Maddie Sue?"

Maddie Sue shrugged.

Cam looked back at Ronnie with such hesitation, he almost twitched. He reached out to the boy. "Can I hold you?"

Gwen quit breathing. She thought Deb, stirring stew by the fire, and Penny, closing the shutters, did the same.

Ronnie tilted his head sideways, looking very shy and, after too long — after Gwen had begun to hurt for Cam — the toddler lifted both hands slowly, an inch at a time, and reached for Cam.

As if he were picking up fragile glass, Cam awkwardly lifted Ronnie under the arms and slowly tucked him up close and hugged him.

Glancing down at a very interested Maddie Sue, Gwen said with a low voice, "Cam, sit down on the floor, slowly, right where you're standing."

Cam didn't hesitate to do so. "My leg's aching anyway. Sitting down is a great idea." He sat and held Ronnie loosely, balancing the boy on his lap.

Gwen stepped toward the table. She sat on a chair beside Maddie Sue and reached under the table to lift the girl to her feet. "Maddie Sue, would you like to sit on Papa's lap, too?"

Maddie Sue shook her head. Cam pretended not to notice, but Gwen could tell by the way his shoulders sagged that he had.

"Let's sit by the fire then, you and me." Gwen lifted Maddie Sue, walked to Cam's side, and sat down beside him.

Cam talked quietly about horse riding to Ronnie. He smiled at Maddie Sue and talked a bit longer. He talked about riding in the snow and the long, steep trail, and how far he and Penny had walked.

Then he started another story about a pony he'd had as a boy. Maddie Sue edged closer, interested in hearing the story. Cam noticed and shifted Ronnie to the knee away from Maddie Sue, making it so the little girl would see the open seat.

Sure enough, Maddie Sue stood and walked the two tiny steps it took to claim the seat.

Gwen had to fight not to cry. Cam kept on talking, telling his story, but she could hear the roughness in his voice, like it was all he could do not to hug both children tightly — except he knew how that would surely frighten them.

She should probably move and leave Cam alone with the children, but Deb and now Penny were hard at work on a meal. And if she moved, Gwen was afraid Maddie Sue might decide to move, too. Besides, it was one of the sweetest moments Gwen had ever seen. She thought of her own father and how he was so busy being a big important man in town that he rarely noticed he had children.

What she would have given for just a few memories as precious as this. Her father holding her, caring about her. She hoped the day would come when Maddie Sue understood just how fortunate she was.

The shutters banged open, and Trace crawled in. The noise popped the kids off Cam's lap. He wanted to growl at Trace but fought back the urge.

Gwen was up and moving away from him, too. Despite the awkwardness she must've felt when he first came in, he realized he'd lured her close as well, as if she were one of the children.

"He had that planned from the minute he picked it as a hideout," Trace said. "That's a fine back door to a hideout if a man knows how to jump off a cliff and live. I've seen his ski tracks, and we all knew he could jump a gully, but honestly I didn't really think he'd do it."

Trace's words brought all their troubles back, and Cam's moment with his children was over. He stood and it was like his whole body had stiffened up. He hoped it didn't show what a struggle he had getting to his feet. His leg felt as though on fire, yet by now he was sort of used to that. Now he ached in every muscle. This was what came of a man being trapped inside the house for a month.

"His skis won't work once the snow's gone," Penny said. "No back door without those. And the way the snow is melting, I wonder if he'll try using that cave again."

Trace opened a bundle, which Cam recognized as the kind of things a man might keep in a cave. A man who had lost nearly everything and had survived a winter in the wilderness.

"He killed my brother and his wife." Cam ground his teeth thinking Raddo might run off and never be found again. "He's going to pay for that."

"He killed my pa," Trace said, sounding as grim as death.

Deb and Gwen each picked up a child and carried them out of the room. Cam wondered just how grouchy he sounded.

Utah said, "Don't matter who he killed. It just matters that he did it. And now he's plotting again with us in his cross hairs. He needs to be put down like a rabid wolf. No one's safe while he's alive."

"But we have to use our heads," Penny said, sounding just as angry as the men, but sensible. Trust a woman to ruin the mood. "He's not going to stop coming. We know that."

"And we know he's as good in the woods as any man alive, judging by that skiing of his," Cam said.

"No, not so good," Trace argued. "I found him with no trouble when he kidnapped Deb last winter. Wolf sniffed him out. Raddo can ski, and that's a strange enough skill to stump us, but when it comes to the woods, well, once the snow's gone, I can best him. I *will* best him."

"We'll best him together." Cam moved around the bunkhouse, trying to work the stiffness from his limbs.

"Why'd you yell after him that you were a witness?" Penny slapped Cam on the back of his head.

"Hey! You're only supposed to do that to remind me I'm behaving poorly around the children or barking out orders."

"Didn't you say we could all slap you?" Trace asked with a grin.

"Why bring a killer's gun to fix on you?" Penny looked willing to slap him again, so he picked up his pace walking and kept as far as he could from everyone.

"Because I want Raddo to know Deb and Trace have friends aplenty. He can't take us all on." Cam thought of the low-down viciousness of the fire Raddo had set, and the way the man had just soared off a cliff and glided away. He knew not to underestimate Raddo Landauer ever again.

Then he thought back to finding Raddo's blood on the ground. Cam had only grazed him. Yes, Raddo was moving fast down the slope, and yes, Cam was ducking return fire, but the truth was he'd had a chance and he missed. The hunger for revenge, the defeat, and the savage hope the bullet would slow the man down all added to an ugly anger that tangled into something no good man should feel.

And he couldn't even ask God for forgiveness, because Cam knew that if he got another chance, he'd fire just as long and hard and with no remorse.

He probably wasn't fit to have children in his care, and thinking that did set him to praying.

"I'm going to head up the trail toward Carson City." Trace gathered bread and some beef jerky after a late midday meal.

"What?" Deb clutched her hands together at her waist.

Cam was immediately suspicious. "You think you can catch him after this long of a head start?"

Trace glanced nervously at Deb. "He's wounded some."

"That didn't slow him down much that I could see," Utah offered with quiet sarcasm.

"You can't go alone." Anger stirred in Cam. "He killed my brother, Trace. He's mine to hunt down." Cam ached in every muscle and joint. He wasn't sure he had the gumption to go on a manhunt right now, yet he'd do it despite the pain.

Trace shook his head. "He killed my pa

and left me an orphan in the wilderness, completely alone for years. That makes him *mine* to hunt down."

"I'm not saying you don't owe him." Cam came to Trace's side. "But my brother, his wife. When I make him pay for it, he'll pay for your pa, too."

"Have you heard talk of me guarding that trail, the one where your brother died?"

"Yep, the Guardian. You're darned near a living legend, Trace."

Trace grabbed a leather sack out of his bedroom. Cam thought it looked a lot like his. And Trace's things had all been burned to ash.

"I was ghosting around those first years out here, driven hard by a need for revenge." He packed the sack while he talked. "I was alone, and I had no choice but to hole up and survive that first winter. I was mighty turned around and was a while finding that wagon trail in the spring. I got to the place my pa had died. I thought to wait for a wagon train, then fall in with it. Before a wagon came along, I saw some men slip in through the woods. They hunkered down and I knew, sure as I lived and breathed, they were the same outlaws who'd attacked the wagon train I was in. I'd found the men who'd killed my pa."

Deb came to Trace's side and wrapped her arms around him. Cam had him on one side, Deb on the other. Trace was standing by the things he'd gathered to the table. He was surrounded and it didn't even slow him down.

Trace patted Deb on the back and resumed his packing. "I opened up on 'em and drove 'em off."

Cam wondered how many men Trace had killed. He hurt for the kid. That kind of thing haunted a man.

"After I'd saved that wagon train, I felt like I'd found my purpose in life. Rather than find a train and head on west, I stayed to guard the trail. I helped, too. They came back over the next couple of years, and I'd drive them off again. The attacks finally ended. It chafed that any survived, but I'm glad I don't have any more blood on my hands. I figured they'd all gone off to harm other people, and I didn't know how to track them down, so I settled in to living out here, ranching. I thought it was all long done, and then it happened again. This time I know that murderin' thief didn't run off. He's still here, still a danger to others. How many has he killed over the years because he survived my gunfire? Well, I plan to stop him. The duty's mine."

231

"No, it's mine. I'm going. You stay."

There was a long pause while Trace glared at Cam. "Are you planning to stay while we rebuild my burned-down cabin?"

"Yep, figured we'd do that, and then I'd head for my place."

"You help with my cabin, and I'll help with yours and bring Utah along. Utah is a fine builder. We'll bring Deb and Gwen along, too. The women can mind the children. Penny'd have her hands mighty full caring for them in a tent and getting meals on alone."

Cam nodded. "Penny's a good builder — I'd like to have her working on the cabin. And I'd appreciate your help, too."

"We can get your cabin up faster than you can on your own," said Trace. "And you can get more time in with your children, getting them used to the idea of being left with you. You can spend more time with them right now while I go after Raddo."

"I still don't think you should go alone, Trace. That Raddo is a dangerous hombre."

"I don't plan on facing him alone. I know the sheriff in Carson City. He's a tough man who keeps his town orderly. The trail's improved, the snow's shrinking. More important, the thaw hardens it so I can ride over top of the drifts. I can get through now and tell the sheriff what's been happening. He'll help me."

"What if Raddo goes to Carson City? What if he's hiding somewhere along the trail, looking to waylay you? That's how he operates."

Deb pinched Trace hard in the arm. "You need to be more careful now that you're married, Trace. You've got a wife who's counting on you to come home safe."

"I'm a wily old coyote myself — though I think I'm more wolf than coyote. He won't be sneaking up on me in those woods."

Cam perked up. "Are you taking Wolf? He'll keep watch better'n any man."

"I think I will. He won't be happy in a town, but he'll take to the woods outside of town. I reckon Wolf will wait for me there."

"Then you can go." Cam clenched his jaw because it didn't set right. "The only one you've got left to convince is Deb."

Trace froze, then turned to look down at his wife's scowling face.

She crossed her arms and narrowed her eyes.

"Good luck." Cam crawled out the window. He was going to encourage Utah to let them build a back door to the bunkhouse.

Raddo didn't have a horse. Trace had taken

it and the two that belonged to Meeks and Dalt when he got the jump on them last fall. But Raddo did have the skis, and he could fly on those.

When he'd cleared the line of sight of the men shooting at him, he stopped and checked the bullet wound. He'd been running and twisting, firing behind his back, and the man firing at him had been after him fast.

He unbuttoned his shirt, glad the weather was mild, and saw the wound that cut across his belly. A long cut that had slit him from side to side. Ugly but not deep. The skin gaped open and bled freely.

He felt no ribs broken, and none of his insides were shot up. He untucked his shirt, ripped a few inches off the bottom, wrapped it around himself and knotted it across the wound. The tight squeeze made him gasp in pain.

He was soaked in blood, enough of it to frighten him.

He knew the sheriff in Carson City was looking for him. Riley had gotten to town with Dalt last fall, to lock him up, with Meeks draped over his horse, to be buried. Raddo was sure the sheriff had heard all about the third man in the group. He knew those men after him right now wouldn't stop hunting him. He'd threatened them too many times. They were too smart to believe he'd stop.

He was out of money and too badly hurt to push this aside and get on with tracking down and killing those witnesses. He burned with anger at how many times he'd been thwarted, how many times hounded. He wanted to fill them all full of lead, only he didn't have the strength right now.

He'd planned to handle all this on his own, but he needed help. And the one man who'd give it was Luth.

Luth had said more than once that he was done lending a hand to Raddo, but so far when Raddo pushed, Luth had helped him. If he didn't do so for old times' sake, he did so because Raddo knew too much. Luth didn't dare deny him.

But it was a long way to that crazy fortress Luth'd built for himself on Lake Tahoe. And the trails were opening up so he might meet riders. He was covered with dried blood, with no clean clothes to change into, and he didn't dare let anyone see him this way. He had no money to buy a horse, and there were few around to steal.

With the skis, though, he could maybe make it in a day. He started right in and put a lot of space between himself and Riley's men. Later, he'd pick a likely spot and get rid of the skis in order to hide his trail.

Partway there, he came upon a trail that was easier to manage. It was still covered with snow, but it had seen some spring wagon traffic. He could stop worrying about his ski trail being spotted.

He hoped anyway.

Yet it didn't really matter because he had no choice. All he wanted was to make good time while he still had the muscle to do it. He felt cold satisfaction to think of just how unhappy Luth would be to see him. And how quickly he'd hand over new clothes, plenty of money, a fresh mount, and maybe even a doctor.

Luth knew better than to deny Raddo anything.

CHAPTER 16

Cam finally stopped nagging Trace, but it didn't set right to let the man go off alone hunting Raddo. But go he did — with Adam along to help Deb feel better.

Cam went and changed into dry clothes and, much as he hated to admit weakness, sank down on the bed for a time. He fell asleep like someone had whacked him on the head with a mallet.

A noise woke him. He had no idea how long he was out. But he was groggy, the room fuzzy, so he figured he'd been in a deep sleep.

He got to his feet, and white-hot brands stabbed him all over. It was all he could do not to holler out loud from the pain. He limped a while in the bedroom, trying to get the worst of it worked out so he could move normally.

He stepped out of his room to find Gwen and the children at work on something by the fire. No men were in the cabin.

"Let me pour you some coffee, Cam." Gwen looked right at him, and he remembered the strange, sweet feelings that she'd awakened in him.

The children clung to her skirts, yet Maddie Sue gave him a shy smile. His beautiful little girl asked him, "Are you my papa?"

She'd been told plenty of times that he was, but earlier today was the first time she'd ever spoken the words to Cam.

He came closer to her, but not too close, and remembered how she liked stories about his horse. Taking a seat on the floor near the fireplace, he made sure his eyes were level with Maddie Sue's. Gwen smiled encouragement at him and, coffeepot in hand, went back to the table and started pouring. Gwen had done so much to help him get to know the little ones. That soft feeling he had for her grew and warmed. Penny sat at the table next to Deb, both of them sewing things that were so small they had to be for the kids.

To look less awkward, Cam scooted around so that his back rested on the hearth. He knew everyone in the room was doing their best to stay quiet and not distract Maddie Sue.

"I am your papa, sweetheart. I was gone

for a long time . . . uh, with the war."

Somehow Gwen managed to kick him without the children seeing. "He means *with work,* honey." She must've set the coffeepot aside, because her hands were empty now. She rested one hand on Maddie Sue's head, the other on Ronnie's. "He missed you so much, and he knows you don't remember him from before, but he loves you."

Cam didn't know if Maddie Sue had any idea what *war* meant, but now wasn't the time to explain. "My work is going to keep me home now, so I don't have to be away from you anymore."

Suddenly Gwen sat on the floor and gathered the young'uns onto her lap. Cam noticed Deb whisper something to Penny, and then they both climbed out the window to give them time alone with the children.

There was the ringing of an ax chopping away outside — Utah getting started felling trees for the new cabin. Cam needed to get out there and help, but not just yet. He couldn't bear to end this moment. In fact, he appreciated being given time with his children so much that he found his heart opening to his friends in a way it rarely did.

Gwen said, "Tell your papa what we did today, Maddie Sue."

His little girl grinned and clasped her

hands together under her chin. Her legs kicked. Ronnie laughed a full, deep laugh and stuck both hands into his mouth.

Maddie Sue whispered, "We made cookies."

Trying to be easygoing and cheerful instead of the no-nonsense, take-charge man he really was, Cam leaned forward just slightly and smiled. "I love cookies."

Maddie Sue clapped her hands.

Ronnie pulled his drool-soaked fingers from his mouth and clapped along. "Cookies!"

Cam took his cue from them and clapped too, though softly. "Are there enough for me to have one?"

Maddie Sue giggled. "We made lots."

"Maddie Sue, you can reach the cookies. Why don't you go get one for your papa?" Gwen nudged her off her lap.

With the prettiest dimple-cheeked smile Cam had ever seen, Maddie Sue asked, "Can I have one, too?"

"You sure can, honey. And get one for Ronnie."

His daughter's eyes lit up. She ran around the table. There was a plate by the dry sink. She grabbed two tiny fistfuls of cookies without counting and rushed back to them.

She almost sang when she said, "One for

Ronnie."

He squealed, snatched it up, and stuck it in his mouth.

"One for Gemma."

Cam knew he had a big foolish grin on his face. Again he vowed to himself he'd change. No more yelling. No more Major Scott snapping orders. Gentle and kind, cheerful and soft-spoken — those were the things that won the heart of a child. And he could do it, even if no one had ever used those words to describe him before.

"One for Papa."

Cam felt a strange heat in his chest, as if his heart might actually be melting. Yes, he could definitely do this. "Thank you, Maddie Sue." He took a big bite. It really was a delicious cookie, but he'd have behaved the same if it'd tasted like the bottom of a hoof. He smiled again and found it almost hurt his cheeks. He hadn't spent enough time smiling in his life. Maybe Maddie Sue could teach him how. "This is the best cookie I've ever had in my life." That it came from Maddie Sue's own little hand made that the absolute truth. "And you helped make them?"

Maddie Sue nodded, and that was her only answer because both she and Ronnie had their mouths full of cookie.

"They most certainly did," said Gwen. "They both poured in the flour and sugar." She gave each of them a loud, smacking kiss on the tops of their heads. "They stirred and then helped drop them onto the baking pan."

Cam could just imagine it. Gwen probably took three times as long to make the cookies because of the children's "help." He would need to learn her patience, learn to include the children even if that slowed him down.

"Thank you, Maddie Sue." He turned to Ronnie. "And thank you, too. You're good bakers, both of you."

Then he looked at Gwen and remembered again. This moment of happiness with the children was due to her and her generosity. She'd helped him get to know his children even though she loved them as her own and knew she'd lose them when they left with Cam. She was gracious even when it would wind up breaking her heart. No one Cam knew had sacrificed more, certainly not for him.

It all awoke something in him that had already begun to stir. He needed to talk with her. He tried to think of the proper words as he leaned against the fireplace with his legs extended. What could he say in front of the children?

At that moment, Maddie Sue jumped off Gwen's lap and went to sit on Cam's knee. She just plopped herself right down there, then turned to look at him over her shoulder with a cookie-crumb smile.

He very slowly reached up one of his big, rough hands to rest on her back. "Thank you again for the cookie, Maddie Sue. It's the best thing anyone ever gave me."

The girl's eyes grew wide, blinking several times, and stayed locked on his face.

"I want you to know that I love you. I've missed you so much while work kept me away from you. Being with you is all your papa wanted while he was gone."

Maddie Sue watched him closely, as if judging his honesty. Then she looked away, her head down, and for a minute Cam thought he'd said things wrong. Was she going to get up and run back to Gwen?

As his heart threatened to crack wide open in pain, Maddie Sue slowly, inch by inch, leaned sideways and rested her head against his chest. Ronnie jumped up at that moment and threw himself at Cam, clambering over Maddie Sue and Cam's legs, kicking Maddie Sue and anything or anyone else in his path.

Maddie Sue screamed and started fighting the little boy. Cam laughed and caught Ronnie and moved him to straddle Cam's leg that Maddie Sue wasn't using to sit on. Maddie Sue found her place again, once more resting her head against him. Ronnie finally settled in, leaning back on Cam's shoulder, and chomped on his quickly disappearing cookie.

Cam kissed Maddie Sue on the head and wrapped an arm around Ronnie to hold him closer. He looked up and saw Gwen watching them, a smile of pure pleasure on her face.

Thinking again of her self-sacrifice, he mouthed the words *Thank you.*

She nodded her head, gesturing at the children. Cam saw that Maddie Sue had fallen asleep. He looked at Ronnie. He'd swallowed the last of his cookie. The little guy was relaxed now, motionless. Cam sat still for a while longer, his breathing slow and steady, until soon Ronnie nodded off, too.

Cam would get to sit here and hold them for the full hour of their nap if he wanted to.

Gwen got up and went to the dry sink and started working at something. Cam couldn't see what because the table blocked his view.

And because he was too busy holding love in his arms.

CHAPTER 17

Raddo knew just exactly how much Luth hated him.

It made him chuckle as he slipped up to the back door of Luth's mansion. Raddo was the only one who knew the way in. Luth had told him about the secret passage and probably regretted it ever since.

Raddo had been in the woods on the edge of the clearing around the house, waiting for dark. He'd been to Luth's house before, so he knew how to get close without revealing himself.

He knew about the sentries. He remembered everything Luth had told him, and a few things he'd found out on his own.

He watched the daily help leave. Luth never allowed live-in servants. He had too many secrets to hide.

Now that it was full dark, Raddo made his way inside the place. He'd've come in anyway to get warm and to find himself some food. But as soon as he looked down the hall past the kitchen, he saw a light shining from under a door. It was the library. The waiting was over.

Raddo moved like a ghost. The house must've been solid because not a floorboard creaked. He turned the well-oiled doorknob and stepped in.

Luth's head snapped up. Anger twisted his face, then was quickly hidden. "Raddo. You could've hollered for me — no need to sneak in."

That was a lie. Luth had made it clear long ago that he didn't want to be seen with any of the old gang. Yet that didn't include Raddo, no matter how bad Luth wanted it to.

Luth's eyes slid down to Raddo's bloody shirt. He'd stopped bleeding long ago but had no clean shirt to change into. He was still wearing the clothes, his only outfit, he'd had on when on the run the night he'd kidnapped Trace Riley's woman. That was months ago.

Besides the bloodstains, Raddo was filthy and ragged. That he looked so pathetic in front of his old outlaw partner made him furious. Luth was dressed like a rich man, money showing in the gleaming rings on his fingers, the silk of his shirt, and the fine wool of his suit. He had a crystal glass at his right hand with some dark liquid in it. Whiskey probably. Luth always had a taste for it. But fine whiskey, not the rotgut they used to drink back when they were raiding wagon trains.

The room was lush with oak paneling and velvet curtains. The lanterns were kerosene and ornate with silver and blown glass. Raddo envied it all so much that it was a good thing he needed Luth's help or he'd've killed the man where he sat.

"I need a place to lay low for a while. A man put a bullet in me." No use mentioning his plans for revenge, nor the women, and for sure not the children. Luth had done the same plenty back in the day, killed anyone who stood in his way. But these days he liked to pretend he had scruples.

"Sure. I'll put you up." Luth smiled like a brother, but Raddo heard the edge in his voice. "You can heal up and rest, get some hot food in you. But then you need to get out of here, Raddo. I can't hide you for long."

Luth ruled his world with an iron fist, and Raddo figured he could hide someone forever. Even so, Raddo didn't call him on the lie.

"Don't worry, Luth, I won't stay but a day

or two." Raddo's belly burned like a wildfire. He'd lost too much blood and had gone too far skiing. Miles and miles and miles. He was near to passing out from hunger and pain. He wouldn't start hammering on Luth tonight. Instead he'd take those two days, then he'd take two more, or four, or seven if he needed them. And then he'd give his big brother the bad news.

Raddo was going to need a lot more than food and a place to rest.

Gwen woke up in the darkness. This time she recognized the sound of water running. She recognized something else, too. Someone was outside her door. In fact, there might have been a quiet knock.

Slipping silently out of bed, she wondered who it was. Hoped it was who she'd wondered about.

She cracked open the door, for a second thinking of the man who'd attacked them and calling herself a fool. And then she saw Cam standing there, his eyes full of questions.

He took her hand and drew her to the window and opened it. He glanced down and saw that she slept with her boots on. They all did to stave off the cold — if their boots had time to dry before bed. He plucked her coat off its hook and helped her into it, and then he climbed out the window. She followed him into the night.

Closing the shutters behind them, he walked on. Gwen was amazed by the mild weather.

Once they were out of hearing distance from the house, he turned to her and whispered, "Gwen." And he pressed his lips to hers.

Her first kiss, and it stirred her all the way to her heart.

She tilted her head and kissed him back. His arm slipped around her waist.

Cam's smile faded as he pulled back a little and looked into her eyes. "I've got me a wild idea, Gwen."

"W-Wild?" Gwen could think of only one thing, and it wasn't an idea. It was another kiss, longer and warmer and . . . wilder.

"When it comes time to take the children home with me, seeing as how they love you more than anyone on earth, you could come home with us, too. As my wife."

And that froze Gwen harder than any High Sierra winter.

Cam froze at the words that'd just come out of his mouth.

He'd meant to kiss her. Talk with her.

Maybe give her a bit of romance. He'd come a-courtin' just as Penny had suggested.

It was far too soon to be talking marriage.

Even before the words traveled from his lips to his ears, his brain reminded him that he didn't even like Gwen much before the chinook wind. Yes, she'd been wonderful helping him with the children, and more than wonderful ever since the evening of the chinook. Then yesterday he'd finally had a couple of fine moments with his children.

Today he'd worked outside. Moving had eased his aches some. He was feeling better than he had since before he'd stepped in the bear trap. But he hadn't spent much time with the children, what with all the outside chores.

And today he hadn't been able to tell if they still cared for him.

He remembered the word *self-sacrifice.* Gwen had helped him get closer to the children, but the truth was, he'd been here for months — trapped at Trace's ranch since that first blizzard. And until he'd gotten hurt, Gwen hadn't helped. She'd only worked to cure the children's dislike of Cam since he'd become housebound. It'd been a long time coming when it was as plain as a campfire on a moonless night that those children were *his* family and belonged with *him.*

He felt his temper winding up, building, tightening. He looked down, hoping she'd been stunned enough that she hadn't noticed anything strange in his expression.

"I saw that look," she said. "Cameron Scott, you don't even like me. In fact, you can barely tolerate me."

Somewhere inside, the thought rattled him that he'd felt too much with those kisses. So much so that he was scared and overreacting. And maybe Gwen was, too.

He tried to speak calmly. "Now, Gwen, that's not true. I'm getting so I can tolerate you mostly."

The growling sound lifted his eyes to see where it'd come from — in case Gwen had gone off and been replaced by a hungry grizzly fresh out of its cave after a long hibernation.

Nope, still the pretty blond woman who'd always been rude to him, at least until that bear trap took a sizable bite out of his leg. Then she'd started being polite a good chunk of the time — like maybe half the time.

"I'm supposed to marry a man who can tolerate me *mostly?*" Her voice rose at the end.

"Shhh." Cam pulled her farther from the house. "Don't wake up . . ." Cam quick thought of all the people he didn't want to wake up. Deb, who'd probably stand right between him and Gwen. Trace was gone, thank heavens, because he'd probably punch Cam . . . for sure if Deb told him to. Utah might consider Gwen under his protection.

He moved even farther from the house.

Penny might be on his side. And he knew exactly why. Penny was worried about the children's happiness, and she'd be looking for a solution to their screaming when Cam took them home.

The solution to all his problems was standing right here, growling.

Cam leaned down until their noses almost touched. In a sharp whisper, he said, "I was thinking of the children, Gwen. They love you. When this snow shrinks enough to let me go, I am leaving here with them. These last few days have been the best I've ever had with them, and that's because of you. But they are nowhere near ready to leave you. They'll cry and be miserable without you. In time they'll learn to love me and accept Penny and me for their family, but we'll have some long, unhappy days before they do."

Cam's temper started rising again. The

only thing he kept low was his voice.

"But they *will* adjust." He caught her upper arms in his hands and pulled her closer. "They'll forget you eventually because they're young, just like they've already forgotten Abe and Delia. In the end, though, that's going to be hard on them. It's a cruelty I hope to spare them from. And bringing you into my family struck me as a good idea."

"You want to talk about something striking you?" Gwen asked through clenched teeth.

He ignored that. "After you stood there and let me kiss you and then kissed me back, in that very moment I thought of us being together as man and wife. I don't consider a proposal an insult. It's natural for an honorable man to speak of marriage to a woman he just shared a very pleasant kiss with. Pleasant enough I'd like us to share many more."

He watched every breath, every flicker of her lashes.

She sighed. "I apologize for being so rude." Gwen clutched her hands together at her chest. "But we can't marry, Cam. It's out of the —"

"Why not?"

That silenced her. Why not indeed? And

he wanted to kick himself for not letting her say no, so he could walk away and forget he'd gone mad just now and proposed to her.

Did he even want to be married to her? Would the children, with Gwen along, go on loving her always and wind up rejecting Cam? Was he making a proposal that would tear his own heart out?

"I can see you're not being unreasonable, or rude."

"No, I reckon I was both."

She cleared her throat and stared at the top button of his shirt as if it held the meaning of life. Finally she met his eyes and said, "I need time to think about it. My strongest reaction right now is that it's not what I want. You are proposing a marriage of convenience where I care for the children without the benefit of a loving husband."

"Gwen, I —"

"Wait, Cam." It was her turn to interrupt. "The thing is, I have always had hopes of a marriage based on love. And there is no love between us, and I don't see how that will ever change."

It might change fast if she'd kiss him again and marry him and then kiss him again and they shared married things. Mighty fast.

"Based on that kiss, I think there's a very

good chance our feelings could grow into . . . uh, well, into something . . . good." For some reason he could not get himself to say the word *love*. It felt like a flat-out lie. Not when he could kiss her one minute and resent her enough to want to start yelling at her the next.

But he knew the yelling was an old soldier's reflex. He had to get over that for the children's sake. And for Gwen's sake, too. Penny wasn't inclined to take much guff from him, either.

"I love the children, though, Cam. I don't want to ever let them go. I admit, your offer is tempting." She reached out and gently took his hand.

He liked her smooth skin, even with calluses — a woman who worked hard. Her hands had both strength and tenderness.

"I am a burden to Deb here. But at the same time, I work hard, and if I leave, a lot more is laid on her shoulders. Of course, the children are a lot of that work, and they would be gone. . . ."

Cam felt as if she were making a list of both the good and bad of marrying him. And he found it wasn't flattering. True, he'd said he could tolerate her mostly, so he supposed she wasn't being all that unfair. In fact, she was speaking with blunt honesty, and he did appreciate that . . . to a point.

"I love those children as if they were my own, and giving them up will grieve my heart for the rest of my life. I don't believe I would ever get over it. They will most definitely forget me, but I will never forget them."

All this talk and soul-searching because he'd had the lunatic notion to propose to her. Oh, he'd planned the kiss, but not the rest of it. Then he'd thought of how much his children loved her. And then he'd thought . . . well, his thoughts had led him straight here.

"Gwen, let's start right now thinking of what the future could hold. I told Trace before he left that I'd stay and help him build another cabin. Trace said he and Utah would trade work and come along to my place. You, Deb, Penny, and the little ones can come while we build a cabin and barn at my place. And we still need to get to the bottom of Raddo and make sure we've got him locked up good."

"We have time, then."

"Yes, all the time there is." He thought that had a romantic lilt to it. He could be romantic if he thought of it *before* he opened his mouth.

"No, Cam, not all the time there is. Good

grief. We only have the time until your cabin is finished, because that's when I have to either leave the children or stay with you. And the men here build fast."

Cam had to admit she was right. So much for being romantic. Heaven knew he'd never had much practice at such a thing.

Nodding, he said, "We have two weeks at the most here. We started cutting trees today. Another two weeks at my place. By then we can decide about you staying there with me."

Gwen didn't say yes right then, but she didn't slap him on the back of the head, either.

Cam went on. "I need to figure out where I can run cattle and horses on my land. I scouted some last fall and have a few ideas. I've got money put by, so I'll buy a herd. I'm a hand at training horses, and I want to build a reputation for that. Which means I'll need good breeding stock. So . . . well, I'd like you to be part of that, so I hope you will make your decision soon."

He reached out and rested a hand on her cheek. "I like looking at you in the moonlight, Gwen. I've known you were beautiful from the first moment we met, even when you were running away from me to hide in your room and taking my children with you."

"I did not run away."

Cam arched a brow. Gwen didn't defend herself any further.

"But in the moonlight your eyes glow like there's a fire burning in you. It's as if you were born to spread warmth and love. Your skin is cast blue in this light, and it gives you an angelic quality, with your blond hair turned white like a glowing halo."

"Cam, my goodness. No one's ever said anything so romantic to me."

Maybe he had a chance at learning how to behave yet. He smiled, and she smiled back. Because he couldn't think of anything else to do, he leaned forward to kiss her again. And she most certainly did not resist him.

He pulled back long before he wanted to. "I think we could make a good life for ourselves. I already appreciate how you've helped me bridge the gap between me and my children. Affection will grow in our marriage because we already have respect for one another. And we'll be able to make a home and a family for our children. Ours, Gwen. Right now they are the children of your heart, but with marriage they'd be yours legally, as well. Let's spend the next weeks getting to know each other in a kinder way and seeing about a future together. Can we agree to that?"

There was a long silence. Too long in Cam's opinion, when her only possible answer could be yes. Especially because he kept his hand on her cheek, and she allowed it. This was not a woman running scared.

"We can agree, Cam. We can agree to consider it. Now, I think I'll return to my room and see if I can sleep for a bit longer before a very busy day begins."

"The chinook always brings work." Cam gave her one last kiss, took her hand, and together they walked side by side back to the cabin.

They climbed inside. He headed for his room, glanced back before he entered, and saw her staring out the window. In the moonlight he could see her profile as she gazed out with a faraway look in her eye.

He hoped she was gazing into a future that included him.

A shiver rushed down his spine, and he wasn't sure if it was longing or fear. Truth be told, it was a little of both. He knew he'd proposed for the wrong reasons. A spur-of-the-moment impulse, laced with a bit of practical good sense.

Neither impulse nor practicality were

good reasons to propose marriage, and he suspected his parents, good people with a solid marriage, wouldn't have approved.

But he'd asked her regardless, and even now with a chance to think about it, he knew he'd ask again — just maybe not so soon.

As Cam crawled back into his bed, he pictured Gwen glowing under the stars, bathed in moonlight, and realized his future would be much brighter if she said yes.

CHAPTER 18

Why on earth hadn't she told him no, flat out, the instant Cam asked?

In fact, she had . . . well, she thought she had. Had she? Maybe at the beginning, but definitely not at the end.

He'd turned very reasonable, practical — pointing out the positive side of his proposal, and distracting Gwen from the negative side, which was that they didn't get along.

He'd thrown in a kiss or two, or three . . . or more. Although *thrown* wasn't the right word. More like eased into, coaxed, *enticed.* Yes. Enticed covered it perfectly. Those enticing kisses had muddled her thinking. And he'd gotten away with convincing her to agree that she would spend some time thinking about the idea of marrying him.

So she went and told him, "I need time to think about it," instead of, "Are you out of your mind, Cam?" Now why hadn't she said *that*? Or how about just telling him, "No! Not in a thousand years."

This was what stuck in Gwen's head as she went back to bed and tried to get some sleep. The utter lack of "no" coming from her. And the kisses that, considering how much she'd enjoyed them, were the exact opposite of *no.*

She thought of all Cam's practical talk of how she loved the children and how he was taking them whether she came with him or not. And she considered herself a practical woman. Then she thought of how she'd always longed for love. Must she live her entire life in a chilly marriage of convenience — with a grouch? On the other hand, she was anything but chilly after those kisses.

Her thoughts leapt back and forth. She'd decide to say yes, change her mind, decide to wait, decide to say no and say it long and loud and right now. She stared at the dark ceiling, praying for all she was worth, trying to figure out if saying yes would save her or destroy her.

By the time Ronnie stirred, it was a mercy to get up and end this dreadful night.

She slipped out of the bed she shared with the boy and Maddie Sue, though once in a while one of them crawled in to sleep beside Penny on the floor. She picked up Ronnie and left the room, hoping Maddie Sue would wait a few minutes longer to wake up. That would give her time to dress the tyke, get him to the outhouse, then start breakfast.

When she stepped out through the window, it was into a changed land. The ground was still white, but the whole south side of the bunkhouse was visible. Water no longer dripped off the roof, which meant the roof was probably clear finally.

On her way back, splashing through running water with Ronnie in her arms, she saw that the snow had melted and receded from the east side too, leaving a narrow pathway all around the house. She held Ronnie on her hip and walked around to the front. The huge drift that only yesterday had run the length, height, and width of the bunkhouse had melted away from the building, with the same icy pathway formed by dripping eaves. Gwen was able to move along the side of the bunkhouse to the front door. The snow was still high in places, though, and the door swung inward for just this reason. But she noticed the door was only partially blocked now. If they wanted to, they could probably start using it again.

Ronnie flailed his arms, squealed, and struggled to get down — her sign to get back inside. Hugging and tickling him, thinking about losing him and Maddie Sue if she said no to Cam, and thinking about agreeing to a loveless marriage, Gwen's heart wrenched. Fighting tears and holding Ronnie too tightly, she strode back to the south side where the shuttered window had served as their only way in and out for over a month.

The sun was strong enough that she could feel some warmth from it on the south side where the shadows weren't cast. The breeze was cool instead of bitter, the sky overhead blue and cloudless, and it seemed to be staying that way.

Gwen approached the bunkhouse, feeling almost foolish for using a window to get in and out of her home. She reached through the window with the wiggling Ronnie and wasn't much surprised when Deb caught hold of the boy, giving her a hand. Gwen then climbed inside to find Penny up and dressed, Maddie Sue in her arms. Gwen took Maddie Sue from her just to give the little sweetie a morning hug.

"Look, the sun's shining! Look at the water running." Penny smiled as she peeked outside.

"It's been a hard winter." Gwen handed Maddie Sue back.

"Nope," Penny said. "A normal one, I'm afraid."

"Didn't you just move into the area right before the first blizzard?"

"True, but I lived in forts all over the West, including up in the northwest. Farther north and higher altitudes than this. So I know winter."

Maddie Sue shouted, "Potty!"

Penny headed for the privy with her.

The men sat at the table eating. Deb and Penny had gotten breakfast while Gwen wandered about outside. Utah and Cam were there. Gwen's breath caught, and she immediately looked anywhere but at Cam.

Trace was missing, of course, along with Adam. Utah had stayed behind because he was the better builder. Gwen knew Deb was worried about Trace, but he'd warned her they might be on the trail for days yet.

"We are going to chop more trees," Utah announced. "Yesterday we found plenty that have no snow on them. If it keeps melting at this pace, we could start building real soon. I'm hoping we can build on the same spot as before."

"I don't like the way the water's flowing," Cam said to Utah. "We might need to find a different site or Trace'll be facing a river where his front door oughta be."

"I'm not sure there's anywhere gonna be any different than that, but we'll give it a good look," Utah replied. "We may end up being glad the cabin burned down."

"I doubt that." Cam finished up the last of his fried eggs, biscuits, and venison bacon, then took a drink of steaming coffee from the tin cup beside his plate. He rose from the table and headed for where the coats hung near the fireplace.

Gwen's eyes shifted to Cam, who was pulling on his leather gloves. He glanced up just as she did, and the spark in his eyes was intense enough she felt like he'd touched her.

He tore his eyes away. Would she ever receive true affection if she agreed to marry Cam?

Deb said, "We'll have fresh coffee waiting at midmorning, and we'll keep it hot and ready all day. Even with the change of weather, you'll be out for much longer hours in the cold. You'll need a few breaks to warm up."

The men chorused their thank-yous, words that never failed to amaze Gwen. Her pa had never wasted his breath on such a word as *thanks*. She watched as they traipsed out the window.

She didn't mention that they could leave

through the front door if they wanted to. But she'd been preoccupied with eating her own breakfast and thinking about the next meal to get on for the hungry men. And they really had gotten good at hopping through that window.

Maybe it wouldn't hurt for the snow to melt back a little farther before they started using the door.

After a week of rest and plenty of hot food, Raddo was feeling more like himself again.

He'd had to stay in the same room until Luth's daily help left for the night, but he needed the rest to let that slit across his belly heal — so the time he spent idle suited him.

Yet the time for being laid up was over. He was ready to talk to Luther Payne.

Luth was probably a millionaire now, Raddo figured. Leastways he lived like one. And was as ruthless a killer as Raddo had ever known, and he'd known more than his share. Luth and Raddo had been the last ones to cut and run when that vengeful ghost started guarding the trail. Folks had called him the Guardian, and he'd put a cold and full stop to their wagon-train raiding.

A shame, because it'd been easy money.

Easy, that is, if a man didn't mind blood on his hands. And Raddo and Luth didn't.

The Comstock Lode had been running full bore by then, so they'd quit the hunt for small wagon trains that peeled off the main trail and started robbing miners. Luth had the notion to do some claim jumping, and he'd killed the right man, taking over a claim that'd paid off soon after. Then he got his neighbor's mine, and no one thought to ask questions because Luth was smooth.

Raddo and the two men left from their gang had done the same. The four of them were the only ones the Guardian hadn't killed, wounded, or scared so bad they quit the country.

Of the four of them, only Luth had struck it big.

Raddo had hit enough silver to keep his hand in, though it kept getting harder to find and the work was wearing him down. While Raddo worked like a slave, Luth killed his way into part ownership of one of the larger mines that kept swallowing up the smaller ones.

No reason Luth couldn't have given Raddo a share of that.

Ever since then, Luth had done plenty of cold-blooded things here and there to expand his hold on the big mine. The only men left owning it now were those who knew better than to trust Luth or challenge him. They survived in spite of the partnership.

Luth also paid good money to keep folks scared of him. It was well known that if you heard gossip about Luther Payne and brought the names of the gossipers to him, you'd be rewarded handsomely. And those doing the gossiping would find trouble enough to quit the country.

Luth had everyone scared into silence.

Except Raddo. Raddo made sure Luth knew there was evidence that would come to light if Raddo died suddenly. Luth knew it, although Raddo had mentioned it but once, when Luth had balked at lending a helping hand.

So, after all these days of being a layabout, Raddo climbed out of bed and got dressed in a fancy suit and went downstairs to face his big brother.

When they were youngsters, it was said he and Luth looked enough alike, at just one year apart, to be taken for twins. Today there wasn't much resemblance left. Raddo lived hard while Luth had gone soft, at least to Raddo's way of thinking.

But they were of a size, so Luth had shared out of his overstuffed closet. It'd been a long time since Raddo had worn a suit of clothes like this. Early on, after Raddo'd started his claim and found a decent amount of silver, he'd lived nice for a while . . . and then the mine played out.

Now he ran his hands over the fine wool and silk shirt. His rough hands snagged the silk, causing Raddo to frown. He preferred denim, broadcloth, and leather. But for one night he figured he could stand it.

Raddo shaved. With a full beard it took a while. Then he hacked his hair short using the cut-throat razor. A butcher job, but he looked a sight more civilized than when he'd had a beard and gray-streaked hair hanging down to his shoulder blades. He stared at himself in the mirror with some surprise. He hadn't seen a mirror in years. He barely recognized the man staring back. With a sick twist to his stomach, he realized he'd become old. Near sixty probably. Birthdays weren't something he paid much mind to.

He looked around the big room and snorted. Even stuck here in the back corner of the attic to avoid servants, the furniture was grand.

Luth had warned him about locking the door. "I'm not making you a prisoner or anything, Raddo," he'd said and handed over the key. "Come and go as you like, but

I wouldn't advise it in the daytime."

Raddo had been in pain and played out, and Luth had come to the attic in the evenings to talk for a bit and play cards. They'd eat some food and talk about old times.

Luth had provided his brother all this, including a short stack of gold and silver coins. Raddo suspected Luth wanted him to take the money and run. Well, Raddo had no intention of doing that. Not yet anyway. Not for that puny pile of coins.

Raddo found Luth in his office. He walked in without knocking — the door wasn't locked. Luth sat like a king behind that big old desk of his, easing back in his chair as Raddo approached.

"It's finally time, is it?" he said.

Raddo nodded. "Yep, time to get back on the trail and hunt down a couple of folks I need to bury deep. Then I'm quitting the country. I'll need a stake to do it, to start a new life somewhere else."

Luth ran his eyes up and down Raddo, now cleaned up and dressed nice. "I see you found the clothes."

"Sure did, and I took out the stitches you set. I'm ready to ride. Once these folks are dead, I aim to travel far and fast. And I want to set myself up good. I don't need no mansion like you got, Luth, but I figure you can share more generous than you done. I helped you gather the seed money that started all this." Raddo gestured to the lush surroundings.

Luth held a cigar in one hand and rolled it left and right. His eyes were cold as they studied his brother. The lantern on his desk flickered and danced, reflected in those hard eyes. This wasn't the first time Raddo had seen firelight in Luth's eyes. It was like looking straight into his soul and seeing the flames of hell.

Silent for so long that Raddo heard the ticking of a grandfather clock on the far side of the office, Luth finally nodded to himself and pulled a key out of the belly drawer of the desk. He used it to unlock the bottom drawer on his right and took out a leather bag the size of a woman's reticule. It clinked loudly when Luth tossed it, and Raddo grabbed it out of the air.

He tugged on the bag's cord and peeked in. Gold coins worth twenty dollars apiece, and there were a decent number of them. Maybe a thousand dollars all told. He'd never had this much money at one time in his entire life.

He wanted it. But he wasn't surprised to find he wanted more. Just how many bags were in that locked drawer?

He looked up into the barrel of a gun. Luth had that in his desk too, it appeared.

Raddo tensed. "I know you're not afraid of killin', but you're mighty careful about it. You'll have your hands full cleaning the blood off your fancy furniture."

"I don't want to kill you, Raddo. But I know you. I know that look in your eye. There's a thousand dollars in that one little bag." Luth scooted his chair backward to the shelves behind him. He never took his eyes off Raddo, nor let the gun waver. "I've been thinking the day just might come when my sins would find me out."

Luth reached behind him and fiddled with something, and a small section of shelving swung out. He pulled out a good-sized satchel and set it on the desk with a heavy thud, which told of its weight. Sliding back to the drawer he'd unlocked, he took out a second little bag.

"Two thousand dollars in gold, and you'll find another five in this satchel. It's what I have laid out for myself should I need to run. If I thought I could live on it, then you should be able to live on it. But I'm attaching some conditions to this money."

Raddo ignored the gun. He didn't have one, and if Luth wanted to fire he'd do it.

But Raddo thought Luth knew better than that. "What kind of conditions?"

"I don't want you going after those couple of witnesses. This isn't the same wild land we ran in with no law for hundreds of miles. Now there's plenty of lawmen. They'll hunt you down for murder, and they won't stop until they've got a noose tight around your neck."

Raddo thought of all the folks he'd killed in the wagon trains over the years. A shiver ran down his spine. He thought of that one witness, the man who'd fired a bullet into him, the one who'd yelled about recognizing him. That was a third witness. And there were others with him in that cave, two at least. He couldn't say who all they were, but there was a mighty strong chance they'd seen him, too. His desire to make sure they were all silent forever ate like a gnawing rat at his insides.

"I'll give you this money," Luth went on, "and the chestnut horse in the stable behind my house, plus leather to outfit it. The condition is, I want you gone for good."

"I have things left from our times together." Raddo had mentioned this before. "Things that connect you to me, and both of us to the crimes we done. I don't take orders from you."

"I've been putting up with you blackmailing me for nigh on to ten years now, Raddo. And I've paid plenty of times for your silence. I know you can bring me down, but I don't see how you do that without destroying yourself."

"That's why I'd never do it unless I was trapped with no way out. I've got things set up so my information comes to light if I die, too." Raddo smiled right into the teeth of that gun.

"I'm not going to kill you except to save my own life."

"Now, Luth, I'm your brother. I'd never —"

"Enough." Luth cocked the gun, and the *crack* echoed in the room. "I'm not telling you to go away to protect myself. The plain truth is, the only way for you to stay alive is to go straight. I've done it. Or at least when I am not straight, I'm sly about it. I've given you enough money to live high on the hog for the rest of your life — if you go somewhere back east and live quiet."

"Me, back east?" Raddo shook his head. "Hard to imagine it."

"Live a quiet life on the money I'm giving you, and no one will connect you to the wanted western man Raddo Landauer. I'll bet your witnesses saw you with a beard and

276

wearing your western clothes. They'd never recognize you as you are now. Take this money and go save your own life."

Seven thousand dollars. Raddo could picture it. Him on a ranch, a few cattle, a fine horse, plenty of money. And good food on the table every day. He'd never lived so well in his whole life, not for one single day. When he and Luth were growing up, there'd been food at home, but their pa was a cruel man who made them pay too high a price. They'd learned to stay away from the house while Pa was there, though they could slip in late at night once Pa had gone to bed. Ma left their window unlocked. They'd live off the land and from time to time sneak into the house and get a bit of food from Ma. Now, with this money, on a ranch, with a few cowhands, life would be easy.

He gave Luth a hard nod and reached for the satchel.

Luth pulled back so that Raddo couldn't get within grabbing distance of his gun.

"There are two changes of clothes in there. Out in the stable you'll find a warm coat and some other supplies wrapped up in a bedroll. There's only one horse and one set of leather. Take it all. I'll go call off the sentries and unlock the front gate."

Raddo unlatched the satchel and tossed

the bags of coins inside. "I'll be on the trail now. Get some hours in before sunrise."

"Go east, Raddo." The gun's aim was true. "I want you out of the house and out of the territory tonight. I've got contacts everywhere, so I'll know if you're still around. And don't go after those folks. You'll end up dead. I don't care about much in this life, but I do like the idea of my brother being above ground. Leave this trouble — and me — behind for good."

Raddo closed the bag and grabbed its handle. "You won't see me again, Luth. And maybe, when I'm far gone and feelin' safe, I'll even burn the evidence I have against you. But it won't be anytime soon."

"Then I'll pray for the day you feel safe, little brother."

Raddo laughed as he headed for the door. "Not sure your prayers are a comforting thought, considering you must be in league with Ol' Nick himself."

There was no response as Raddo strode away and kept going straight out the kitchen door toward the stable. He'd only gone a few steps when he saw Luth walk out behind him, on his way toward the massive stone wall he'd built around his mansion, where he lived all alone with just his three sentries.

Luth was a fool. Rich, but not wise to sink all his money into a house he couldn't be driven out of. Left over from Pa's cruelty, no doubt.

Raddo rode out through the gate, with Luth standing there waiting to lock it behind him.

Luth thought his brother to be gone for good. Well, he was. But he wasn't going east.

Those witnesses wouldn't forget, and Raddo couldn't let such folks go on living.

He rubbed a hand over his smooth-shaven face and thought of the fine suit of clothes he wore. He wondered for just a minute . . . could it work? Could he really just ride away, come up with a new name for himself, and live in peace?

Peace didn't appeal to him all that much, but neither did dying.

No, he didn't believe it could work.

They'd seen his face.

They knew he'd done murder.

They were folks who had the feel of never giving up.

After they were all dead, Raddo would ride hard for Denver. The thought of going much farther east than that made his skin itch.

He thought of Luth's unwavering gun and felt that shiver of fear crawl up his spine

again. Luth was the meanest man Raddo
had ever known. Tough, ruthless, downright
brutal if need be. Raddo didn't care to
tangle with him anymore. Best to just ride
out.

But he wouldn't be riding east.

CHAPTER 19

"Trace is back!"

Deb's head came up at Cam's shout from outside the cabin. All the noise from the building crew ceased.

Deb smiled like the rising sun and raced for the window, skidded to a stop and laughed, then spun around to leave through the front door. They were learning to use it again.

Gwen laughed, and Deb glanced back, her face alight with both pleasure and relief. Trace and Adam had been gone for most of a week.

Deb had done her best to act normally, but the truth was that she'd been worried sick. In fact, Gwen had found her tossing up her breakfast one morning. The stress was just too much.

With Ronnie in her arms, and Maddie Sue by the hand, Gwen left the bunkhouse to welcome the travelers home. She saw Trace gallop into the yard, swing down from the horse, and hug Deb after she leapt into his arms. Adam rode in at a more rational pace.

Gwen saw love light up her sister's eyes. Trace returned it. He spun her in a circle. Gwen's eyes sought out Cam, who didn't notice because he was scampering down the corner of the cabin. Its walls were up now, and the roof was framed.

If she married Cam, she'd never have the love that Deb had found, and she wanted it so desperately. She kissed Ronnie and swept Maddie Sue up in her other arm. She hugged them both tight.

"Papa!" Maddie reached out toward Cam as he strode toward them.

Cam's head came around, and for a second it was clear in his expression that he feared Maddie Sue was reaching for Trace.

But she wasn't. She was reaching for him. A smile bloomed over Cam's face. With quick steps, he closed the distance between himself and his daughter.

That was when Gwen made her decision.

Now to tell Cam . . . and then live with her answer.

"You've got my cabin up while I've been hither and yon." Trace slung his arm around Deb and walked toward the mostly done structure.

Utah, climbing down behind Cam, laughed. "You oughta stay home now and then, boss."

"But you moved it from where we had it before."

"I didn't like the way the water was flowing," Cam explained. "You'd've had long weeks of trouble with mud every spring."

"I didn't see what the spring thaw would do there," Utah added.

"We didn't move it far," Penny said, coming out of the mostly finished cabin. "Did you catch up with that coyote?"

And that put an end to the light talk. Deb's smile faded to worry. She held Trace tighter.

"Let's go in and have a cup of coffee. I'll tell you what I found, and that's mostly nuthin'."

A dead end in Carson City. Ski trails clearly visible until he reached a stretch with no snow. There the trail ended as surely as if the man had learned to fly. Or maybe he just took the skis off and walked.

The men and Penny went back to building. Penny preferred it to kitchen work by a Rocky Mountain mile.

"Deb," Gwen said quietly as she pared the rough, withered skins off a mountain of potatoes, "I've made my decision about Cam."

Deb was slicing side pork, and at Gwen's solemn voice she dropped the knife and turned to give her a wary look. Then Deb washed and dried her hands and pulled Gwen into her arms. "Now, tell me what you're going to do."

The room was full of commotion. They were clearing the supper table, washing dishes, and the children were overly loud, as they often were at the end of a long, tiring day.

"I'd like to speak to you outside for a moment, Cam." Gwen's voice was barely a whisper, but he heard it clear as day. Everyone did.

The noise in the room died like a robin in a May blizzard. Cam looked at her, his eyes wide, or maybe not — he couldn't see himself. Maybe he only just thought he was reacting like a scared mustang.

A second or two passed, and then the noise roared to life again, louder than ever. Not a single person there looked at her.

Gwen stood by the front door. Cam came to her, opened the door, and she slipped outside. He stayed right on her trail.

The days were longer, but the moon

wasn't yet up. Much of the snow had melted, and the white of it had always made the night brighter. While there was still plenty of snow left in the forest, mostly it was a black night.

Cam's heart pounded. From her tone, he knew she had something important to say, and he was afraid he didn't want to hear it.

The breeze was cool, so he led her to the new house. They'd worked until dark and had the roof in and the shutters and doors all hung. There were several rooms framed up inside the place. The cabin was much as it'd been before, but there was the finishing work left to do. Even so, they were only a day or two from leaving for Cam's land to start building there.

"Last night," Gwen began, "when we were reading the Bible after dinner . . ."

They read from the Good Book every night — if they could keep their eyes open.

"We started the book of Joshua." Cam spoke for the first time and realized how silent he'd been.

She nodded. "The verse that struck me was, 'Have not I commanded thee? Be strong and of good courage; be not afraid, neither be thou dismayed: for the Lord thy God is with thee whithersoever thou goest.' "

"It's an encouragement," Cam said, remembering how it'd made him feel to know God was always at hand.

"That verse helped settle things in my mind, and I'm ready to give you my answer now to your proposal."

It seared through Cam's mind that she was turning him down. She wanted the children, but she realized God would go with them and they would make it with or without her. She was getting ready to pat him on the head and tell him *Be not afraid.*

Cam swallowed hard and opened his mouth to start arguing with her.

"Yes."

He clamped his mouth shut.

"I will marry you, Cam. I have my doubts, but where I go, God will be with me. I love the children, as I know you do. And I am drawn to you, and I enjoy it when you kiss me. That isn't perhaps a firm foundation for marriage, but God's promise is a firm foundation for life. So, I've decided to take this step in faith."

She was drawn to him. She liked kissing him. It uncurled pleasure in his gut, but it also felt hollow somehow.

Closing his eyes, he prayed silently for wisdom and as much courage as Gwen had. "It seems to me that's a verse I might use myself."

A smile curved Gwen's lips. "You have no lack of courage, Cam. When have you ever been afraid?"

"I do show all the signs of being mighty brave. Especially when I go to hollering and giving orders to everyone. But I'm trying to live a new way, Gwen. I'm trying to be less of a ruler to the people around me. I was trained for that in the army, but that's not how a man should behave toward his family and friends." He leaned down and kissed her. "Nor the way he should treat a wife. And a man starting a new kind of life, well, he needs a lot of courage to keep from slipping into old habits. So I'll claim that verse right along with you."

This time she kissed him, her arms winding around his neck.

He lifted his head. "It's yes then, pretty lady? You'll marry me?"

"It's yes, Cam. I will."

"If we're to go to my home tomorrow or the next day, I'd like us to go as husband and wife. Can we ride into Carson City and get married? Trace said the town of Dismal is closer, but there's little chance a man of the cloth or a judge will be there. In fact, he said the folks who live there chose it *because* there's no man of the cloth nor judge. They do have a sheriff, though."

"Carson City sounds fine to me. Can Deb come? I hate to slow down the building, and she didn't wait to marry until I could be there, but —"

Cam stepped back and took her hand. "Let's go invite everyone. We'll see if they'd rather build straight through or take a day away from this place — most of them for the first time in months — and go to a wedding in town."

"Don't ask the men which would appeal to them most." Gwen smiled. "Their answer might pinch my feelings."

He laughed. "C'mon."

He wrapped an arm around her waist, and they walked slowly, close together, to the house. Things had quieted down. The youngsters must've gone to sleep, because everyone sat quietly while Adam read aloud from the book of Joshua.

Adam stopped when Cam stepped into the room with Gwen. Cam looked down at her. They should have planned this. Whose job was it to make the announcement?

Gwen's face turned pink. She could act unusually shy around people she knew well. So Cam decided to jump right in.

"Gwen and I are getting married."

The room exploded. Everyone jumped to

their feet. Deb was first to reach them, and she had eyes only for her sister. Though she didn't look quite as joyful as everyone else.

Penny threw her arms around Cam. "You're a smart man, big brother."

Trace shook Cam's hand around that hug. Penny giggled and moved on to hug Gwen.

Ronnie started crying from the bedroom. Everyone dropped to complete silence, but the celebration didn't stop. Cam had his hand shaken with such enthusiastic slaps on the back that he figured he'd be sore tomorrow.

Details were discussed. Turned out everyone wanted to go to Carson City. They didn't even mind watching a wedding.

Utah muttered, "Keep it short."

Cam couldn't imagine how a wedding could be overlong, so he didn't bother worrying about it.

The wedding wasn't the first thing they did when they arrived in town. Cam took Gwen to the Land Office, where she filed a claim for 160 acres. Cam knew the exact piece of land he wanted.

Apparently it was completely legal for a woman to claim a homestead as a single woman, then get married and keep the land. With his long years of military service, Cam had to homestead for only a year to fully own his land. And that had started last fall, even though he hadn't lived there yet. He had to get the cabin built within six months and live there the rest of the year to qualify. He'd own the land in full by year's end.

Because Penny had done work on a military base that suited the land agent, he'd given her two years off the five years she needed to claim her land. Six months of that too were already gone.

Now Gwen would need to stay on the land for five years, but she wasn't going anywhere. It delighted her to add so much to the family holdings. Of course, they needed much more to run a decent ranch. Or so she was told. Three homesteads at 160 acres each made 480 total, which sounded vast to her. Then Cam told her he had his sights set on about five thousand!

They headed to the church next, and now here Gwen stood, a toddler in her arms. This wasn't how she'd pictured her wedding, and yet she'd be switched if she didn't like it.

She hugged Ronnie tight. It'd been her idea that they each carry one of the children up to stand in front of the parson. They were doing more than just getting married — they were forming a family. Besides that, holding the wriggling toddler kept her mind off the vows she was taking and the man she was marrying. When she thought about it, she got a little sick to her stomach.

She'd prayed about this decision. Prayed long and hard, and decided it was the right thing to do.

And since God hadn't seen fit to hit her with a lightning bolt, did that mean He agreed? She listened for thunder but heard nothing.

"Dearly beloved, we are gathered here to-day . . ."

Gwen listened to every word. This was a vow before God. She would make her promises and keep them for the rest of her life.

"Cameron Scott, do you take this woman to be your lawfully wedded wife?"

Gwen edged closer to him. If she was nervous, if she had doubts, then it was up to Cam and her, as a team, to get through them together.

"I do." Cam's deep voice pulled her out of her unfortunate daydream.

It had to be her turn now, so she listened intently.

". . . for better, for worse, for richer, for poorer, in sickness and in health, to love, honor, and obey, till death . . ."

Love, honor, and obey. She hoped Cam would keep letting her slap him on the back of the head when he was doing wrong by the children. She wasn't sure if that fit into their wedding vows or not. She was tempted to stop the parson and ask for some exact definitions.

A discreet nudge of his elbow against her ribs bumped out of her, "I do."

"Now whom God has joined together let no man put asunder. I now pronounce you man and wife. You may kiss the bride."

Well, Gwen knew how to do that. Whether she should be proud of that or not was a question she would *not* be discussing with the parson.

Cam leaned down toward her, threading past Maddie Sue in his arms and Ronnie in hers, and gave her a light, sweet kiss.

And then Deb dragged her away from her favorite part of the ceremony and hugged her. Trace slapped Cam on the back and said he'd never had a brother before.

The parson shook Cam's hand, and there was general chaos for a very short while as they were wished well by everyone.

Utah said, "I need to get some supplies from the general store."

Adam headed after them, and then Trace went along. Cam took a step toward Trace when Gwen grabbed his arm and tugged him back.

"Stay with me, husband. We can go to the store together."

Penny and Deb each grabbed a child and said something about fabric. They left, the parson on their heels.

"Did you want to tell me something?" Cam seemed content to stay there with her. But all Gwen could think of was that she needed fabric, too. Would Deb buy the things the children needed? Surely that was Gwen's job now.

"We can meet for the noon meal, I suppose." They were alone in the church. "I just grabbed you because it seemed like a newly married couple should spend their first hours together." She thought of her errands and that she had no real need for the company of a man. "Maybe first minutes anyway."

"Do you need anything in town?" Cam asked.

Gwen nodded. "Remember I gave you the money your brother had hidden in his wagon? The outlaws didn't find it. It was gold and silver coins, so it survived the wagon-train fire, and later the cabin fire. We've tried to spend it on the children's needs."

"How could you spend it when you've been living under a snowdrift for months?"

Gwen smiled and gave him a quick kiss. "Trace and his men got to town a few times before the hard weather hit. Trace has paid for everything. But we were cooking and cleaning and sewing for him, so it seemed fair enough. Deb went to town once and managed to spend your brother's money on the children. We've been careful with it because that money should be used to support the children, and we want it to last."

"I'm sure you were good stewards of it, Gwen." He pulled her close and hugged her. "I'm not going to fuss at you about caring for my children."

"We also found money hidden by a few others. Abe taught them how to build boxes that were hard to find under their wagons, so the outlaws missed out. We found some letters, and I remember everyone's name who was on our small wagon train. We had hoped to send what we found on to the families. But all the names of kin were on letters lost in the cabin fire. We don't know who exactly is due the money or where to send it all."

"Things have been mighty hectic, with the attacks and the blizzard and the building. There's more of that to come, but we'll make time to study what you have and return the money to the rightful heirs if we possibly can."

"Right now I need a bit of money to buy clothes for the little ones. They've grown out of all their things. Deb is heading for the store that sells fabric." She blushed and added, "A wife should make her husband clothes, too. Are you interested in coming along to choose things?"

Cam gave her a generous handful of coins. "Not really. I'd like to take my horse and get it reshod, Penny's too. And the horse you're riding is Trace's. I'll buy you a mare. Mine's a stallion, so I'm looking for good stock. We can get to growing the herd. I'd like to go to the blacksmith and the livery stable."

Places Gwen had no interest in.

"I oughta get to a barber, as well." He ran his hands through his hair. It was clean and it'd been tidy before he messed it up just now, though his hair hadn't been touched by a scissors since long before he'd come to Trace's.

Nodding, she said, "Going our separate ways is the only solution if we're to meet for a meal. It's nearing noon already."

Cam wrapped his arms around her waist and pulled her close. "I'll walk you to this fabric store and then leave you with Deb and Penny. But since we have a moment alone . . ."

He bent down and gave her one of those wonderful kisses from before. Not the sweet, quiet kiss that marked the end of their wedding vows.

Then he let go, hooked her hand through his arm, and they walked out of the church, both of them smiling.

Gwen decided God had been listening, after all. The lack of lightning bolts was exactly as He intended. She was confident God approved of the decision she'd made today.

CHAPTER 20

What harebrained decision had caused John to come west working for the Chiltons?

But here he was, and there was no going back.

He was surprised by how good it felt to do actual detective work on this case. So far he'd been more of a traveler.

Pushing aside his distaste for the foolish Chiltons, he asked questions, starting with the sheriff, then on to the general store, a city office, five banks, three newspapers, and plenty of saloons.

No one seemed to recognize the name Deb Harkness.

One man at a dry-goods store said Trace Riley sounded familiar . . . maybe. And then in the fifth saloon he tried, he spoke with a cattle buyer and struck gold. Well, he struck a witness at least.

The witness said he'd bought cattle from Trace over in Sacramento and spent some time talking to him around a campfire.

"Do you have any idea where he lives?" John asked. He felt foolish asking for directions for some reason — he couldn't recall ever doing it before this trip — but he forced himself. "I got a letter from this Deb Harkness, and it was sent from Dismal, Nevada."

"Ain't never heard of the Harkness woman, nor Dismal. I'd've remembered if Riley mentioned it. But there're lots of little towns scattered around in the mountains." The man talked like an uneducated frontiersman. He had a patch over his left eye, with an ugly, slashing scar that ran down the side of his face. He had a week's growth of whiskers that were more gray than brown. But he dressed in a black suit with well-shined boots and a flat-topped black hat like a man from the city might wear.

"Ambrose!" the buyer shouted.

A man dressed in typical western garb stirred from where he was dozing in a chair by the fireplace. He carried a Colt Peacemaker that looked as if it'd been through the Civil War. Same for the boots and Stetson hat. And his brown pants and shirt were worn to near rags.

The saloon was quiet this time of day, and the coffee they served was black and strong enough to warm a man right down to his toes. It suited John perfectly.

"Need somethin', Patch?" Ambrose stood, scratched himself, then meandered over to John and the buyer.

"You've been up around these parts a while, right?"

"Yep. Dug silver for a time. Showed tourists around Tahoe. Hauled rock for a big house on the lake. Cut wood."

"This fellow needs to find Dismal, Nevada. Claims it's a town around here."

John arched a brow. *Claims?*

"Yep, I know Dismal right enough. Mighty small, but it has a fair to middlin' general store, and some folks friendly enough to share a bottle and play a hand or two of cards. But not so friendly I don't watch my back trail when I ride away from town. Dismal is the kind of town where a man feels lucky he ain't got nuthin' much worth stealin'."

"Can you tell me how to get there?" John asked. "I'm looking for a man who's said to live in the area. Trace Riley."

"I know where Riley lives, too. On land just downhill of the south banks of Tahoe. Well, not just. Reckon it's an hour or two ride south and maybe some west of the lake."

"I appreciate it." John was starting to wish he'd never asked. The man's eyes were shadowed, and judging by his breath, the shadows came from drink. His directions were worse than nothing. Where in the world was Tahoe? There couldn't be any lake up this high. "I'll find my way when the snow clears on the trail to Ringo and Carson City."

"That's the main trail, and it oughta open up soon. A month, no more."

"A month! It's May already!"

"Is it?" Ambrose looked doubtful.

Patch slapped Ambrose on the shoulder. John braced himself to catch the man when he fell.

"Ambrose has done his time as a guide. He knows a trail or two that'll be clear by now."

Perking up, Ambrose's eyes cleared for the first time. "I do know a game trail that's sheltered from the worst of the snow. It closes up too, but by now it'll be passable." He nodded and got a sly look in his eyes. "Not many around that know it, and it branches off here and there. You'd get lost for sure on your own, but for a price I'd be glad to take you through."

John had decent instincts, and he didn't think Ambrose was dangerous, not a man to be afraid to go riding with. Just an aging drunk. He might look at a trail he knew well, see two of them, and follow the wrong one. But that was less of a risk than waiting a whole month. John thought again of the Chiltons' bonus offer. He wanted that money.

And a month's wait would make it impossible to earn it.

"You're hired," John said. "When can we leave?"

"I want my money first. I need to buy supplies, rent a horse, and get a good night's sleep."

No doubt the supplies would be bottles of whiskey, and the good night's sleep would be Ambrose sleeping it off. Nope. Paying the money now wasn't an option.

It crossed John's mind to offer the man his packhorse, but then he decided against it. The minute they made it to where they were going, he planned to pay Ambrose his money and then send him straight back home, and he couldn't do that with him riding the packhorse, because the no-account might just steal it.

"We leave right now or I find someone else to guide me. Ten dollars to take me through. It can't be more than a couple days' work. You'll ride back here owning the horse I buy you with ten dollars in your pocket."

Ambrose looked annoyed, or more correctly, he looked thirsty.

"Let's go find you a horse and get saddled up." John decided to keep the man moving. "We'll swing by the store and get what supplies we'll need."

He saw Ambrose's eyes light up, and John knew he'd have his hands full keeping Ambrose from including a bottle in with the supplies. But John was used to having his hands full. He clapped Ambrose on the shoulder and, trying to be subtle, steered the man outside.

Gwen rode home side by side with her brand-new husband.

They'd enjoyed their day in Carson City. Gwen had bought sparingly, worried about how much money Cam had and how much room they had to bring things home with them.

She'd come with her sister and sister-in-law to the diner the parson recommended and found that Cam had bought two spare horses. One for Gwen to ride and one to be used as a packhorse. And he had a fair amount of supplies already packed up.

They had to build a cabin, so she supposed he was getting ready for that.

The meal was quick because the little ones were overtired and fussy. It was a relief to be heading for home. Wolf had followed them to Carson City and afterward vanished. Then suddenly the wolf-dog joined them again on the trail for the return trip.

They'd go back to Trace's, where Cam and Gwen had more things to pack. When the new cabin was built, they'd head for the Scott family homesteads.

It was still daylight when they arrived. The men quickly unpacked the supplies and hauled them inside for the women, then headed for the mostly finished cabin. Penny went along, too.

"I'm better at outside chores than inside," Penny said. "I hope you don't mind me abandoning you, but I can be more help on the cabin than with dinner."

"You're a fine cook and seamstress," Deb insisted.

"I'm passable and that's always been enough. But I can swing an ax better'n any of those men but Cam and Utah." Penny smiled sheepishly at Deb. "No offense, your husband is a fine hand with tools, but he makes no bones about all he needs to learn about building."

"Go on with you." Deb grinned. "And no

offense taken. Although speaking the truth can pinch on occasion."

The women all laughed, and Penny hurried outside.

The children had slept while riding home and were rested now and full of energy. Gwen and Deb were kept on the run through the late afternoon cooking, storing supplies away, and tending the little ones.

The men came inside to a fine stew, better for having fresh beef rather than venison, after a winter's worth of living on food they'd stored away in the root cellar.

And Deb had made a cake with white sugar to celebrate the wedding.

The meal was quiet except for Maddie Sue and Ronnie. It had been a long day for everyone.

A chair had been left for Gwen next to Cam, and she'd enjoyed being near him.

As they ate the cake and drank the last of the coffee, Trace said, "I think the cabin is done enough that Gwen and Cam can sleep there tonight. Utah even knocked together a bit of furniture."

"It'll need more finishing, but it can be used," Utah said.

"So you won't have to . . ." Trace fell silent.

Cam didn't speak. Yet he'd obviously been

working there, so how could he not know what had been done?

Penny cleared her throat and picked up where Trace left off. "You'll have a . . . that is, we lit the fireplace. It should be warm and comfortable . . . for you to — to sleep."

Gwen felt heat climb up her neck. Ronnie sat in her lap and was chasing crumbs around with his fingers from the cake Gwen had shared with him. She became very busy scraping what little was left on her plate into a bite and feeding it to the boy.

Then Ronnie was gone from her lap. Since she hadn't been looking, she didn't see Deb come to her side and pluck him up.

Penny got Maddie Sue. "They're ready for bed."

Gwen thought for a second that Penny was talking about her and Cam.

The women carried the children to the bedroom.

Cam took Gwen's hand. "Good night."

He led her outside, where Gwen could breathe again. Once they were well away from the house, the moonlight shining down on them, Gwen smiled at her husband. "That was embarrassing."

She had a feeling there might be more embarrassment to come. Deb had talked with her about wedding nights, but Gwen still felt very unprepared.

"Let's stay out here for a bit." Cam pulled her close, his arm around her waist, and they stood side by side. "It was the moonlight that first gave me notions about you, Gwen. The moon will always be something special between us, at least for me."

Gwen rested her head on his shoulder. "That's nice, Cam. I hadn't thought of that exactly, but I was remembering the first night of the chinook when we watched the water running, the moon and stars shining down on us. That you say it now makes it special for me, too."

"We'll finish the cabin day after tomorrow. I've talked with Trace. We'll stay here tomorrow to work and to pack. The next day you and I, with Penny and the children, will head for our homestead. I want to get there before everyone arrives. We'll be roughing it until we get a cabin up, but we can get a roof over our heads fast. And I lived in an army tent plenty of times. We'll be fine. Probably as comfortable as we've been packed into that bunkhouse."

Gwen smiled. "It is crowded."

"I bought a few head of cattle too, back in Carson City. There was a man who was ready to thin his herd, and he spoke of a cattle drive in the fall. He'll sell to me for a lower price than he'd get in Sacramento, but he'll still come out ahead by not having to hire extra hands and spend a lot of days on a dangerous trail."

"Sounds like both of you made a good deal." This was all very interesting, but she got the feeling Cam was just giving her time to relax.

He turned her to face him. The moonlight shone on his ruggedly handsome face. He'd left his Stetson behind in the bunkhouse, and most all of his things. Gwen hadn't bothered with a bonnet, either. She'd been too nervous about leaving with him.

He wrapped his arms around her, bent his head, and kissed her. It was different receiving a kiss from her husband now. Purer, more honorable, and it carried with it the weight of vows given and received before God and man.

He deepened the kiss, and her arms slid around his neck. They forgot about moonlight and shining stars. They forgot about children and building a cabin and buying a herd. Or at least Gwen certainly did, and there was no hint of distraction coming from Cam.

After long, sweet moments, he raised his head barely an inch. She felt the warmth of his breath with every murmured word.

"Would you like a longer walk, Mrs. Scott? Or are you ready for our wedding night?"

When they left the bunkhouse, she'd been the furthest thing from ready. But the talk, the warm breeze, Cam's sweet kisses, and his strong, gentle arms had changed everything.

She stepped back and took his hand in hers. "Let's go in."

Raddo left Luth's foolish walled mansion and rode a few hours away before he made camp to rest up a bit more and make plans.

Still there, he lay awake thinking about going east and remembered how that man fired at him. Killing mad, he'd emptied his gun.

It wasn't Riley, although Raddo had seen Riley there, also firing away. But nothing like the other man. Raddo had seen him good. Must be one of Riley's hired men — probably one of them from last fall when Riley's men had taken the girl back and caught or killed Raddo's saddle partners.

That cowhand, the way he fired and fired and fired. The way he shouted, as good as daring Raddo to come back and fight . . .

No man's gonna talk to me that way and live.

Not only a determined man, but one

who'd keep looking. There was no use riding away or changing his name, not while a man like that was after him and had seen his face.

Raddo had to go back. A chill of fear made him hesitate. Luth was meaner'n a rattlesnake, and rich enough to have his killin' done for him. Raddo would have to hope Luth didn't find out.

Four men had seen him in that cave, and they'd watched him run. It burned bad to look like a coward in front of them. But he'd been outgunned and stood no chance against them.

While he knew he needed to kill them, they were a tough bunch. They'd survived his burning down the cabin. They'd tracked him and survived the bear trap. They'd found his lookout. And he hadn't managed to kill a single one of them.

But then he'd been reckless. He hadn't paid them enough respect. From now on, then, he'd take his time. Catch them out alone, one by one. With the snow melting fast, he wouldn't be leaving such clear signs with every step. He'd harass them if he could and maybe some of them would quit the country. If they did, he'd let them go . . . maybe.

Stirring on the hard, cold ground, softened

only by a blanket, he let his anger build. Luth was sly in his killing. Raddo would be sly, too.

He'd had plenty of rest and was healed up now. Impatient, he got to his feet, broke camp, saddled up, and rode out. He'd had all the sleep a man needed. It was time to end this. And then afterward, with Luth's money in his saddlebags, he'd ride for Colorado.

By the time Luth learned about what he'd done, Raddo would be long gone.

Gwen woke up from her second night as a married woman. Today was the day. Today they headed home. Her own home. She even owned some land.

Being married was nicer than she'd dared to hope. Stirring, she bumped against Cam and smiled. Both of them were up with the sun. In fact, everyone was, for there was always plenty to do.

"You awake, Gwen?" Cam hugged her close.

She shut her eyes and enjoyed his strength and the gentleness he'd shown her. "I am, I'm just thinking of all we've got to do today. I need to get on."

Cam kissed her, and she held him tight.

"Let's get on, then. Today we're going

home." He kissed her again, longer this time. "I told Trace we'd like to come over on Sundays and we could worship together. Would that suit you?"

Gwen smiled and lifted her head so fast she whacked him in the chin with her head.

"Ouch."

Gwen grimaced and rubbed her head. "I'm sorry. Deb suggested it to me, and I wanted to see if that was all right. I'm not sure how long a ride it is, and I wouldn't ask it of you if it was too long a trip. But yes, I'd love that."

"Butting me in the head is a strange way of saying thank you." He sounded cantankerous, but he had a gleam of humor in his eyes. "Let's finish the last of the packing. We'll eat breakfast and then hit the trail."

"That suits me right down to the ground." She kissed his chin.

He growled and made her kiss him on the lips instead. Then he kissed her back.

They didn't get on with the day as quickly as they planned.

CHAPTER 21

Deb flung her arms around Gwen's neck. "I'm going to miss you so much." She glanced at the children.

Gwen saw the pain — felt it herself.

Deb sniffled. "I love those sweet babies. Cam is a fine man. Penny has taught us more about surviving in the West than I'd ever hoped to learn. But you are who I'll miss most of all, Gwendolyn."

"No one's called me Gwendolyn since Ma died." Gwen smiled, but that didn't stop the tears from brimming. "We've been together for so long. You took care of me all those years, working your heart out while I stayed at home and went to school." Gwen wanted to cry. She held Deb so tight it was a wonder either of them could breathe.

"Someone needed to run our home, Gwen. You know that. And you're so much better at it than me."

"If I'm better at it, it's because I was doing it all the years you ran the paper. And even at that, you do nearly as well as me running a home."

"Regardless, I'm so glad I was able to let you attend school. Let you grow up without having the burden of adulthood quite so young. I was going to be working no matter what — Ma needed me to help, and later when she was gone, there was no one else. Surely not Pa. And being able to protect you made me happy."

"Now I have to leave." Gwen's tears wouldn't hold back.

"I'll miss you, Gwen, but we both have good men. Not men like Pa, but men who will protect us and help carry the load. I can let you go without fear." Deb pulled back, lines of worry creasing her forehead. "Without much fear at least."

"Without fear, Deb — you were right the first time."

Most of the worry lines faded then. "And to marry and leave home, that's as it should be. 'A man shall leave his mother.' Cam did that long ago. 'And a woman leave her home.' It's only right."

"I know." Gwen sniffled and let go with one hand to drag a kerchief out of her sleeve. "I know it's the way of life. But that doesn't make it easy to walk away from the one I've always depended on. And I'm taking Penny with me, which leaves you alone with —" she glanced over her shoulder to make sure no one could hear — "all these men."

"I won't be alone exactly." A light in Deb's eyes told Gwen there was something big going on. She leaned close. "I haven't wanted to talk about it yet, what with the work of building the cabin and worrying over Raddo . . . but before you go, I have to tell you, Gwen." Her already quiet voice dropped to a whisper. "There's going to be a baby soon here at the High Sierra Ranch."

Gwen gasped. Deb slapped a hand over her mouth. "I'm not quite ready to tell Trace yet. He's so protective, I'm afraid he'll wrap me in cotton wool. Honestly, I'd like to put it off until I can just hand him the child."

Gwen giggled, and Deb joined in.

Cam, coming up from behind them, asked, "What're you two laughing at?"

Gwen blushed. She had no experience keeping secrets from a husband. And then she looked at Maddie Sue in Cam's arms. Comfortable there. Loving her papa. It was such a beautiful thing to see, it almost set her to crying again.

"We're just talking about missing each

other and happy memories, and we got to laughing." Deb hugged Gwen once more.

"And crying?" Cam looked from one to the other.

Gwen thought he seemed a little scared, like he didn't know what a man did with a woman's tears. She squeezed Deb tight, then let go and slid her arm around Cam's waist.

A high-pitched whine turned Gwen's attention down to Cam's feet.

"Wolf is . . . is . . . whining?" Gwen had never heard that sound coming from him before.

"I have never heard that sound from my dog before." Trace held Ronnie, but he had a deep furrow across his brow, worried about Wolf.

There was some debate about whether Wolf was a wolf or a dog. Some of both for sure, but maybe a little too much wolf. Except right now.

He reared up on his hind legs and licked Maddie Sue's toes. Then he dropped to all fours and went to Trace, still whining, reared up and licked Ronnie.

"If I didn't know better," Cam said, nearly knocking off his Stetson while scratching his head, "I'd swear that dog is crying."

Gwen suppressed a smile as she decided

her husband didn't know how to deal with Wolf's tears, either.

"Wolf wouldn't *cry*!" Trace sounded personally offended on behalf of all males.

The dog dropped and went back to Maddie Sue.

"There might be tears in his eyes." Gwen watched the dog, feeling bad for taking away his best friends.

"Wolf is the meanest dog that ever lived, and I've always been the only one allowed to touch him." Trace looked like maybe his feelings were hurt.

Cam lowered Maddie Sue to the ground.

It went against everything Gwen knew about animals to let this half-wild wolf-dog near the little girl. But there was no denying they were fast friends. She remembered that time Cam had shouted, not at Maddie Sue but near her. Wolf had stepped between Cam and his daughter as if to protect her.

Trace let Ronnie down. The two children jumped on Wolf, and soon all three of them were rolling on the ground, giggling.

Well, Gwen didn't think *Wolf* was giggling exactly, but they were all very happy.

"Let them play until the last minute," Trace said. "Unless —" he swallowed so hard, Gwen heard it — "unless you think I should send him with you."

If they weren't careful, Trace might start crying. How would Cam deal with a man's tears?

"No, he's yours. Bring him along when you come to build." Cam looked nervous now. "They're not going to want to go with me. They'll want to stay with Wolf."

"Wolf stays." Gwen decided to take charge of the situation. "The children go. We'll teach Wolf he's not going to be permanently separated from the little ones — he'll accept it."

Ronnie wrapped his arms around Wolf's middle. Maddie Sue kissed the dog . . . right on the fangs.

Gwen flinched.

Deb said to Cam, "We'll see you for the building, then you make sure to come back on Sundays. Our services wouldn't be the same without the three of you and the little ones."

"We're planning on it," Cam assured.

"We've got finishing work to do on the cabin. We'll follow along soon, tomorrow or the next day, to help build yours. I'll bring Wolf along." Trace smiled at his wife. "Deb too. That's not too long a separation, is it?"

"Thanks for including me." Deb backhanded him gently on the arm. "No, that's not too long at all."

He pulled her close with one arm around her waist.

Deb looked up at her husband. "Can I help build? Without the children to care for, I've got time on my hands." And time to be lonely. Gwen heard that even if Deb didn't say it out loud.

"We'll find plenty for you to do." From his tone of voice, Gwen thought Trace heard Deb's unspoken words, as well.

Deb snuggled up to Trace much as Gwen had to Cam.

"We'll be getting on, then." Cam shook Trace's hand and gave Deb an awkward pat on the arm. "We're burning daylight."

Gwen and Deb grinned at each other as Penny brought the horses up, including a packhorse tied to Cam's saddle. Penny was wearing trousers as usual, with her slouchy broad-brimmed hat pulled low on her head. Two long braids dangled down her back, blending into her shirt.

Gwen and Deb had made her a dress, but Penny wasn't inclined to put it on. She wore it for the hour they spent in worship every Sunday, and she'd worn it to town. She even wore it occasionally while washing her real clothes.

Gwen loved her new sister. She looked down at her own bedraggled dress and how poorly it was suited to horse riding and couldn't help but envy Penny's common sense and unconventional ways.

As she mounted up, it struck Gwen hard that this was the moment she was really leaving home. Not the bunkhouse. Not the new cabin. Not Trace's High Sierra Ranch.

Deb.

Deb was her home and had been for most of her life. A biblical moment because, once married, a woman was called by God to leave her home. And Gwen surely was.

Not wanting to distress Deb, Gwen fought back tears and the uneasiness of starting a new life with a husband who at times could treat her like a private under his command. Cam could be kind, too, and gentle . . . but would he ever love her?

She waved goodbye. Her eyes met Deb's and she knew — and she saw Deb knew — that their separating hurt like an open wound.

Gwen turned to face forward, to face her future without fear as God called her to, and fell in beside Cam. Gwen carried Ronnie. Cam had Maddie Sue. The trail was wide here, so Penny was on his other side.

The five of them rode away together, leading a heavily laden packhorse, Gwen leaving her home behind, unsure if she would ever find another.

They rounded the first curve in the trail and heard Wolf howl like his heart was breaking right there in his chest.

Raddo rode along toward Riley's ranch, high above the trail, on a game path that was finally clear of snow. He peered down as he'd done all winter from many different lookouts. Wondering who he'd get to kill first, he settled in. They were all outside.

Or were they? He'd counted them over the winter many times, and he noticed one of the women was missing.

He was far enough away he couldn't make out details, but he saw four horses saddled, mounted, and ridden by two men and a woman. The fourth horse carried a big pack.

Raddo was a long way off and at a bad angle to the riders, but his eyesight was keen enough he saw two little ones riding in front of the woman and the man riding in the center. Two men, a woman, and two children. He'd have to dig to get his spyglass, yet it wasn't necessary. He saw all he needed to from right here.

As they rode out of the ranch yard, excitement built within him. They were on the trail to Carson City. His first chance to thin the herd had come quick. Out on the trail they were much more vulnerable than they were at the ranch.

He'd thought he'd pick them off one by one and had spied on the ranch enough through the winter to count eight adults. Five men and three women, though one woman didn't come outside much. In fact, he'd seen all three women outside together only a few times.

Eight adults meant a lot of firepower, so he'd need to go about this carefully and use every bit of his skill. He'd accepted as much and was determined to be as patient as a cougar on the hunt.

Now here he was with a good chance to thin the herd with one mighty strike. He knew a spot ahead where the trail to Carson City narrowed and the woods came right up close, meaning they'd have to ride along it single file. He'd be able to come down the mountain near there and get within comfortable gun range.

With a smile, he doubled back on the path to follow along, anxious to solve about half his problems in one, swift, lethal attack. He'd do it without reloading his gun. And then he'd turn his attention to the group left at the ranch.

He could take the two men with his first

bullets. They'd be on the ground dying before any of them knew what was happening. That left the woman alone.

He reflected back on the wagon-train raids. Women were weak and worthless. He ignored the sharp chill of fear when he thought of a few who weren't.

No matter. Right now he needed to ride well ahead on the trail to Carson City, so he'd have time to climb down and get himself in place. He kicked his horse and picked up the pace. It wasn't long before he left them far behind.

Gwen felt a sharp chill of fear. She had no reason for it, but she couldn't ignore it. "Cam, I feel like I'm being watched."

Turning in his saddle, Cam studied her, then the forest beyond.

"I'm checking this side," Penny said.

Neither of them panicked. They'd ridden too many dangerous trails together and knew better.

"How good a position could Raddo get along this trail if he wanted to dry-gulch us?" Gwen eyed the wide trail.

"The forest is back a ways," Cam said. "A sharpshooting man would have trouble making his bullet fly true, especially if firing from cover. And if we're talking about

Raddo, then that would be his way. This isn't a likely spot for an attack, but I understand your feeling. I wasn't worrying about it because of the trail. Now I'm thinking that may be wrong."

"Nothing I can see over here," Penny said. "And the woods are thin on the edges. If someone was watching us, he'd have to be up the mountain a long way, because we'd spot him down low. Then where the forest thickens, he'd have trouble with a lookout spot until he found a big boulder he could climb on."

"Well, the trail's like this all the way to my place."

"Is it?" Penny asked. "We've only taken it that one time when we headed to Trace's ranch to fetch the children. That was on snow-packed trails, right at the beginning of that big blizzard that trapped us at Trace's. I don't remember every detail of the trail, but I think there's at least one stretch where the trail gets real narrow."

Gwen watched them both. Competent and skilled in surviving this hard land. "I shouldn't have worried out loud. I know you both are better than me at reading signs and scouting a trail."

Reaching for her hand, Cam squeezed it tight. "You did the right thing. Don't ever ignore even a tiny whisper of fear like that, Gwen. Such a feeling isn't usually your imagination. You heard some little sound out of place — you might not even realize it exactly — but a noise out of place makes you edgy."

"Or a shadow moves wrong," Penny said. "Or a bird takes off too fast. Or the wild critters in the forest suddenly fall silent. Trust your instincts."

Gwen nodded and felt less foolish. "You both need to teach me all the ways of the frontier. I need to learn to read a trail, chop down a tree, and hunt, shoot, and skin a deer."

"Gwen, I —"

"I know you'll take care of me, Cam. I plan on letting you. All three of us will be working long, hard hours. I'm better in the house, so that's where I'll handle things. But I don't want to go through my life ignorant. I don't want everything to have to rest on your shoulders like a heavy weight. Not the weight of the work, but the weight of you knowing your wife is helpless should anything happen to you. That's a burden to a man, and to a woman."

Cam met her eyes. Three seconds passed, then five. "You're right. We need to do it for both of us. For Penny too. But never forget you're the best cook, and you're best with the little ones."

Gwen looked down at Ronnie, dozing in her lap. Maddie Sue's head was resting heavy in the crook of Cam's arm. She was fast asleep.

"Penny's as good as I am," Gwen said, being polite because it wasn't really true.

"Not as good," Penny interjected. "Decent. I could get us fed, keep the clothes washed, care for the children. I can sew some, but it's a much harder job for me, and the end result isn't nearly as nice. What you lack in woodland skills I lack in the kitchen. You have things to teach both of us, too."

Cam nodded. "And we'll be busy at first building the cabin and barn and corrals, rounding up a herd. We may not have much time for teaching, but I promise — you won't be shirking while we labor. You're going to have everything inside the house on your shoulders to handle. Yep, we'll all be working plenty hard to get the ranch up and running."

Gwen smiled. "You're right about the work ahead of us, even with Trace and Deb and the men coming over to help for a few days. In the meantime, I plan to trust my instincts."

Cam smiled at her. "You're gonna make about the best little ranch wife a man ever had, Mrs. Scott."

Gwen felt heat climb up her neck and onto her cheeks. She turned to face forward and hoped Cam couldn't see her blush. It seemed like the exact opposite of what a frontier ranch wife would do.

They rode along, and now Gwen didn't just wait for a chill of fear. She watched, listened, even smelled the world around her. Gwen was going to learn and do it fast. After all, she was a strong woman, and this country needed strong folks like her to settle it. She was glad to do her part.

Raddo didn't bother watching the trail. They were coming, and that was all he needed to know. There was no other route to Carson City, which had to be where they were heading.

Hurrying so he had time to descend the mountain and be ready when they passed by, he followed a high-up trail to the narrow stretch. Once there, he tied up his horse and left it behind, then started heading downhill. Although the snow here was melting fast, there was still plenty of it because of the cool shade of so many pines. Water was running everywhere, and the half-melted snowdrifts that had turned to ice overnight made the going treacherous.

But Raddo was used to it. He picked his way carefully, scouting without exposing himself to any oncoming riders. Finally he found a good spot where he could fire from cover.

The trail ran straight for a long way right here, so he'd know when they were approaching and have plenty of time to study them and take aim.

He settled in once more. With distant surprise, he realized he wanted to kill them. It felt like hunger. He'd never minded killing folks, for that was his way of earning himself a living. It was a job, nothing more. Yet now it felt different. Powerful. He thought back to the wagon train in the fall. He'd killed no one since then.

It'd been too long.

For the first time he wondered if he could live a quiet life somewhere, enjoy Luth's money. No risk, no adventure. No power . . .

If this same hunger he felt now came on him then, what would he do? Who would he kill to satisfy that feeling gnawing at his insides?

He didn't know, but it'd be fun planning it.

Spotting the group as they came around a

curve, he slipped quietly behind a boulder that had a covering of winter grass in front of it. He could see them, but they'd never see him.

He burned his gaze into them. His vision was sharp as a snakebite. As he cocked the gun, his lips curved into a smile.

CHAPTER 22

"We haven't really talked about your land." Gwen seemed to like to talk while they rode.

Cam smiled at his wife. His arm tightened on the slowly rising and falling chest of his sweet little girl. Ronnie was sprawled against Gwen's body, such a sturdy, handsome little boy. His looks were a perfect mix of Abe and Delia. Cam felt blessed that his brother lived on through his son.

And Ronnie . . . his full name Cameron. Abe had paid Cam a high compliment with that.

"The turn is just ahead." Cam hugged Maddie Sue, but not so tight he woke her. He'd learned that lesson.

"I didn't really understand its location from looking at that map at the Land Office," Gwen said.

Cam looked up at the long, straight trail leading to Carson City, and he felt a chill. Like Gwen, he couldn't say why, but the woods came down so close to the road they'd have to ride single file.

The trail they were on was still wide, though mountains rose up on both sides of them, just back far enough there was no one who'd risk a shot from cover. And Raddo was the type of coward to only shoot from cover.

Straight ahead, the trail turned into a near tunnel.

A hundred more yards and they'd be in rifle range.

He hoped the men came first. He'd pick them off like it was a turkey shoot.

He'd wait until they were right under his guns so that even if those behind the first kill turned to run, he'd have more than enough time to shoot them all.

He took his pistol out of its holster, cocked it, and let it rest on the boulder in front of him.

If he emptied his rifle and there were more who needed killin', he could clean things up with his six-gun.

Easing back the hammer on his rifle, he took careful aim and waited.

"I picked out a home site last fall, but the land you homesteaded, Gwen, is what I'd planned to encourage Abe to claim." He looked from Gwen on his right to Penny on his left. "What do you think? We considered homesteading on the land Gwen got. I think there's a better home site on that land."

"I remember it. We debated it, but decided to claim the pieces we did because of grazing land, and we could only have two sections. Yes, let's move everything to Gwen's land. I'll have to build my own cabin, but we can put one cabin straddling the property line of your two holdings."

"You're not going to live with us?" Gwen asked, sounding dismayed.

Penny smiled. "I've got to have a building up on my own land to prove up on the homestead. But I'll be eating with you, and we'll all work together. I'll be around so much, the spot where I sleep won't make much of a difference. We cached a lot of supplies at the place we picked last fall, before we came to Trace's house. We'll have to go there and pack up our supplies, including a wagon. I hope no one found it and helped themselves."

Cam peered ahead at the trail that narrowed to a tunnel. He didn't like it. "We expected to get the little ones and come right back." He glanced at Gwen. "But I managed to round up a wife, too."

She smiled back and rode easy.

A trail that veered off at a right angle to the road to Carson City opened up beside them and headed straight east. Cam looked at that tunnel and wanted no part of the gauntlet, even though they'd ridden right through it twice on the day they got married. He was glad the homesteads weren't any closer to town.

"We turn here," Cam said. Together they rode to the east, away from the tunnel of a trail. He breathed easier.

Raddo was so furious he could hardly breathe. He'd've given in to a full-fledged howl of rage except he bit it off so as not to give away his position.

Had they seen him? He hadn't noticed them make a sudden turn. No, it was all done calm-like. They'd never planned to come this way.

He'd run across that gap in the mountain and never once thought of it as a trail. The snow was melted, the grass thick on it. If it was a trail, it didn't have a single wagon track on it anywhere.

He wanted to punch someone, take out his frustration. He'd assumed they set out for Carson City. So where were they heading?

Raddo had no idea. And now, by the time he made the long, hard climb uphill to fetch his horse, they'd be well away before he could get within shooting distance again. He was in such a rage at the moment, he thought about just charging after them, right out in the open, and start blasting with his six-gun.

Instead, he took a deep breath and forced himself to wait, pushing back the fury. He had to handle them right. Two men, a woman, two children. The children didn't count, and the woman would be easy pickins, but even a weakling could pull a trigger if given plenty of time.

Three adults. That added up to a lot of guns that could level on him when he started shooting, if he just rode in and attacked.

No, he'd get a handle on his temper first.

He'd climb to his horse and then go after them quietly.

And he'd figure out where they were heading.

Calmer now, he began the long trek up the hill. It reminded him of his gunshot wound. Though it was healed, he still ached. And he tired easily.

Finally he approached the spot where his horse was tied up . . . and it wasn't there.

The branch he'd tied the animal to was broken, and a good-sized chunk of it lay a few paces down the trail with hoofprints heading the wrong direction.

A killing rage erupted.

Raddo set out after his horse with plans to work off his anger, and do it soon.

CHAPTER 23

Settling in at Cam's place — Gwen's place too now — took all day.

She was thrilled when Cam pointed out where, a few dozen yards into the woods, they'd build themselves a cabin. It was much closer to Deb than she'd dared hope.

"There's an open glade in there. We'll ride in later, and I'll show it to you. It's a beautiful place. It'll straddle the line for me and you, Gwen. Penny's cabin will be within shoutin' distance."

They went to the open valley near where Cam wanted to build and unloaded the packhorse. Then they rode on to where he'd cached his supplies over the winter. They found the covered wagon Cam and Penny had driven west, almost melted free of snow from where it'd spent the winter.

Cam began uncovering the supplies he and Penny had left. When he picked up a case of building tools, Gwen saw the coiled muscles bulge in his back and arms as he made easy work of setting the heavy crate in the wagon box. She knew life came with no promises, but she'd married a man who would work at her side. Something her pa had never done. Gwen's father wouldn't have lasted two weeks in the West. She suspected that a woman searching for a husband to protect and provide for her should head west right away.

"I'm not putting the cover on," Cam said. "That way, the wagon is ready to go as soon as we load it. Penny and I left four cows and two extra horses here over the winter. We'll leave them here until the new herd comes."

Cam and Penny had a surprising pile of supplies.

"I'll get the two horses in the pasture and hitch them to the wagon. Come with me to check the cows."

"The livestock looks good," Penny said.

"Look, we've got two babies." Cam pointed, smiling. He scooped up Maddie Sue in one arm, Ronnie in the other. "Do you see the baby calves?"

The little ones giggled and asked questions. Gwen was amazed at the patient way Cam answered every one of them.

"I hope to get one more calf. I have three

cows in there and a bull, all Herefords."

"Hereford, is that what they call a red cow?" Gwen asked.

"Yep, red cows with white faces. They're supposed to gain better than a longhorn. See that big old bull? He's the ruler here. He followed behind our wagon coming here, gentle as a lamb, but he almost looks like he wants a fight. I hope he hasn't gone too wild over the winter."

They looked at the corral built last fall. It was up against a steep mountainside covered with lush winter grass. Not so steep, though, the cows couldn't climb it to graze.

The tall grass bent in a spring breeze sweeping across the slope. The cows ate placidly.

The herd of six cattle stood together about a hundred feet away. They watched the strange people curiously, chewing. One of the calves jumped up and skittered behind its mama. Two sturdy draft horses drank water from a small pond below a spate of water gushing from a rock wall.

"I picked this place hoping it'd work all winter, but left thinking I'd only be gone a few hours, so I didn't worry if the snow didn't make it a decent pasture. Because I'd be back to take care of things. A day maybe." He shook his head and laughed.

"What if you'd made it to our place and back?" Gwen's throat tightened as she thought of it. "What if you'd been here with the little ones, pinned down by the storm all winter without enough shelter and food?"

Cam turned to her. "The Lord stayed us, Gwen. He kept us at the High Sierra Ranch and protected us. It's like our verse from Joshua, 'Be not afraid.' "

Gwen smiled. " 'Have not I commanded thee? Be strong and of good courage; be not afraid, neither be thou dismayed: for the Lord thy God is with thee whithersoever thou goest.' "

Cam gave her a crooked smile. "I reckon I've been dismayed a time or two. Over my injured leg, but mostly over the children and whether I could ever earn their love."

Maddie Sue tore off along the corral fence, thrilled to stretch her legs. Cam grabbed her as she ran past and hoisted her high, then kissed her noisily on the neck. She giggled and squirmed. Not that long ago she'd've screamed and cried.

Gwen repeated part of the verse. " 'The Lord thy God is with thee wherever you go.' "

Penny said, "Only God could find us all the way out here."

That melted the smile off Cam's face. "We

know that's not true. We've had outlaws find us too many times. It seems to be only Raddo, working alone. We have to figure he'll find us here, too."

Gwen looked around them. They were in a broad, grassy plain that sloped until it was more sideways than flat. The trees stood back a fair distance. And where the snow had melted, the grass was thick and would be lush come summer.

"I can feel him out there." Gwen winced at her tone. "I'm sorry to sound so bleak. 'Be not afraid.' This life will be hard enough without living in fear of that scoundrel."

Cam lowered Maddie Sue to the ground to play again with Ronnie. "Out here, anyone who's not wary is a fool. If it isn't outlaws, then it's wolves or green-broke horses, stampeding cattle or wild, unpredictable weather. Being on guard constantly is just the way of life in the West for those who want to survive. I try not to waste time being afraid, but staying on your guard isn't fear — it's good old common sense. And with or without Raddo, we have to be on guard."

Gwen nodded in agreement.

Cam turned to the field and whistled sharply.

The bull lowered its head and pawed at

the ground. A second calf broke and ran like a deer for the far corner of the corral. Its mama didn't even quit chewing.

Both horses took a hesitant step, then a second before walking calmly up to the fence where they sniffed Cam's outstretched hand. He gave their ears a good scratch and talked quietly to them. Tossing lassos around their smooth necks, he led the horses to the wagon and hitched them up. He left the packhorse in the fenced-in meadow and tied the horse he'd ridden here to the back of the wagon.

"I'll drive the wagon and take the children with me. Gwen, you and Penny ride horse-back."

Gwen smiled with all the force of spring. "Let's get going." She mounted up and watched Cam boost the children high onto the wagon seat.

They both settled in beside Cam on the high bench.

Gwen nudged her horse and trotted up beside them on the right while Penny rode to the left side of the wagon. She planned to love everything about making a home in this beautiful, wild land.

Raddo had taken a while catching his horse,

and the sun was low in the sky by the time he did.

He studied the trail left by those two cowpokes and the woman. He should be able to find the group he'd spotted. No man could hide from Raddo Landauer in these mountains.

Tomorrow he'd scout out where the travelers had stopped. He needed a place to sleep tonight. He went hunting for a hole. He'd lived in caves all winter, but he'd lost his best spot when Riley and his men had tracked him.

He needed a new place. The bears had birthed their cubs, and the babies were old enough they'd begun wandering, which meant they no longer returned to the same place to sleep at night. Raddo appreciated not having to fight a bear for the roof over his head.

After sleeping the night away, he rode over the back trails to a different lookout to see the setup at the Riley place. A new cabin in the few days since he'd been gone.

He itched to go burn down the cabin again. It ate at him to see them wipe out all the harm he'd done.

Three men and a woman, that was all he saw. There must be another woman around somewhere. Raddo was sure he'd seen three women and five men over the winter.

The numbers made him nervous. He wanted to be sure he'd seen everyone and knew right where they were. Raddo was an old hand at biding his time, which was why he still lived and breathed. But he needed to see about the three riders who'd headed out yesterday, and then take care of them while they were separated from the group. He dropped back from his overlook and retreated to his cave. His pack had plenty of food in it, thanks to Luth's supplies.

He built a fire and cooked some jerked beef and a pot of boiling hot coffee.

It was time to make sure no witnesses survived. He had to get this done, then head east, at least for a year or two.

He saddled up his horse and headed for the trail of those three riders.

Raddo had waited long hours to back-shoot a man and rob him. Today he had no patience left in him.

They said that patience was a virtue. Well, this wasn't the first time he'd lacked a virtue, and it wouldn't be the last.

Cam pushed back from the breakfast table, eager to get back to work.

A table was one of the things they'd stashed here last fall, along with four chairs.

Of course, the table was outside, and the meal was cooked over a campfire. But the table had to be somewhere, so they'd set it by the fire. He had Maddie Sue on his lap.

He and Penny had started chopping down trees yesterday near where he planned to put the cabin and worked long into the evening. It helped to widen the open area in the woods and let in more sunlight. And they'd already put in hours working this morning before breakfast.

"You got enough energy left to fell more trees, baby sister?"

Penny smiled. "I can outwork you any day, big brother."

Cam came to where Gwen sat with Ronnie on her lap and handed her Maddie Sue. He rested a hand on Gwen's shoulder, and she looked back at him. "That was a delicious meal, Mrs. Scott. Thank you very kindly."

"It was my pleasure, Mr. Scott. I heard axes ringing, so I knew you'd be working up an appetite."

"And we're off to work up another one." Cam leaned down and kissed her pretty lips. "I wonder if Deb and Trace will show up today or tomorrow."

"I hope the weather holds. The five of us packed that tent pretty tight."

Cam and Penny had rigged the wagon

cover into a tent with speed and skill. They'd done it plenty of times before.

"Holler if you need anything," Cam said. "Preparing a meal and tending an open fire — with two little ones to watch over — might give you all you can manage."

"I'll let you know," replied Gwen. "Thank you."

He nodded. "We want to chop down some trees on the far side of the valley for Penny's cabin. We're hoping to get all the wood cut and start with putting up the walls before Trace shows up. Tackle both cabins at once."

"I trust your judgment on our cabin site, Cam. You say it's a pretty spot?"

"More than pretty. It's beautiful. It's not that far into the woods, either. But carrying both little ones in and out would be a big job for you, and if I take you now —"

Gwen stopped him with a kiss. "Go on," she said quietly. "I'll see it when Deb gets here. In the meantime, back to work with you."

He kissed her in return, surprised that suddenly he didn't want to go to work. He'd've liked very much to stay right here, play with Maddie Sue and Ronnie, and spend time with his wife. Maybe take a long walk and show her the place where they'd live that straddled her homestead and his so perfectly.

"All right, I'm going." Cam fought back the urge to tell his wife just how much she meant to him. The words clogged in his throat, so he pushed them away until later. There'd be time for sweet words, playing with children, and long walks once they had a roof over their heads.

He couldn't wait to take a stroll with Gwen in the moonlight around their own cabin. That's when he'd tell her how he truly felt. It'd give him time to work up the courage.

Until then, he walked with Penny across the wide valley, imagining the day he and Gwen would start their life together in a new, freshly built home.

CHAPTER 24

Raddo wasn't stopping until they were all dead.

He reached the spot where those travelers from yesterday had been riding and turned after them, on the hunt.

Raddo listened like a nervous cougar, watching the trail for any danger with cat-like eyes. He caught what he could as he galloped along, following their horses' hoof-prints. They'd broken a new trail. The ground here looked unworn, yet it was wide enough and clear enough that horses and wagons could pass through easily.

Where were they going? There was nothing out here that Raddo could think of. Then he heard the distant sound of chopping. Someone was swinging an ax.

Amused, he shook his head as he slowed his horse. It wasn't gonna be much trouble finding those folks now.

Quietly as he could manage, he followed

the new trail toward the chopping sound. He felt certain he'd catch them by surprise, as they obviously weren't worrying about being found. And the only reason for that was because they didn't know they were being hunted.

His amusement turned into a chuckle. The chopping was just ahead, although the bends in the trail made judging the distance based on noise tough.

He'd begun to wind his way down through the wide valley before he started spying on them, but then he spotted a game trail coming out of the woods on his right — the south side where it headed up the mountains. The south was where the chopping came from. He noticed how the woods were well back from the valley he was riding through.

Raddo took the game trail. He might get all three of these varmints before even one of 'em got a shot off.

It'd be a nice first step, he decided.

Gwen heard the trees toppling, the axes chopping, the sounds of building for the future. The sounds of their new home taking shape.

She took the children out of the tent to wander, staying mindful of the campfire.

The trail was so wide here, Cam called it a valley. Gwen's land came first. A square 160 acres that Cam said blocked the whole valley off to traffic and gave them charge over more land, because no one would want to live where they couldn't drive cattle to market. The markets were to the west, and Gwen's claim closed this valley in that direction.

Cam's land was east of hers, while Penny had claimed her land straight north of Cam's. Together, those two holdings blocked the main trail. On top of that, Penny's land and Cam's both had access to free-flowing springs, like the one Cam's small herd had used for water all winter long.

Now Gwen stood outside the tent, which was a sturdier affair than she'd expected.

They'd tucked the tent right next to the forest. It was backed up to boulders and the beginning of a stretch of rugged mountains that ran all the way west to Lake Tahoe. Trace and Deb said it was a breathtaking sight, but Cam, Gwen, and Penny had yet to see it.

Letting the children stretch their legs for a while, Gwen stood in the sunlight enjoying the blessed warmth after so many weeks of cold and snow. Then seeing that the fire was dying, she moved to build it up again.

Raddo tied his horse to a tree, a stout one this time, and went on afoot.

The game trail headed on up the mountain. He left it behind, and the going turned hard. The trees and underbrush were packed so tight together, a man could barely pass through. Old fallen logs crisscrossed everywhere, and it was a bear to climb over or go around them.

Yet Raddo was no newcomer to the wilderness. He made his way slowly, picking where each foot should land to keep him moving forward. Soon the chopping grew louder. He started downhill. The chopping covered any small sounds his boots made as he stepped on twigs and leaves.

A few moments later, the edge of the woods came into view. He could see down to a dirty white tent. Out in front of it stood the woman. The easiest one to pick off.

He'd've rather gotten one of the men first. Thin the more dangerous part of the herd before anyone had warning he was here. The children played in the dirt around the woman's feet.

He'd shoot her, but not the children — he wouldn't waste his bullets on them. The two men would come a-runnin', and they'd have to cross the open valley to get to her. He'd pick the first one off and try for the second. Even if he missed the second, at least then it'd be one-on-one.

She was on the north side of the valley, he the south. And the chopping was on this side. Thinking it through, Raddo holstered his six-gun and dragged the rifle off his shoulder. It had to be near a hundred feet across the valley, but he was a hand with a rifle.

He closed in on her a few more feet. A twig snapped, then another. But it was nothing compared to the chopping noise.

Then the woman's head came up.

Something had happened. Gwen couldn't say what, but Cam told her to trust her instincts.

She took each of the children by the hand and rushed inside the tent. She found the six-shooter Cam had bought for her on their wedding day. It wasn't flowers or candy, but his trusting her to fight with him, or for herself, made her proud. He'd given her confidence in her own bravery and ability to fight.

It was a wise gift from a man she felt so much for.

She raised the gun, but not straight up.

No sense blowing holes in their tent. Instead she aimed at the woods all the way across the valley, well to the side of where the axes were chopping.

Penny told her the pistol wouldn't hit anything from a distance, but that was fine. Gwen didn't want to go shooting something she couldn't see — Penny had also warned her against that. Still, she aimed the gun where her instincts told her to aim.

And she fired.

The chopping stopped.

A bullet whizzed past Raddo's head.

He threw himself flat onto the ground, banged his head on a fallen tree, and jammed his rifle, muzzle-first, into the dirt. Dazed for a few seconds, he lay there and got mad.

When she'd disappeared inside the tent with the children, he wondered what she was doing. But he couldn't see inside it. And the next thing he knew, she fired a gun right at him!

Shaking his head to clear it, he brought the rifle up and tapped on the muzzle to clear the dirt. He swung the weapon around and aimed across the valley, knowing it'd be sheer luck if he hit her. But maybe he could scare her a little.

The chopping had stopped. The men would be coming soon.

Cam grabbed his rifle and took off running.

As he ran, he did some thinking. *Gwen! I have to get there. Run. The children! Run . . .*

Penny caught up to him at a flat-out run. Neither of them said anything.

The gunfire had come from near the tent.

Cam picked up the pace, and Penny kept up as if he'd been slowing her down before.

Gunfire. Gwen. Maddie Sue. Ronnie.

Please, God, protect them. And forgive me for not protecting them enough.

He remembered his boast about not being afraid when Gwen had spoken that Bible verse.

"Be not afraid, neither be thou dismayed: for the Lord thy God is with thee."

Now he knew himself for a fool, because he'd never been so afraid in all his life.

It was a sturdy tent, but not when it came to stopping bullets.

Gwen grabbed a bowie knife out of a box of cooking supplies. She marched to the side of the tent, away from the open valley, and slit the tent from roof to ground.

Next, she led the children out of that death trap and did so without letting go of the gun or the knife.

Still acting on instinct, she grabbed the children and hurried toward the trees and rocks where the valley turned to forest, only steps beyond the tent. The trees provided shelter whether you were hunter or prey. Gwen had to figure in this situation, gun or not, she was considered prey.

Gunfire rang out, and bullet after bullet pierced the tent's canvas.

She ducked behind a pile of boulders, placed the children against a rock wall and had them crouch down, using her body to shield them from the vicious flying lead and praying they stayed quiet.

More bullets pinged off the rocks after they passed through the flimsy tent. From the direction he was shooting, Raddo — Gwen figured it had to be him — couldn't see into the tent. But even firing blind, he'd have shot her and the children to ribbons.

She looked up to see a small overhang. The bullets whined as they ricocheted, but none came near them. She'd found a good spot. She'd remember this if she ever had to cut and run again.

They were not only well-protected, but no one could sneak up on them from behind or draw a bead on them from higher ground.

The gunfire went on. He was intent on

killing her and the children, thinking they were hiding in the tent. Thinking they were nothing but harmless little rabbits.

Fury poured through her. To open fire like that on a woman and children!

She cocked her gun.

This time, the bunny rabbit was going to shoot back.

Rifle fire exploded after that first shot!

Cam, half-mad with fear, plunged forward. He had to get there. He had to stop this. He figured the first shot was Gwen's, a warning shot. She'd heard something or seen something.

But this was rifle fire, and it was coming from across the valley. Where was Gwen? Was she already dead? Were the chil— ?

"Cam!" A shout! The most beautiful shout he'd ever heard.

He was only paces from running right out into the open. He threw himself backward and slid down the steep slope — clawing at the earth, grasping at prickly scrub brush.

He caught sight of the forest edge. He rolled over, desperate to stop the slide.

Raddo emptied his rifle twice and reloaded. That was enough.

He'd meant to fire only a couple of rounds

354

into the tent, but a killing fury had taken over, and he'd sprayed that place with lead. He remembered how long it'd been since he killed someone. He'd never gone so long between kills before and realized how much he'd missed it.

No one could still be alive in that tent. Now he raised his sights a bit and watched for the men to dash out into the open.

Cocking his rifle, a slow smile curled his lips. Two more to go.

Cam's dive to the side of the trail made him slam into a boulder.

Well, he'd wanted to stop.

The wind was knocked out of him, and he gasped like a landed carp. His ribs ached something awful as he struggled to get to his hands and knees.

He knew Penny hadn't gone past him, which meant she'd gotten stopped uphill somewhere.

"Penny, did you hear Gwen shout?" Cam tried to keep his voice down. No sense pointing himself out for Raddo. And who else could it be but Raddo?

"Yes, I heard. My guess, she's letting us know she's all right, or she'd be screaming like mad for help. And with Raddo firing away like that, I doubt he heard it."

Cam nodded but then felt a wave of dizziness come over him. He prayed the children were unharmed. He gasped and wondered if the dizziness was from his not breathing properly.

Forcing himself to stay calm, he took some deep breaths and stared out across the valley. He and Penny were on the same side as Raddo. If Gwen didn't need them at the moment, they should stay here and go after him. Cam guessed Raddo's location within feet from where those shots had come from. He holstered his pistol and slung his rifle around in front of him.

He turned to plan his next move with his sister. Penny wasn't there.

But Cam knew exactly where she'd gone.

They weren't racing toward the woman and children. That meant only one thing — they were coming for him.

Raddo lost the fury that'd driven him this far.

At least two men had been working in the forest. Neither had shown himself. Now they were hunkered down, probably skirting around and looking for a chance to open fire on him.

Raddo backed away from the boulder that shielded him. He'd head in a different direction and walk until he found a trail that took him up the mountain. He'd lay down false tracks, then make his way out of here.

He'd done it many times before. He had a knack for slipping away.

Picking up the pace, he stumbled and fell. He clawed his way back to his feet. Then a few steps later, his feet got tangled in thick underbrush and he fell again.

He lay still, listening for others' footsteps, and made ready to draw and shoot.

Losing his cold cockiness, he got up and pushed on, then a minute later broke into a run. Because that was how a man like him lived for another day. Even in retreat, no one would corner Raddo without dying.

Gwen had called out once in the middle of that rain of gunfire. She almost did it again. She almost shouted to Cam the words *I love you.*

She probably should. He'd be hunting Raddo, facing danger, and he could do it knowing that he was loved by his wife.

Instead she stayed silent. She bit back the words to keep from giving her location away. Raddo might've missed her single shout. He might believe she was dead. It was the best protection she could give the children. She kept them close and kept them quiet. Raddo would never find her in this crevice in the rocks. She had her gun in hand, ready to fight, ready to signal Cam with it if need be.

Gwen settled in.

Wherever Cam was, she wouldn't see him coming until he was only steps away.

She waited and wondered and listened. And she hoped those instincts didn't fail her.

CHAPTER 25

Cam had won some footraces in his day. He wasn't fleet of foot like Trace, but that man was a freak of nature.

He found a trail in the woods and rushed along it toward the gunfire. Penny had gone ahead, but Cam was determined to catch her in time to help with the shooting. He was now certain that Raddo had been lying in wait somewhere along that tunnel section of the trail to Carson City. Turning off the trail had saved their lives.

Raddo might've stayed in place, but then the man was nothing but a yellow-bellied coward. Chances were he was running now. But running where?

Cam charged on, moving as fast and as quiet as he could. He hoped Raddo wouldn't see him coming. And if he did see him, Cam wanted Raddo to have a fast-moving target to aim at.

■ ■ ■ ■

Raddo heard someone coming.

A cruel smile spread across his face. Had he gotten the woman or not?

Even a weak woman left out here alone — a woman with a horse — could find her way to Carson City. If he wanted her dead, he'd have to do it himself. He'd survived all these years through wagon-train attacks and stagecoach robberies and silver holdups around the Comstock Lode, all by leaving no witnesses.

It was his one rule, and he gave it sole credit for his survival.

Those two cowpokes were coming toward him through the woods on this side of the valley.

He was swept up by a wild, crazed need to see if his bullet had found her heart. He quit trying to slip away, turned and ran straight out of the woods and across the valley.

The woods swallowed him up on the other side without a single shot fired.

They hadn't seen him.

The dense woodland full of rocks and undergrowth made it impossible to find any tracks. They'd be searching for a long time.

He still saw a chance to weed out a whole lot of his enemies.

He'd glance into the tent, make sure he'd finished her.

It'd be quicker and cleaner if she was dead, though Raddo wouldn't mind pulling the trigger one more time before he went after the men.

Gwen slipped deeper into her crevice in the rocks. The children had crawled forward onto her lap. She didn't like not sheltering them, but they'd been riding and running all morning and now were falling asleep. And that was what she wanted. If they made a noise or cried out, talked or giggled, it might give their hiding spot away.

She listened, keeping her senses wide open, and prayed. The verse came back to her that she and Cam had spoken of.

"Be strong and of good courage; be not afraid, neither be thou dismayed: for the Lord thy God is with thee."

Was it possible? Could a person go through this life unafraid?

But what did it mean? Did God expect a woman with two babies to care for to not be afraid when a man opened fire on them? Did God really think anyone could be so brave?

She remembered something her ma had told her many times — the Bible is about souls. Read the Bible and think of God as interested in your soul.

Gwen tried to do that now. And she found a surprise.

In her soul she was not afraid, because her soul was right with the Lord. Her faith was firmly in God's Son. She almost smiled at the thought.

Tucked in here, protected by solid rock on three sides, with two strong people fighting for her . . . and yes, with a gun in her hand.

She was not afraid.

While it sure wasn't her wish to leave this earth today, she didn't fear what came after this life. She didn't fear where her soul would spend eternity.

Her heart soared as she clung to the words of that verse.

"Be not afraid."

She held it firmly in her heart and trusted in God's Word.

As the children slept, she eased them to the ground behind her. She wondered if she dared to leave them for a minute to get a blanket out of the tent so their bed wouldn't be so hard. She didn't see how an outlaw across the valley could see her if she kept behind the rocks, then behind the tent, and went in through the slit she'd cut in the canvas.

She eased forward, just enough to get past their little arms and legs sprawled in sleep.

And then, like a slap, her instincts said *Stop*. It was as clear as the voice of God. She lifted the gun she'd laid aside and vowed to stay put.

Raddo stepped out right in front of her, and with one quick move he kicked the gun out of her hand.

Then he leveled his gun on her. "Stay right where you are."

He cocked the gun with a harsh metallic *crack*.

"Don't kill the children. Please." Gwen spread her arms wide, a useless attempt to block a bullet. "Instead of shooting me, take me with you. Right now, fast."

"I don't plan to haul you anywhere. I want you all dead."

"I'm ready to meet my Maker, Raddo. Are you? What do you think hell is like? A warm place to play cards with your vile friends?"

She saw him hesitate when she mentioned hell.

"If you want to keep on living, then take me as a hostage. You're not going to live through this otherwise."

Raddo swallowed hard and looked at her. She doubted he was worried about where he'd spend eternity. Instead he was thinking of saving himself. Then the look on his face changed to hunger, as if he were sitting before a feast.

"I find I like killin'." He leveled his gun on her.

A roar ripped through the air.

She flinched from the impact of the bullet . . . that never came.

Raddo went down. Eerie, otherworldly snarls tore through the woods. Not the roar of a gun, but the roar of a wolf.

Gwen grabbed for her gun.

Cam charged into view.

Gwen looked down at Raddo, who had a wolf-dog growling and snarling at him. Raddo's gun arm was clamped in Wolf's jaws. Wolf threw all his weight against the gun. It fired, then fired again.

Wolf yelped in pain. Raddo cursed as he staggered to his feet. He hurled the dog aside.

Gwen shot him. Cam's bullet hit a second later.

A third gun fired.

Penny raced up, her gun drawn, but the

third shot had come from a different direction.

All three whirled and faced a man striding toward them from the direction of the tent. Smoke curled out of his gun's muzzle.

Both children wailed in terror.

The newcomer holstered his gun swiftly and smoothly, then raised both hands high in the air. "Don't shoot, folks. I'm John McCall, and I'm on your side."

Gwen took one distraught glance at Raddo, dead at her hand. She looked at Cam and saw his face, white with fear . . . for her, for the children. Gwen threw the gun aside, rushed to the children, and held them tight. She wept as hard as they did.

Cam bent over Raddo, laid a hand over the man's heart. His hand covered two bullet holes. Cam waited a few seconds before lifting his hand and wiping it on Raddo's dangling sleeve. Wolf had torn the fabric away.

"He's dead." Cam looked back at Gwen. His eyes held such regret, such relief.

Such love.

"I would have thought the bullet wounds through the heart would have been all you needed to see," McCall said.

The newcomer seemed very calm for a man who'd just shot someone.

McCall nodded at Penny, his hands still raised. "I don't blame you folks for being nervous, but I'm gettin' mighty tired of that gun leveled on my chest."

Penny hadn't let down her guard.

Cam launched himself at Gwen. His arms came around her and the children, and his lips pressed against her temple. The cold sweat of tension was replaced by the heat of his breath, the warmth of his strength.

For only her ears, he whispered, "I'm holding my whole world in my arms."

Gwen looked past him to see Penny, who had a dead aim on the newcomer.

The children's cries lessened, and Gwen fought hers down.

"I mean you no harm." McCall was careful not to make a threatening move. None since he'd shot Raddo, anyway.

Gwen didn't care much about what the man had to say, so long as he kept that gun holstered.

He made a gesture toward his hat, a black broad-brimmed hat with a shining silver band around it. He seemed to be going to tip it, then thought better of moving while Penny had her gun trained on him.

The man looked dirty from the trail, but was dressed in a fine black suit. His shirt, though travel-stained, was sharp and fit him well.

Penny's gun never wavered. Gwen watched McCall as he looked at the children with keen interest, and then his eyes shifted to Penny.

"John McCall?" Penny lifted her gun slightly, but she sure didn't aim it away. "I've never heard that name, nor seen you around before. What brings you here? And this gun stays pointed at your chest until I'm satisfied you're not with Raddo."

"I just shot him, didn't I?" He sounded mildly amused.

"A man like Raddo ran with his own kind. Maybe you betrayed him? You saw you were outnumbered, so shooting him makes you look like you're on our side and gets rid of a partner who might talk to the sheriff and set you up to hang for his crimes."

CHAPTER 26

John tilted his head to one side, thinking. The woman had a point.

And he didn't just mean a gunpoint.

He sure wished she'd lower that barrel. His gun was holstered, after all.

Her hand looked mighty steady — a good thing in this case, because a nervous woman might have the slightest twinge and finish this against his favor.

"Wolf's been shot," the other woman said. "Cam, hang on to the children. I've got to see to Wolf."

John looked at the dog. It honestly could be a wolf. John didn't know much about wolves, but what he'd heard was really bad. The critter stood, head down, a low growl in its throat as scary as that leveled gun.

Blood coursed down the dog's flank.

John looked at these folks. Cam must be the father of the girl. Cameron Scott was the name he'd been told. The woman, Deb

Harkness maybe? Considering the holding of each other and the whispering, the two seemed to be involved.

And he had no idea who this beautiful brunette warrior was, aiming her gun at his heart. Her coffee brown eyes judging every breath John took.

Cam held the children as the woman scrambled to aid the dog.

"Let me help." John took a half step forward.

"Stay right where you are."

That mouthy woman again. And dressed like a man, too. Her hair was blowing free and wild, a rich brown with streaks in it that looked like they'd been burned in by the sun. Pants or not, no one in this world would mistake her for a man, not for one second.

John stretched his hands wide and turned his back. "Take my gun. Search me if you want. The man there needs to hold the children. You need to be ready to shoot at me. The other woman needs help. A second set of hands for doctoring would be a benefit, in case that wolf decides to chew on his doctor. Let's use mine."

His gun was jerked away. And he wondered if that wasn't the stupidest thing he'd ever done.

But he really didn't think this warrior woman would shoot him.

Unless he did the littlest, tiniest thing wrong.

Her hands slid down his leg and pulled the knife out of his boot. She found his hideout gun in his other boot. She reached down the front of his shirt and yanked the hunting knife out of the sheath he wore on a leather thong around his neck. She missed the knife in his hat and the small gun up his sleeve. And a few other things.

Still, she'd done better than most.

"Now you can help." She was a little too close behind him when she said it, and her warm breath brushed his neck.

Something very strange happened.

He had no idea what it was, but two things struck him almost as hard as a bullet.

He'd never felt quite like this before.

And he would love to see this woman in a proper dress.

Cam watched Gwen as she worked to help Wolf. She'd pressed him to the ground. The deep-throated growling had stopped.

Now Wolf lay quiet as she touched his wound. It had to hurt, yet the beast bore it in silence.

Cam's heart was finally beating something

near normal again.

He'd live the rest of his life haunted by the sight of her under Raddo's gun. Her arms spread wide, protecting the children. Seconds from death, with him too far away to save her.

He thought of himself as a warrior, yet he was nothing compared to her. His chest swelled until it hurt, it was so full of pride, respect . . . love.

She'd fired a warning shot, then called out so he'd know she was all right. She'd saved herself. Saved the children. Saved him, because he'd've run out of the woods right into Raddo's guns.

He'd seen her, the children pinned between her and a mountain, her arms spread wide, shielding them with her own life.

And she was his. And he'd never let her go.

"He's been shot in the flank," his little warrior said, "but it doesn't look too bad. We should be able to care for him ourselves with no trouble."

Wolf lay calmly, but Cam saw the critter's eyes blink when Gwen poked at his bullet wound. That was one tough dog.

The stranger knelt beside Wolf. He bared his fangs and went back to that low, vicious growl. John McCall, whoever he was, stepped back.

Cam decided the man wasn't a complete fool. But then he'd bet Raddo would've stepped back too, and no bigger fool had ever lived.

Cam exchanged a glance with Penny, another woman who made him so proud he could bust. He turned his attention to the crying little ones and realized he was holding them — and they were clinging to him, burying their faces against him. Letting him protect them.

He talked quietly to them, not a single snapped-out order. They calmed under his voice and his touch. He was tempted to cry himself.

McCall stepped away from Wolf, hands at his sides. And Cam noticed he did a fine job of making sure Penny stayed a few paces away. He was smart about Wolf, and smart about the gun.

"If you're not with that outlaw, what are you doing here, McCall?" Cam asked, keeping his voice low. He wanted to growl like Wolf, but he had small children to shelter, and Gwen had her hands full tending the animal. She didn't have time to slap him on the back of the head.

Gwen spared Cam a glance and gave him an approving smile. Then she got up and hurried away. Cam worried, but then re-membered they'd taken care of most of the danger . . . he hoped.

"I've been sent here to rescue Cameron Scott." McCall's eyes slid from Penny, the gunslinger, to Raddo, lying dead on the ground, to the retreating form of Gwen, the doctor and warrior, to the growling, bleed-ing wolf-dog. A glint in those piercing blue eyes spoke volumes about just how danger-ous he thought this place was.

"Rescue me?" Cam arched a brow.

"My brother needs no rescuing, mister," Penny replied with a voice as crisp as a winter wind. Cam couldn't remember her ever sounding like that before.

Gwen came back with a long strip of cloth. "Get off our land," she said to Mc-Call.

Cam remembered her treating him much the same way when he'd first come here. She'd have tossed him out on his ear if the blizzard hadn't trapped them.

McCall nodded. "I wondered if you were Cameron Scott."

"Yep, I'm him."

"I am looking for a two-year-old boy." He glanced at Ronnie. "What's his name?"

Dead silence.

Finally, McCall answered his own question. "It's Cameron Scott."

More quiet followed.

"Yes, his name is Cameron Scott," Gwen said at last. She knelt down and began bandaging Wolf. "Named for his uncle. We call him Ronnie. And he's fine and needs no rescuing, either. What gave you such a notion?"

McCall's eyes went back to Raddo.

Cam figured Gwen's bandage on Wolf would last about ten minutes . . . if she didn't let him go for ten minutes. But maybe ten minutes was enough. The pressure would stop the bleeding.

"I was told his parents are dead. I was sent to bring him home."

"Home?" Cam shook his head like a dog shedding water.

"Yes, home to —"

"The Chiltons." Penny cut him off, leveled the gun again, and cocked it.

"Did you get the diamonds and the silver coins?"

Florence stopped as they rounded the last corner and glared at Edmond as she raised the heavy satchel she carried.

"Of course I got it." She'd have been more likely to forget Edmond than the diamonds. She had a few other valuable things he didn't know about.

Creditors had come banging on their door just after dawn. Florence had expected it sooner or later, and she'd been prepared to run.

They'd had to leave much behind, but they'd each grabbed a satchel. Edmond's was packed with clothes and other necessities.

Florence's was filled with gold, silver, diamonds, and jewelry. She'd carefully rat-holed enough for them to be away for a while.

"And you have the gold and the family jewels?" Edmond panted as he leaned against the wall of the old stable. They had horses waiting here.

Ignoring the question, Florence executed her plan. "We can't ride long and hard like we need to. Neither of us is fit for that. We should have kept up our skills."

"We only have to get to the next town that has a train station."

She wanted to growl at the half-wit. "Our creditors will have the law after us. The main road runs north and south through town, so he'll expect us to go that way. We're heading west."

"There aren't any trains to the west."

She felt more in charge now that he'd

started whining. "No, but there are stage-coaches. We'll ride west until we find one. After a time we'll reach a river, get to the sea that way, and take a ship around to San Francisco."

She had pictured it in her head many times. They'd take on false names, travel separately rather than as a couple. The clothes packed in their satchels were of poor quality and would make a fine disguise.

"San Francisco is the nearest port to our grandson. We'll find him and bring him back home. We'll gain access to his trust fund, then return to life as normal."

"But the neighbors will have seen the creditors. We'll be ruined."

They very possibly would be. Florence tried to remain calm. "We say we got word of Delia's death and our grandson needed us. We left in a terrible hurry and forgot about making arrangements to pay bills. Then we'll pay everyone and settle back down. If that doesn't soothe the feathers of the old biddies who like to gossip, then maybe we'll just move. See what New York or Boston society has to offer." Florence wondered if they might never come home again. Leave their bills behind and start fresh in California — or somewhere else where nobody knew them.

Edmond nodded. "Let's saddle up and get out of here. I enjoyed sailing the ocean before. Of course, it was on a luxury ship heading for Paris. I wonder how this ride will be."

Florence wanted to slap him. What difference did it make how the ride would be? The ride would take them away from this town, which was all that mattered. Yes, she knew she carried enough gold and valuables to pay off all their debts, but then the last of their money would be gone. How would they live?

It flitted through her mind that if they'd been kind to Delia and accepting of that dreadful man she'd married, Delia would have stayed back here, stayed close to them. No doubt lived in a fine home. Delia had always been softhearted. Florence had learned she could get the girl to do almost anything for a bit of affection or a kind word.

But fawning like that was distasteful to Florence, and she'd been angry at Delia all her life because Florence's mother so clearly preferred her grandchild to her own daughter.

If Florence had handled the headstrong girl right, Delia would have supported them.

But to go begging to her own daughter?

And to act as if Abe Scott was anything but a disgrace? It was more than Florence could bear.

Florence had hoped to hang on until that Pinkerton fellow returned with their grandson, but time had run out.

After giving it careful thought, she'd put aside enough money for such a day as this. They could travel in comfort — or in as much comfort as the ships sailing around the tip of South America could offer.

She suspected they were in for a stormy ride.

They didn't have much choice.

CHAPTER 27

Gwen had Wolf bandaged.

Cam and John had Raddo draped over a saddle.

Penny had the children fed.

They were all going to town.

Gwen knew Wolf didn't much care for town. She ran her hand over Wolf's coarse grayish-brown fur and asked, "Where did he come from?"

Cam tied Raddo's hands and feet to the stirrups to keep the body from falling to the ground. "Do you think he ran away from home?"

Gwen chuckled. Penny laughed. Cam's work was a bit too grim to join in, but Gwen thought his shoulders lifted a bit, as if the laughter of others made Cam's burdens a tad lighter.

"Ran away from home?" John asked. "A dog?" He looked at them like they were all crazy.

Gwen could hardly blame the man. Too bad he'd come to kidnap her children.

He'd gone back and fetched his horse, then told them he'd been on his way to Trace's house when he saw Raddo heading this way. John had hoped to talk to Raddo and get directions from him.

"I realized after only a few minutes that he was sneaking along on your trail, and it looked as though he was up to no good."

John McCall finished tightening his cinch and straightened to look at them. "I heard the shooting and came as fast as I could."

Gwen let go of Wolf. He immediately swung his head to his flank and started chewing on the tight cloth binding.

Maddie Sue ran to Wolf and hugged him. Ronnie was a step behind and tripped, fell, and tackled the poor dog and Maddie Sue . . . who screamed.

Wolf took it well, though he did look over his shoulder at Gwen. He had huge pitch-black eyes. They gave her what seemed to be a long-suffering look.

The chaos made Wolf too busy to chew any more on the bandage, so Gwen let them all play.

"I know just how you feel, Wolf." She ran a hand across the dog's head. He licked her hand.

Hoofbeats pounded the dirt.

Cam, Penny, Gwen, and John all came around. All four of them were armed. Guns drawn, aimed, and cocked.

"I thought you handed over your weapons," Penny snapped at John.

A second later, three of them exhaled.

Gwen yelled, "Deb!" She lowered her gun and waved.

McCall said, "If you aren't going to shoot these folks, I'm sure not." He tucked his gun back up his sleeve.

Penny gestured at the pile of weapons she'd taken from him. "Get the rest of your stuff. I reckon if you wanted to shoot us, you had plenty of chances."

"Obliged, Miss Scott." McCall touched the brim of his hat as if to tip it.

"It's my sister and her husband." Gwen stepped out to meet them, though she hated moving away from Cam. She needed just a minute with him. Just one. Or two. Five maybe. She had a few things she needed to tell him.

"And both hired men," Cam said in a regular voice. Then he raised it and yelled, "We got Raddo!"

And then they all had a long, hectic story to tell.

"What's this?" McCall's voice turned

them all around. He lifted the sleeve Wolf had torn off, which now hung in tatters around Raddo's arm.

"What are you looking at?" Cam went over to the body, still draped over the saddle.

"There's a tattoo on his arm."

"A tattoo?" Gwen headed there, along with everyone else.

"Appears to be a line of words." John leaned closer. "I think it says . . . 'Luth,' and then it becomes faded. Must be many years old. But it looks like it says, 'If I die . . .' "

Trace pushed John McCall aside. "Let me see that."

Cam nodded. " 'If I die' . . . that sounds mighty important. Let's write down what it says."

"Did you search him?" Utah lifted Raddo's arm to study the tattoo. He spoke with such authority and so matter-of-factly that Gwen wondered if he'd spent time as a lawman somewhere along the way.

Utah, Trace, and McCall studied the tattoo a long while. Finally, Trace said, "It's early enough, I'm going to haul Raddo to town. I'll go because I've met Sheriff Moore. I turned Raddo's two saddle partners over to him last fall. McCall, since one of those bullets in him is yours, come with me and

Cam to take Raddo in. You can help explain what happened."

"I'll go instead of Cam," Penny said. "I witnessed it from the beginning. McCall here only got in at the end."

"Fine with me," Trace replied. "Three's plenty — we don't all need to go."

The group heading for town moved out. Deb was busy talking with the children.

Wolf's bandage was long gone.

Utah started chopping trees. Cam grabbed his ax, but before he could leave, Gwen stopped him.

"Cam, can we talk for a minute?"

Turning, he dropped the ax and reached for her. Her hand was warm, solid, alive. She'd stood before Raddo's deadly gun and lived. He was glad not to leave her right now.

"I think it's time to show you our home site. Deb, can you mind the children?" Cam didn't notice if she said yes. He was focused on Gwen alone.

He wove his fingers through hers. She liked that closeness. He liked it himself.

The dense woods swallowed them up. They had to pick their way along, but Cam didn't mind lifting her over a fallen tree. It gave him a chance to hold her close.

They found the little clearing. The trees

arched overhead like a cathedral ceiling. Lush grass danced and swayed in the spring wind. A trickling stream sang and stumbled along a rocky corner of the clearing.

A perfect circle in the woods without any trees and brush, as if it'd been opened up and cleared by the mighty hand of God.

They stood there in silence for a while, holding hands, enjoying the moment and the view.

Finally, Cam said, "I wanted to talk to you for a minute, too."

Gwen turned from looking around the pretty glade. "What about?"

He reached to take both her hands . . . and remembered. "Gwen, honey. My wife . . ." He pulled her into his arms and kissed her, breathed her in.

It was a long while before he could bear to lean away even that smallest inch to speak. "I was searching for Raddo on the far side of the valley. I saw him when he ran across. When I realized he was going after you . . ." His voice trailed off, and he shuddered.

Gwen's arms came around his neck, comforting him when it was she who'd been in such danger, she who'd stood as a shield between his children and certain death.

She nodded. "I thought I'd never see you

again, Cam. I thought he'd kill me and the children. And I knew losing them would tear your heart out."

Before she said more, he jumped in. He wanted to go first. Say it before she did. "I love you, Gwen."

There was the tiniest gasp as her arms tightened around him, the grip of a little warrior.

He forged ahead. "Before I met you, I didn't even know a man could feel what I feel in my heart for you. I want to —" His words were stopped by her mouth.

"I love you too, Cam. I *love* you. The joy that is ringing through me is like music straight from God. I'm so blessed to be your wife."

Nodding, he decided he hadn't finished saying what he wanted to tell her. She'd interrupted him with that kiss and those heavenly words. "When I thought I might lose you, Gwen, I knew — finally, almost too late — how important you are to me, how deep my feelings run for you. And I'd never told you. I've been so selfish and stubborn. So busy giving orders, I —"

Gwen swatted him gently on the back of the head.

He stopped, looked down at her, and smiled.

She smiled back just as brightly.

"Do you know," he whispered, "that I am now *imagining* you slapping me like that when I hear myself acting like a tyrant?"

A soft chuckle escaped her. "Then my work is probably done."

Grabbing her around the waist, he lifted her and swung her around in a circle, in that God-made chapel in the woods.

"Your work is just beginning, wife. Because I want to be a better man every day. A kinder man."

She kissed him softly. "Cam, you were born to lead. That isn't a sin. Yes, you need a gentler voice. But I married a warrior who's fought for his country and for his family, and I never want you to change that most basic part of yourself."

"You're a warrior too, Mrs. Scott."

She grinned. "A reluctant one, I'd say. But I will fight against evil for you. I hate knowing I k-killed a man." Her lips trembled, but she firmed them and went on. "But I believe God blesses people — or at least understands and forgives them — when they fight to protect their family and their home from a man in league with the devil."

They held each other close and let time pass, feeling the tension ease after today's madness.

"I figured something out today, while I hid in those rocks with the children. I figured out what it means to 'be not afraid.' "

Cam's eyes went wide. "You did? Because I decided it wasn't a verse that made much sense. I was never so afraid in all my life than today."

She kissed him again. "It's not about the world we live in — it's about our souls. Be not afraid, because whatever happens in this life, if we put our trust in God, He is with us and our souls are safe. Believing in God is the great fortress, the great refuge. We fight here on this earth, but God will protect us whether we live or die."

Cam shook his head. "That sounds wrong . . . God protecting us while we die? That doesn't seem like protection to me."

"Think about it, Cam. Whatever happens, God promises to be with us. So, *Be not afraid.* He goes before us in this life and the next. I'd say it sounds exactly right."

Cam said, "And I'd say you're the one with true courage. The one with the warrior's heart. I see what you're saying now — once the trouble is over — but I didn't when I was in the middle of it. I'll probably forget again."

"If you do, I'm here to remind you."

He kissed her until the joy she felt rose up and filled their little round chapel and she had the sense that, though their vows were legal and binding before, right now, from this moment, she was fully married.

Her dream had come true. A marriage to a man she truly loved.

He stepped back, took her hand, and turned her to look around the clearing. "Come and see where I want to build."

Cam's vision of their cabin reached out to a vision for their life together. As he spoke of his dreams, Gwen shared her own.

They disagreed on most everything, and then they'd laugh and find a middle ground. Once in a while they'd stop for another kiss.

"Will you be happy here, Gwen? I just realized I chose this spot without you. We can search longer if you want. Penny's picked her site, so we can build her place first while I . . . uh, while *we* scout around."

"You've found a beautiful spot for our home. If we searched and searched, we might find something just as nice, but we could never find anything better."

"And in the end, it doesn't matter where we live." Cam pulled her close.

"It doesn't?"

"No, because my real home is wherever you are. My real home is in your arms."

That earned him a kiss that lasted so long he could've gotten a couple of trees cut down in the time it took.

When at last they spoke again, Gwen pressed a hand flat on his chest. "And my home is right here in your heart."

Two reluctant warriors, glad to finally set aside the danger that had stalked them and to have found faith, home, family, and love.

ABOUT THE AUTHOR

Mary Connealy writes romantic comedies about cowboys. She's the author of the TROUBLE IN TEXAS, WILD AT HEART, and CIMARRON LEGACY series, as well as several other acclaimed series. Mary has been nominated for a Christy Award, was a finalist for a RITA Award, and is a two-time winner of the Carol Award. She lives on a ranch in eastern Nebraska with her very own romantic cowboy hero. They have four grown daughters — Joslyn, married to Matt; Wendy; Shelly, married to Aaron; and Katy, married to Max — and four precious grandchildren. Learn more about Mary and her books at:

maryconnealy.com
facebook.com/maryconnealy
seekerville.blogspot.com
petticoatsandpistols.com